DONKEY

JOEY TRUMAN

Whisk(e)y Tit
VT & NYC

Part 1

If you know what motivates somebody you know their soul. This is impossible. I am acting in good faith. I can never know what motivates anyone. If I did, it wouldn't be in good faith. You see how easily this world corrupts? The good die young? Only because living makes you bad. Every minute of life is another minute of corruption, every bad decision splintering into a million more bad decisions. This is impossible. I tell you I am acting in good faith. You have no choice but to believe me. This is impossible. Yet it must be true. Otherwise society would collapse. That is. If society is acting in good faith, this is impossible. You want to know what is impossible? I will show you. Just do me one favor. Take it in good faith. Otherwise this too is impossible. It started like this:

Chaz was eating a hot dog. Don't get me wrong: it was ten in the morning. We were standing next to the exhaust pipe of a truck. It was cold enough that the exhaust just puffed out in a constant white poof. Settling at our feet. Getting caught between our legs. The tailpipe hot against my leg. Little drips of water falling out the hole. I was wondering: What the fuck am I doing here? Watching Chaz eat a hot dog. Standing in smoke. Burning my leg. Ten in the morning. Outside a gas station. On the outskirts of town.

I backed up. To get away from the exhaust. The hot pipe. I had only moved in because I could barely hear what Chaz was saying. He talked so quiet. The truck was so loud. He was moving his mouth like he was talking. It was only when I moved in that I noticed he wasn't talking. He was just eating the hot dog. He smiled at me. Showed me the hot dog. Proud.

Mustard. I don't know what he was proud about, the mustard, or the hot dog itself. When he went back to eating I went back to standing around. Waiting for what? I still wasn't sure.

A week went by. Waiting for this. A week ago, or whatever. Last week. I got this phone call. "Come do this thing" he said. "In like a week" he said. It wasn't Chaz that called me. It was this other guy. Bonzo, or something. Bronzo. I didn't really hear him right. He said he was friends with Chaz, and needed a guy like me, for this thing. Jonzer. Whatever. The guy we were waiting for, while Chaz ate that hot dog and I stood around looking. Bronzer! His name was Bronzer!

So Bronzer was paying for gas. Getting "supplies" as he called them. Chaz was eating a hot dog at ten in the morning. With mustard. And I was standing there looking. Wondering what the fuck I was doing here.

I knew Chaz a long time. Since before this thing that we were doing. Whatever the hell it was. I guess he was a friend. He started showing up when things started to get really bad. He always had a bunch of thoughts about stuff. Which was fine, I guess. I mean, he talked real quiet, so he was easy to ignore. But when he showed up— around— he always had some work that needed doing. Which is nice. Things being bad as they are. It is nice to get some work. Sometimes. Eat some food and stuff. Pay for things.

This Bronzer guy though. With his dumb phone call:

"Hey dude, you Donkey?"
"Yeah, who's this?"

"Nice, nice. I am [muted name, sounded like Bonzo, or Bronzo] friends with Chaz, okay?"

"Yeah, okay?"

"Um, I got this thing. Care to help? Five hundred smackers, dog."

"I guess. What is it?"

"Don't you mind it, dog. Meet me at the gas station where the highway meets the highway, over by the old airport, next Monday at ten in the morning, ya dig?"

"Yeah, I guess?"

He had hung up. I called Chaz. Chaz didn't know either. Which was that. Now Chaz was eating a hot dog with mustard, and I was standing around looking while Bronzer got "supplies" and paid for gas. Did I mention there was another guy? Sitting in the truck? I could see his head. That was all. The truck was a dual cab thing. Kind of. It had a back seat. But you had to pull the front seat down to get to it. The other guy was sitting on the side with the steering wheel. He looked like he was just looking at stuff too. Stuff in front of the truck. He never moved his head. His head looked round. It looked like he was wearing a stocking cap.

It was cold. I told you this before. Now do you believe me? Mid-January. The sky was bright. No wind. For once. I could have just got into the truck, but I didn't want to. That other guy seemed like too much. What was I going to do? Sit there and look at stuff alone, together? I will take my chances with Chaz and his hot dog with mustard. I looked out onto the plains. The highway meeting highway. A truck passed. The windows frosted with ice. I looked over towards the old airport. No planes landing. A lousy golf course hanging adjacent. I wondered who the hell would golf at a place like that? My brain gave me no answer. Which made me wonder if I even asked it a question. But that was stupid, and suddenly Bronzer showed up carrying a hot dog and a quart of oil. He looked at Chaz, and me, and said:

"A couple of boners! Let's roll!"

Chaz looked at me. Smiled. Licked mustard from his lip. Threw the hot dog doily to the ground. Walked around me. Opened the door. Pulled the seat down for me to get in. I got in. The other guy looked straight ahead. I didn't bother saying hello. His vibe was not very nice. Chaz pushed the seat back. Slammed the door. Then just like that, I was trapped.

Whatever the fuck this was, I was part of it now.

Now Bronzer was eating a hot dog. Driving and eating a hot dog. I could see his eyes in the rearview mirror. He kept looking at me. Then the road. Then he would take a bite of hot dog. Then he would look at me. When he finished eating the hot dog, he rolled down his window and threw the paper doily out. Then he looked at me again. Rolled up the window. Looked at the road. After that, he didn't look at me any more.

Chaz fell asleep. I could hear him breathing heavy. The other guy just stared straight ahead. I could see him not moving or anything out of the corner of my eye. He was wearing a stocking cap. I knew that now. I saw it when I got in. It was black. Which is a good detail, right? I mean, I wasn't sure before, but now I was sure. That is a good detail, right?

The highway we were on snaked around the outskirts of town. Then it went south. I knew where we were. I had no idea where we were going. The plains had very little snow. Badlands, I guess. Gusts of wind blew dust across the highway. There was quite a few antelope bouncing around. I saw a rabbit. It looked like a jackrabbit. The size of it, at least. We drove for a while. I am not sure how long. I kind of zonked out myself for a minute. All I know is that at some point we turned left, and the road got real bumpy. Then it got really bumpy. Then I was wide awake. My back was being rubbed raw by the wool seat cover. The other guy had his arm up, and was holding onto a handle above the window next to him. I didn't want to look over. So I didn't. I could see this out of the corner of my eye. I reached up and grabbed the handle above the window next to me. Chaz was awake. I could tell because he was putting a chew in. Then he said, "Oh shit." Rolled his window down. Spit the chew out. I was blasted by the smell of spearmint, and tobacco, and very cold air. Then he rolled up his window. "Forgot a spitter," he said to no one that was listening. Bronzer looked at me in the mirror.

The longer we drove, the slower we went. The road got bumpier, and bumpier. It started to snow. The sagebrush became pine trees. The open plains became a corridor of trees, and ruts. I started to think that this thing would take a lot longer than I had planned. I thought about the piece of meat I had thawing on the counter. I should have put it in the fridge. I mean, why did I even take it out of the freezer? I had no idea how long this thing would take. That was pretty stupid.

Not only that, but it was one of the better chunks I had in the freezer. Back strap. I was going to make a roast. Nothing to do about it now. But damn it! I made a little wish that it would thaw slower than normal, but that was stupid. I knew it was probably ruined. Even if we got back by nightfall it would be ruined. Maybe not ruined completely, but ruined for a roast.

The truck kept chugging along. At one point Chaz and Bronzer got out to lock the hubs. When they got back in, Bronzer engaged the four-wheel drive. The snow was really coming down now. Bronzer kept shifting from first gear to second gear, then back again. All the while getting dragged into ruts, then getting the truck back out of the ruts. Over, and over, and over. The wool seat cover rubbing me raw. Jarring me, back, and forth, back, and forth. I pulled myself up straight, and adjusted my posture. Holding on to the handle above the window next to me. My pants driving themselves up further into my crotch. My balls, and dick, smashed. The long underwear pulling themselves up out of my boots. My socks somehow sliding down into the tips of my boots. My shirts climbing up my torso. I was very uncomfortable. I wanted to take my coat off, but I didn't want to have to interact with the other guy. I was suddenly very hot. I was suddenly very hot, and there was nothing I could do about it. The window in the back didn't roll down, and nobody else seemed to be having the same troubles I was having. I suffered in silence.

Another hour went by. It stopped snowing. The pine trees grew away. Into the distance. The road got better, and the truck gained some speed. Now instead of getting sucked into the ruts, it kept sliding into the ditch that ran along side the road. Well, not a ditch exactly, just a place where water was flowing. And now, every time this happened, the truck would hit a rock, and bounce us back and forth, and I would hit my head on the ceiling. I was starting to get annoyed. Where the fuck was this dude taking us? Was this thing that we were doing going to be worth the money I was getting? I mean, was I just hired to roof some guy's cabin in the middle of fucking nowhere? I doubt it. I mean, if that was the case, we probably would have started well before ten in the morning. Whatever. There was nothing I could do about it now. I suffered in silence.

We came to a fence. With a cattle guard. A green metal gate. Chaz got out. Shut the door. Opened the fence. Swung it back towards the truck. We drove through. Bronzer put the truck in park. Pulled a lever down by his left leg. Got out of the truck, leaving the door open. The key reminder started ringing. Bronzer took a piss. Chaz got back in the truck. Shut the door. Bronzer popped the hood. Messed around for a while. Came back to the driver's side. Reached in, and grabbed the quart of oil. Disappeared into the front of the truck again. A while went by. The empty can of oil flew off into the sagebrush by the side of the road. He slammed the hood back down. Got into the truck. Put the truck in drive. Drove on.

The hills around us were now covered in cows. Antelope mingled among them. Bronzer had to honk the horn a few times. Because the cows were hogging the road. The sun came out in the west. Behind the clouds. Where we were, it started snowing again.

Don't get me wrong, but this thing was taking forever already, and now I wish that I would have eaten a hot dog. Maybe got a bottle of water or something. I was thirsty and hungry. Both bored and anxious. I had to piss, and now my kidneys hurt from all the bouncing around. I was starting to get mad at Chaz. And I think he had fallen asleep again. The jerk. Also, Bronzer kept looking at me in the mirror again. The other guy was the same as usual. Which was also starting to get on my nerves. I noticed the Check Engine light come on in front of the steering wheel. I thought about the quart of oil. Like, why did Bronzer only get one quart if he had to pour it in the engine so soon after we started driving? Were we about to be stranded in the snowing mountains? It'd take us forever to walk back. We would probably die. I was wearing overalls and boots. A stocking cap. Same as everyone else. I think I brought gloves, but now I wasn't so sure. Man, I need to learn to ask more questions. Don't get me wrong, but all this was a pretty bonehead move on my part. And my meat, thawing on the counter.

We drove for about another hour. The road went back into the pine trees. No more cows. We ran into another fence. This one was made of barbed wire and wood that looked like it was found on the ground. There was a No Trespassing sign on it. Chaz got out. Opened it. We drove through. Chaz closed it. Got back inside. Said, "Damn! Chilly bastard out there! Zoinks." We drove for a little while more. Then we came to a cabin.

The cabin was small. Rustic. There didn't seem to be anyone in it. Snow covered everything. There were no tracks. No smoke coming from the chimney. Bronzer pulled up to the front of the cabin. Put the truck in park. Turned it off. Leaned his head against the window next to him. Pulled his stocking cap down over his eyes. Soon he was breathing heavy. Asleep. I said "What the fuck." Under my breath. The other guy turned his face towards me, and scowled. Don't get me wrong, but whoa! The look on his face. He was young. Younger than me. I think he was Mexican. I don't know why I thought that, he just reminded me of a guy I knew that was Mexican. Nice guy, but he spent all his energy trying not to stab people. I mean, don't get me wrong, I don't think he would actually stab people, he just told me that once when I pissed him off for doing I don't know what. I was like, Hey, Man, I'm sorry I rubbed you the wrong way, but I didn't mean to. And he was like, You have no idea how much time I spend trying not to stab people, so watch yourself homey. He called people homey for some reason. Even though we went to school together, and knew all the same people. I never figured out where he picked it up. Nobody else I knew called people homey. But this other guy, the look on his face was the same as this guy that I knew. I held up my hands instinctually. In apology. The other guy went back to looking straight ahead.

Chaz fell asleep too. I could tell because he started snoring. I tried to ignore what was happening. I looked out the window. The snow falling. The pine trees. The cabin. I, myself, tried to fall asleep, but my feet were starting to get cold. The air in the truck had dropped twenty degrees. I could see my breath. I sat on my hands. Then I zipped my coat up. Then I sat on my hands again. I just got colder, and colder. There was nothing to do about it. My ears started to hurt. I pulled my stocking cap down over them more. Then I put my hands back under my legs. At this point I was feeling really claustrophobic. There was nowhere to go. The cold air increasing. This maniac other guy just staring into the distance. Bronzer, with his glances in the mirror. Chaz, and his stupid thing that he got me involved in. I thought about my meat thawing on the counter. How I could be making a roast right about now. Cozy in my crappy little apartment. But instead I was here. Doing god knows what.

I started to panic a little. Trying to make sense of things. But then I realized that this was work. This is what work feels like. Trapped somewhere until the job gets done. And when it gets done, you get paid. Don't get me wrong, I have done enough shitty jobs in my life that this was nothing. After I had this thought I calmed down. My toes were numb at this point. Aside from my face, the rest of me was warm enough. I wouldn't die or nothing. The windows started fogging up. Soon, with no help from myself, I was personally asleep.

The sound of the truck engine starting woke me up. All of the windows were fogged up. There was a smell of hot dog farts in the cab. Bronzer turned the heat full blast. Chaz was looking in the glove box for something. The other guy sat there like normal. Looking straight ahead. When the windows stopped being fogged up, nothing outside had changed. Except there was now about a half inch of snow on the hood. Slowly melting while the engine heated up. Chaz found what he was looking for. Closed the glove box. We sat in silence for a while. The air got warmer. I took my hands out from under my legs. Rubbed them together. Some more time went by. Bronzer looked at me in the mirror. Turned the truck off. Said "Let's go."

Bronzer and Chaz got out. Pulled the seats forward for me and the other guy to get out. Shut the doors. I could barely stand up. My feet were needles. My toes. I stomped my boots in the snow. Bent over, grabbed a handful of snow, put it in my mouth. Bronzer went to the back of the truck. Grabbed a shovel. Handed it to me. Said, "Here, take this." I took it. He marched towards the side of the cabin. Chaz started following him. I waited for the other guy to follow Chaz, but he just stood there. I got the impression he was waiting for me to move. I followed Chaz. The other guy followed me.

In the back of the cabin there was a large field. Don't get me wrong, I don't think field is the way to put it, but there was a big empty space. Bigger than needed to be in the back of a cabin on the top of a mountain. In the middle of the field was a cemetery. With a fence around it. I counted twelve gravestones. All with the name Michael on them. Don't get me wrong, some of them said Miguel, which I think means Michael in Spanish. Some of them were crosses. Some just regular gravestones. They all looked really old. Leaning this way or that way. Bronzer walked straight to the cemetery. Then he held out his hand. Chaz handed him a paper. Bronzer held it up. Like he was cross-referencing the paper with the gravestones. He walked to the back. Held the paper up again. Folded it. Handed it back to Chaz. Looked at me, and said

"This one."

I looked at him. He was really tall. I didn't notice how tall he was before. And very skinny. Don't get me wrong, I kind of made him out to be kind of chunky, I guess. Maybe because of that hot dog he was eating earlier. Chaz was kind of chunky. And he too was eating a hot dog earlier. So, there is that. But he was tall and skinny, and he had the same eyes that he kept looking at me in the mirror with. I mean, kind of pervy. But indifferent. Like he might fuck me, then shoot me after. There was a moment of silence. Then I said:

"What?"

"This one."

"This one, what?"

"Start digging this grave."

Don't get me wrong. I understood what he meant. I just didn't understand what he was saying. I mean, I had never been handed a shovel before, and then asked to start digging up somebody's grave. I mean, I wasn't being obtuse, or even insolent, I just couldn't adjust. And instead of just doing the stupid thing I was asked to do, I said:

"You want me to dig this grave?"

"Yeah, boner, that's why I hired you. Chaz said you were good for it. He said you were a real good dirt slinger. Said you had experience."

"Digging graves? You drove me all the way out here just to dig this grave?"

Don't get me wrong. I am normally not this stupid. It is just I had all these questions about shit, and they started coming out in idiotic ways.

"Just dig." Bronzer said.

"Why couldn't you just have Chaz do it? Or do it yourself? Or Kevin here?"

"Who the fuck is Kevin?"

"Well, this guy."

I pointed the shovel at the other guy.

"Who told you his name is Kevin? His name ain't Kevin, dog."

"Well, nobody told me. I just."

"Just what? Name people Kevin?"

"Well, no. He just reminds me of Kevin."

"Who the fuck is Kevin? Never mind. Just dig."

"Okay, here?"

"Chaz! Your boy's a dunce. You told me he was a rockin' dude."

"C'mon Donk, just dig." Chaz was looking embarrassed.

"Okay, okay."

I put the shovel through the snow. I hit frozen dirt.

"This couldn't wait until spring?"

"Donkey!"

The digging went pretty slow. Bronzer, Chaz, and the other guy stood there looking. The ground was frozen. The gravestone was a regular gravestone. One that said Miguel, which means Michael in Spanish, I think. There was no other words or information. Just Miguel. Every time I dug a little I looked up. Miguel. I would dig a little more. Miguel. This went on for quite some time. I had no idea how far I was supposed to dig. I assumed it was until I hit the coffin, but the fact that I was digging a grave in the mountains in winter, and these three weirdos were watching, meant that I could be digging for anything.

I got hot. I took off my coat. The snow stopped. I asked if anyone had any water. Bronzer just stared at me. I sighed. Kept digging. Twenty minutes. Thirty. Forty. I was just chipping away at brown ice, it felt like. Inches at a time. Don't get me wrong, I can only assume how much time went by. This is what it felt like to me. After about an hour it started to get dark. Then it was dark. Then I couldn't see anything. Bronzer said:

"Chaz, go get the flashlight."
"Nothing doing, dog."
"Why not?"
"There ain't one. I got some matches?"
"Fuck!"

Bronzer brooded for a while. Thinking, I guess. No moon came out. It started snowing again. I could feel it. I couldn't see it. I could kind of see the silhouette of everyone standing around the grave. I was maybe three feet down at this point. I leaned the shovel against the edge of the wall of the grave I just dug. Then I got myself out. Bronzer said:

"Alright. Fuck. Kevin, you think they will know if we stay here the night?"
"Ha! His name is Kevin!" I yelled.
"Donkey! Shut it!" Chaz yelled back.

"I, I mean, it's either that, or drive back now, and we can't leave this grave this way. I don't...[sigh]." Kevin knew the people who owned the cabin. It was all coming together. "Okay, okay. How about this? We just wait for first light, in the cabin. Get the goods, and get the fuck out. Nobody will know the difference, dog." Bronzer said.

"Yeah, okay." Kevin said. "We can't leave this grave this way, and we can't fix it in the dark. Maybe there is a flashlight inside? Or a lantern or something."

"Chaz, you got them matches?" Bronzer said.

"Yep."

"Lead the way." Bronzer said.

Chaz led us to the front of the cabin. With a match or two. Maybe three. I won't lie to you, I can't remember how many. I just know there was no back door to go in, and getting to the front of the cabin was a pain in the ass in the dark, even with Chaz and his matches. But we got there. Which was good. The door was even unlocked. And on the way in, I noticed there was plenty of firewood on the front porch. Which is a pretty good detail, considering we will probably need it, right?

I have to tell you, the cabin was cold inside. Chaz went around lighting matches, trying to find a lantern or a flashlight. He found some candles. He lit a couple of them. Me and Kevin and Bronzer stood around waiting. The candles didn't throw much light. What light they did throw exposed a bare-bones cabin, with a bed, a stove, a cupboard. Not much else. Kevin went outside, and fumbled around in the dark for a while. Came back in with some chopped wood. Tried to make a fire in the stove. There was no kindling. No axe to make any kindling. He took one of the candles and roamed around the cabin looking for stuff to burn. There was nothing. Bronzer took the other candle, and said he would look in the truck. He left for a second, and then came right back inside. The candle had burned out. He lit the candle again off the candle Kevin was holding. He said to me, in my direction, "Donkey, go out to the truck, see if you can find some paper."

I went outside. It was dark as shit. I couldn't see anything. The sky was cloudy, I guess, or there was no moon, or something. I stumbled towards what I thought was the truck. It was. I tried to open the door. The door was locked. I fished around in the bed, hoping to find something to burn. There was nothing but empty cans. I stumbled back to the cabin. I went inside. Bronzer said:

"And?"

"The door was locked."

"Shit! Fuck. That fucking."

"That fucking what?" Kevin said.

"Get ready for a long night, dogs, we ain't going nowhere till the morning. Automatic locks."

"Are you serious?" Chaz usually talked real quiet, but this was pretty loud.

"No, I'm joking. Let's get going."

"You locked the keys in the car?" Kevin said.

"No, I did not lock the keys in the car, I locked the keys in the truck, and it wasn't my fault, those fucking automatic locks, dog."

There was silence in the cabin. The candles took this moment to burn out. Don't get me wrong, this sounds dramatic, but that is how it happened, I swear. Outside, the wind started howling. The cabin shook a little. I zipped up my coat. I put my hands in my coat pockets. "No way!" I said. Someone said "What is it now?" I think it was Chaz. "Oh nothing, just gloves," I said, as much to myself as to whoever had asked me about it. I put my gloves on in the dark. I didn't know if I should just stand there or sit down or what. I kind of wanted to hop in the bed and go to sleep, wait for the morning in snooze town. Bronzer beat me to it. I only know this because I heard a bed creaking, then I heard Kevin say:

"Oh, fuck no, Bronzer, get out."

"What? I'm cold, and tired."

"Yeah, well, your dumb ass locked the keys in the truck, and this my family's cabin, the bed is mine. Get out."

I heard some more creaking. A transfer of ownership, I suppose. And that was that. I sat down. Leaned against the wall closest to me. And waited. I don't know what anyone else did. There was no way to see anything. I heard some heavy breathing. My stomach growled. I thought about my meat again. Just dangling there on the kitchen counter. Waiting for me. The night was going to be long. I guessed it was maybe six in the evening. We would be in this stasis for at least twelve hours. It was reminding me of the time I took the bus from Denver to New York City. Waiting in the lobby of the bus station in Chicago. Nothing to do. Nowhere to go. And if I ditched, I would be completely stranded in unknown territory. Dangerous and exposed. Just to sleep for a couple hours. Forget about everything. All this waiting. Waiting. Waiting. Cold, and exposed. Waiting.

I kept thinking that Chaz would start talking. As quiet as he was, he kind of never shut up. At one point he did say "this sucks." But when nobody responded, he kept his mouth shut.

Don't get me wrong, it was a long night. The wind blowing on the outside of the cabin. Rattling the windows. Mice started running around. Getting confident. Running over my legs. And, I guess, up Chaz's pant leg, because he screamed, followed by "one just ran up my fucking pant leg!" Luckily it never got colder. Sadly, it never got any warmer either. I drifted off to sleep a couple times, only to be woke up when a mouse ran across my face. Or tried to make a nest out of my hair. What were these mice even doing here? There was nothing to eat. Maybe they were smelling the hot dogs that Chaz and Bronzer kept letting loose out of their butts. Both of them would laugh if they let one rip. Then me and Kevin were left to suffer the consequences. Well, me for sure, I think Kevin was either asleep, or just staring off into the distance like he did in the truck ride up here. Lying down. Under a blanket. Probably covered in mouse turds that he didn't know about. In the land of shitty cabin adventures, the cotted man is king. Or something. I mean, the longer the night drew on, the more it was really like waiting for the bus in Chicago. At first

I was just using that thought to entertain myself, but in the end, I felt exhausted. Wondering what the fuck I was doing with my life. Sitting around some useless room, surrounded by assholes. Wishing I was anywhere but here. Knowing I would have to wait until the waiting was done. Cold, bored, and hungry.

I guess, though, that in Chicago I could have gone to the snack machine, and got some chips or something. Maybe a coffee. But I would have had to drag my duffel bag with me, and I would lose my sweet spot. The one that wasn't next to the door, so it didn't get a blast of cold wind whenever someone would come in, which was every twenty seconds or so, and not so much in the middle of foot traffic, where I would have to move every time somebody was walking by dragging a wheeled suitcase behind them. I mean, I guess this time I wouldn't be swindled out of twenty bucks when some guy asked me for a dollar to get a coffee, and for some reason I said, "All I got is a twenty." And he said, "Oh, no worries, I will bring you change." He never brought me any change.

I won't lie, I was a lot stupider then. I can't say I was much smarter now. Some guy says there is some money to do this thing, come do it. And instead of asking a single question, here I am, cold as shit, waiting for dawn in some dumb cabin in the woods on some mountain in the middle of Wyoming. Aside from my pride, I think losing that twenty bucks would be much better than this. At least I could eat some chips, or something. I kept thinking about that meat on my counter. How tasty it would be right about now. Maybe I could cut it up, and dredge it in flour, and fry it for a while. Add some salt and pepper. Eat it while standing over the stove. In my warm and cozy apartment. Alone. Without a Dick, a Moron, and a Maniac. Two thirds of them blowing hot dog farts into the wind when I just wanted to sleep, or be left alone.

Enough hours went by that I kind of forgot what was happening. I fell asleep. For real. Don't get me wrong, I must have been asleep for a while, because I could see around the cabin when I woke up. Kevin was snug in the bed. Looking quite peaceful. Warm. His head was covered by the blanket he had on top of himself. His face poking out. His breath making shallow blasts of steam. Bronzer was next to the bed. Somehow under some of the covers, his back to the bedframe. His ass under the bedframe. Chaz was next to the stove. He was using a log as a pillow. Next to him was a stack of newspapers and kindling.

The cabin was very small. Two windows. One by the door, one on the other side, looking out at the graveyard. There were shelves on the wall. A lantern. A police flashlight with an unopened package of batteries next to it. In one of the corners was a stack of wool blankets piled about three feet high.

I got up and walked over to the blankets. I put one around my shoulders. I looked out the window. Toward the cemetery. The shovel poking out of the grave I was digging. The sun was coming up in that direction. Which I guess was east. The clouds were gone. It looked really cold outside. The shovel had hoarfrost on the handle. I looked over at Chaz, asleep by the stove, the kindling, the papers. My stomach hurt pretty good, I won't lie to you. I was hungry as a starving dog. Which is pretty hungry, I think. I ached like I had a hangover. My neck. I stood there looking at everyone sleep. The blanket was nice.

I bent over and got another one. Draped it over my shoulders. Soon I wasn't completely miserable. Only kind of.

Kevin woke up first. He looked at me like he might stab me. I backed up a little. He stood up. Looked at Chaz. Shook his head. Kicked him. Chaz woke up a little, and moved. Kevin went to work building a fire in the stove. I looked over at Bronzer. He had moved from the floor, and into the bed. He was smiling. Chaz tried to sleep some more, but Kevin kicked him again, and said "Matches." Chaz handed him the matches. There was none left. Just the cover. Kevin made a face like he was about to stomp Chaz's brains out. He turned around instead, and looked for something to light the fire with. He couldn't find anything. He looked at me. I shrugged. He kicked the bed. Bronzer said "What's up, dog?" Kevin said, "Light?" Bronzer said, "In the truck."

I mean, that was that. Don't get me wrong, it sucked. No fire, no tasty food, just the same old shit. Standing around waiting for shit to get shittier. Kevin got really annoyed. I watched him go out the door, then I saw him at the grave site I had been digging. Through the window. He shoveled the dirt I had dug out back into the grave. Did his best to make it look like we weren't there. Then he took the shovel around the side of the cabin. I saw him emerge in the front of the cabin. Because I was looking through the front window. He threw the shovel in the back of the truck. Walked over to the front door of the cabin. Grabbed a log. Walked back to the truck. Threw the log through the driver's side window. Reached in. Turned the truck on. Brought the log back. Put it on the pile. Came inside. Told me to fold the blankets, put them back. Took the logs out of the stove. Took them outside. Put them on the woodpile. Removed the paper and kindling from the stove. Put the kindling with the other kindling. Said, "Okay, time to go."

Chaz, Bronzer, and me went to the truck. I got in the back. So did Chaz. Bronzer got in the driver's seat. Kevin went over to the fence. Opened the gate. Bronzer backed up. And out. Kevin went and broke a branch of pine from a tree outside of the fence. Walked back inside, went into the cabin to double check, then came back out. Went around the back. Used the branch to cover our tracks. Same with the front. Walked into the woods. Ditched the branch. Came back. Closed the gate. Got in the truck. Said, "You better hope it snows before anyone comes up here."

Bronzer looked scared, but he held it together. He did a horrible job turning around. Got us stuck twice. Me and Chaz had to get out and push. Don't get me wrong, but we got the hell out of there eventually. The ride back was both hot and cold. The heat was on full blast, but the window next to Bronzer just ushered in freezing wind. Chaz got most of it, but me and Kevin got it too. As well as the noise. Nobody said anything the whole ride back. Bronzer was sitting on glass. That must have been uncomfortable. The same hours it took getting up to the cabin, it took coming back down. When Bronzer dropped me off at the gas station where we started, I couldn't believe how much better I felt. I mean, don't get me wrong, the dude was supposed to pay me money, but at this point, I didn't care. I started to walk back to my car before I stopped. It must have been about ten in the morning. I turned around. I went into the gas station. The hot dogs were ready.

I couldn't believe my luck. I got two. With mustard and everything.

Donkey

Part 2

Don't get me wrong: the hot dogs were delicious. But because I hadn't eaten in so long, I had to run back into the gas station to use the bathroom. I mean, yikes. I didn't know what to do about it. Socially. There was a guy that was waiting when I got out. I said "Wasn't me." He looked at me annoyed. Bit his lips. Then I guess went in. I was out the door ASAP. I got thirsty this time when I was walking back to my car. I couldn't bring myself to turn around. So I kept walking.

My car was covered in snow. A thin layer. The thing looked frozen. It's a good thing the locks were broken, because something told me the key holes were all frozen. I got in. The air was bright. My breath was a giant cloud. I reached under the seat to grab the keys. I put the keys in the ignition. Did the usual prayer and turned the key. The engine chugged, and chugged, and chugged, and just when it sounded like the battery was dying, it turned over. I let out a sigh. I turned the heat to full blast. Cold air came rushing out. I turned the director to defroster mode. Reached over to the glove box. Opened it. Grabbed the ice scraper. Put my gloves on. Got back out of the car.

I scraped the windows for some time. Don't get me wrong: I'm not lazy, but the ice was just too thick. I was getting nowhere. I mean. Don't think I am being dramatic. This sort of thing happened at least twice a year. And every time it happened, I told myself I would buy a better ice scraper, instead of using this dumb thing that I got from Key Bank, like ten years ago, when I opened up a now-closed bank account. And every year, at least twice, I have gone through this annoying farce. Life is a real can of worms, I mean, if you know what I mean.

I got back into the car. Waited. The heat seemed to be coming out of the defrosters. Not much. But some. Frustrating. Boring. I looked around for a bottle of water, or something to drink. Nothing. Well, there was a cup from Taco John's, half-full, frozen solid. I became cold and impatient, so I kind of forgot about being thirsty at this point. I sat there looking at the windshield. White. Frozen. I took my gloves off, felt to see if things were getting hotter. A little. I put my gloves back on. Got out of the car. Tried my luck with the scraper again. Nothing. I got back in the car. I turned on the radio. Remembered it didn't work. Turned it off again. I stared at the windshield some more. Something was finally happening. The very bottom of the ice looked like it was melting. I watched it for a while. To make sure. I was sure now. I got back out of the car. Scraped on the ice some more. No progress. Although the ice melting on the bottom was progress. I stood there looking at it. I said "Fuck it." I dropped the scraper on the driver's seat. Slammed the door and walked back into the gas station.

The air inside was nice. Warm. I took my gloves off. I slowly made myself a coffee, trying to waste time. My face started to burn. It must be really cold outside, I was thinking. Kind of. I mean, I was thinking that, but I wasn't actually thinking that. I mean, I wasn't like:

"I am burning," my face said.

"It must be really cold out," my brain said.

I mean, it was more like, I knew it was really cold. I poured some imitation cream into the coffee. Huge chunks of it floated on the top. I poured some sugar from a glass sugar pouring thing, the thing with the metal lid, and the one hole, with the flap. I thought this might break up the creamer chunks. It didn't. It never did. Every time I did this, I always hoped that that would happen. It never did. I guess I am either stupid, or always optimistic. Probably both. I grabbed a thin red stirring straw, and tried to break up the creamer chunks. This kind of worked. I gave up, and just stirred the whole coffee, letting the remaining chunks swirl around in the middle of the cup while I put a lid on. I threw the stirring straw in the trash. Went up to the counter. Paid. Took a sip of the coffee. Got a mouthful of creamer chunks. Chewed on them. Like little balls of milk flour. I started to walk out the door, stopped. Put my coffee on the counter. Put my gloves on. Then I walked out the door.

The coffee was really tasty once the creamer chunks were gone. I drank it really fast. I was thirsty. It made me warm inside. I was nearly finished with it when I got back to my car. The ice had shifted. Fallen down. Slid down. I opened the driver's side door. Reached in, grabbed the Taco John's cup. I didn't know what to do with it. I dropped it to the ground and stomped on it. I put the coffee cup in the place where the Taco John's cup was. I grabbed the scraper off the driver's seat. I used the scraper to pry the sheet of ice off the windshield. It came off in one big chunk. I tried to drag it off the car without breaking it, but it fell on to the hood, and broke into a bunch of pieces. I went around the front of the car brushing them off. I went back to the driver's side. Looked at the Taco John's cup. Smashed. The lid and straw still in mint condition.

Mint condition. I mean, it wasn't like some collectible or something, but when I smashed the thing, I mean, in relation to the rest of the cup. Don't get me wrong, I picked the cup up. Dumped whatever ice and stuff that was in it, pop, I guess, onto the ground. Then threw it, and the lid and straw, into the back seat. I got in. Put the ice scraper in the glove box. Looked out the windshield. Finally. Took a drink of what was left of the coffee. It was cold now. Turned the wipers on for a couple of passes. Rolled down my window to see what would happen. A big sheet of ice and snow came into the car and fell in my lap. I got very annoyed. I got out of the car and brushed it off. Then I brushed the driver's seat off. Then I slammed the door. Luckily this made the rest of the snow and ice fall off.

I rolled the passenger-side window down. From the controls on my door. The same thing happened, except this time it didn't fall into my lap, so I didn't care. I couldn't see out the back, and my side-view mirrors were useless with ice, but I was sick of everything, so I put the car in drive, and drove out of the gas station parking lot.

The drive home was pretty same ol'. Don't get me wrong: same shit, different day. The ice and snow on the back window never went anywhere. I would probably have to pour some hot water on it or something the next time I drove, but such is life. Same with the side-view mirrors. But so what. I don't know why, but I avoided the center of town when I was driving home. I was feeling guilty for some reason. Like I was drunk, or stoned or something, and the cops were going to pull me over. But I was sober, and as far as I knew, I had done nothing wrong. I mean, I don't think digging up an old grave is like a thing to be proud of, but we didn't disturb a body or anything. And as far as I knew, the cabin belonged to Kevin's family, the Michaels, or Miguels, which, don't get me wrong, but I think that is Spanish for Michael. I mean, I don't think we were trespassing. Whatever. I took the back roads home. Which took about ten more minutes than it should have, but once I crossed the tracks and could see the ratty limousine that that fucking asshole Sindy rented out to unsuspecting cheapskates that he would drive to the prom, or whatever, I felt so much better than I had in the last twenty-four hours at that point. No, longer. Don't get me wrong, but spare me the details, right? And when I pulled into the front of the house, and was unlocking my door, I felt pretty good.

My apartment was warm. All my stuff was in the same place I left it. My first and only thought was about the meat on the counter. I walked pretty quick to the kitchen. There it was. Sitting in a pool of blood, wax paper soaking it up. The words, Elk BS XXXX, elk back-strap from last fall. I don't know. Don't get me wrong, I unwrapped it. I smelled it. I mean, I kind of smelled a fart, but that was about it. There were no flies or nothing flying around. The air was warm, the meat was warm, but I don't think it was ruined. My heart jumped a little bit. Not everything was lost. The problem, though, is that I was super exhausted. There was no way I was going to make a roast right now. Or anything resembling a roast. The only thing I could think was to slice the meat into thin strips and fry it in bacon grease. I mean, I don't think that I could have put it back in the freezer, or the fridge. I was afraid of getting sick from it.

And that is what I did. Don't get me wrong: I didn't get sick from it, I cut it up and fried it in bacon grease. Sliced it up, even. I think it took me like thirty minutes to do, but I was fading fast. Between the heat and comfort of being home, the smell of cooking food, and the beer I was drinking, I was entering some sort of state of euphoria. I fried all the meat, both sides. Well done. I put it on a plate. Sprinkled salt and pepper on it. Took it into the living room with a fresh beer, laid down on the couch, my coat still on (don't get me wrong, I never took it off), turned on the television, chewed a few pieces of meat, and who knows what next, but I was out cold before I even had a chance to open my fresh beer.

I know you think I am being dramatic, but hear me out: when I woke up, Kevin was standing in my living room. Just standing there. Looking at me. I wasn't surprised for some reason. I think I must have been dreaming about him or something. I mean, he was just staring at me. I wondered if that is all this dude ever did. Stare at things. I sat up on the couch. Wiped my mouth. Took the beer from the coffee table. Opened it. Took a drink. It was warm, but I was thirsty. It was dark out now. Kevin was lit by the television screen. I reached over and turned on a lamp. At this point I could see he had company with him. A girl. Don't get me wrong, I think she was about my age, Kevin's age. Kind of short. I thought she was pretty, whatever that means. We looked around at each other for a little bit. I picked up a piece of meat and started chewing on it. Drinking the beer some more. Eventually I said:

"Hi, Kevin."

"My name ain't Kevin. Your jackass friends were fucking with you, homey. My name is Seneca Michael Miguel. Get your shit, we have some unfinished business."

"Yeah, okay. Hold on. I should get some things."

"Make it quick."

Seneca Michael Miguel said something to the girl in Spanish. Don't get me wrong, I don't know Spanish. I mean, I think Miguel is Michael in Spanish, but I could be wrong. But when he addressed her it sounded like he was calling her Goil. Maybe Gayle, is Goil Spanish for Gayle? Is there a Spanish version of Gayle? That seems really weird to me. But whatever. I got up off the couch. Took my half-empty beer and drank it all. Grabbed the plate of meat and went into the kitchen. I dumped the meat into a plastic bag I found in a drawer. I put the bag of meat in my coat pocket. I found a bottle and filled it with water. I went into the fridge, grabbed a hunk of cheese and a couple beers, put everything in my free pockets. I made sure I had my gloves. I was wearing my stocking cap still. I searched around and found some matches and my head lamp. I went into my bedroom and grabbed a pair of socks. Suddenly I was overflowing with shit, so I found a backpack, and dumped everything in it. I went into the kitchen. Put the bottle of water inside. Zipped the bag closed. Went into the bathroom. Took a piss. Brushed my teeth. Which seemed weird, but now there was a girl involved, so. I spit out the toothpaste. Drank some water from the faucet. Flushed the toilet. Turned off the light. Went into the bedroom. Turned that light off. Then the kitchen. Turned that light off. Went over to the lamp. Turned the lamp off. Grabbed my keys. Put them in my pocket. Grabbed the remote. Turned the television off. Goil fumbled for the doorknob. Opened the door. Seneca Michael Miguel followed. I turned the lock on the doorknob on the way out. Checked that it was locked. Followed Goil and Seneca Michael Miguel to a truck parked on the street. Single cab. Brown. Chevy. I think. Seneca Michael Miguel got in the driver's side. Goil got in on the passenger side. Scooted to the middle. I got in after she did. Seneca Michael Miguel started the truck. It was very loud. Put it into drive. We drove away from my house. This time, though, I brought the meat with me.

Don't get me wrong, I am acting like I knew this would happen. I didn't know this would happen; I just had a feeling that this thing wasn't over. So put that in your bong and take a rip. This whole thing seemed fishy from the get go. But what can you do? Such is life.

The ride back to the cabin was more pleasant than the first time going there. Seneca Michael Miguel had some nice tunes playing. Sitting in the front seat was less bumpy. Goil smelled nice. Seneca Michael Miguel was less intense, I guess because he was focused on driving, and not focused on stabbing me. Our tracks from before were covered in snow. Meaning the road was slightly more slippery. But Seneca Michael Miguel was a good driver. Plus, I was now in charge of opening gates. So I got to stretch my legs. And this time I was neither hungry nor thirsty, and even if I was, I had something to eat and drink. I still couldn't figure out why it was me that they kept bringing along on this mysterious thing that involved digging up a grave site behind a cabin in the mountains, but what can you do? Am I right? It's nice to be included sometimes. Specially since how shitty things had been going.

It'd been a bummer of year. All the oil fields got closed down. The only field work was closing orphan wells, which was easy work if you could get it, but you had to have seniority to get that shit. I was on my second year being a pipe donkey, which made me the equivalent of a busboy in the grand scheme of things. A shop steward. If you want to put it in construction terms. My only job was to clean up messes, and move pipe around for other guys that knew what to do with pipes. Don't get me wrong, I wasn't lazy. I worked hard enough. There just wasn't any work around anymore. Between Alaska, Texas, and fracking, Wyoming gas was inefficient, so like all good capitalist endeavors, when shit wasn't drawing in all of the money, the oil companies just picked up and went elsewhere. Leaving a huge pile of shit for whoever else to clean up after them. And I had no interest in moving to Alaska, or Texas, or Pennsylvania, for christsake. So for the last year I have been putting around Casper, hoping for a new boom, eating my savings, starting to get pretty freaked out that nothing would change. And frankly, things didn't look like they would change any time soon. What can you do? Even the politicians stopped talking about gas and oil. And when those slimy birds stop dropping, you know it's about time to get the fuck out of the mine.

All I am saying is that I didn't mind when Chaz asked me if I was interested in this thing. I was interested. Mostly for the money, but mostly also for something to do. Things were starting to get real dank around here. I was getting pretty sick of dart night at the Rendezvous, with all the asshole orphan jockeys calling me Donkey. Buying all the Red Bull and Jaegers. Like I can't fucking afford a four-dollar drink.

Don't get me wrong, I kind of can't at the moment. But that is no reason to rub it in my face. I mean, those orphan wells are going to dry up too, and then they will see who buys who drinks all night. Me, that's who.

The annoying thing is that Chaz is a pipe donkey too. But nobody calls him Donkey. My guess is because he can't hear so well. That is why he is so quiet all the time. I found this out at one point, but I never told anybody. But he can't hear so well, so I think it is hard to give him shit. Because you have to be sensitive to be given shit. Otherwise, what is the point? If you don't react. You don't give a plant shit because what will a plant do? Cry? You can give a dog shit, or a cat; they will react, but not a plant. You see what I am saying? I mean, that is my guess why they don't call him Donkey and they do call me Donkey. Even Chaz calls me Donkey. Don't get me wrong, but I think I need to get out of this scenario. But the money is so good, but the money has dried up, but this thing, with Bronzer, and Chaz, and Seneca Michael Miguel, and now Goil. My god! What is life?

Sorry, I went a little sideways there. My point is, don't get me wrong, I mean. When we pulled up to the cabin this time there were lights in the cabin. Flashlights. Seneca Michael Miguel had turned the headlights off before we got to the fence. I am not sure if he suspected something like this, or he just wasn't sure what we were coming into, but this is what he did. He turned the truck off. We just watched. I am also not sure why the people with the flashlights didn't hear us coming, but they were acting like they didn't. Or maybe they didn't care. But the flashlights kept moving around the cabin, looking like they were looking for something. Seneca Michael

Miguel reached up and switched the overhead lamp off before opening the door and getting out. He reached into the side pocket of the driver's side door and grabbed something. I assumed it was a flashlight. It might have been something else. Everything was very dark. Aside from the moving flashlights in the cabin. I think I saw Seneca Michael Miguel climb over the fence. I opened my door as quiet as I could, to try and hear things. I heard footsteps crunching in the snow. Then I heard a clanking noise. Followed by a flashlight shining directly at the truck. Someone yelled "Oh shit!" A gun went off. Two beams of light ran off into the woods.

At this point I froze. Then I acted. I ran to the fence, and had a very hard time getting over it. I got tangled, fell to the ground. I tried to get up and run into the woods after the flashlight guys, but I immediately got lost, and the snow got really deep. I turned around and went back. Seneca Michael Miguel was opening the gate. He got in the truck and started to pull forward. He stopped. Turned on the lights. Saw me. Rolled down the window and yelled, "Shut the door, homey!" I walked to the passenger side and shut the door. He drove past me. Then he yelled back through the window, "Shut the gate, homey!" I shut the gate.

Seneca Michael Miguel left the lights on. As well as the truck. I went to the passenger side and opened the door. Reached into my bag and grabbed my head lamp. Goil sat still in the middle of the seat. I turned my head lamp on. Shined it at the cabin, then shined it at Seneca Michael Miguel. He was looking at the footprints. A pistol was in his right hand. He waved me over with it. I went over. He told me to shine the light into the trees. Nothing. Just tracks. I asked him if he thought we should follow them. He said he didn't know. "Give me a second, homey." After he thought about it for a second, he decided we should wait. There was no blood on the snow, and if we followed them now, they would probably wait for us, and brain us the first chance they got. It was better let them get themselves into trouble first, then we would have the upper hand. I got the impression that Seneca Michael Miguel didn't have any desire to follow whoever it was that he had just shot at into the woods in the middle of the night. And frankly, I didn't either. It took very little convincing to go into the cabin and start a fire, maybe get our bearings, as he called it, and check on things in the morning.

This time in the cabin was nice. The fire started easy. It warmed the place up really fast. Seneca Michael Miguel had a cooler in the back of his truck. I helped him bring it in. The thing was full of food and cold beer. He also had a lantern that he lit, and a little jukebox that ran on batteries. That connected to this little thing he had that held songs. It was nice hanging out. But I got the feeling we were being watched. Don't get me wrong, that is pretty dramatic, but damn, Seneca Michael Miguel just shot a pistol at some people that were poking around in his family's cabin, for what reason I can't tell you, and they also just ran into the woods, going where, I can't tell you, and how the hell did they get here? I can't tell you, so maybe I was being paranoid, but shit, you tell me.

I don't know. We stood there drinking beer. The three of us. Next to the stove. Seneca Michael Miguel was not relaxed. I wasn't either. Goil looked really freaked out, but was trying to hide it. Nobody said anything. Nobody looked anybody in the eyes. We were all trying to be quiet. Jumpy. Trying to decide if this noise or that noise was a mouse, or somebody sneaking up on the cabin. Seneca Michael Miguel locked the door of the cabin. Just in case, he said. Trying to be nonchalant. I was glad when he did this. I was thinking what he was thinking what Goil was thinking: I wish the windows had curtains. They did not. And instead of looking for something to cover the windows, Seneca Michael Miguel just turned the gas down on the lantern saying "We should probably conserve fuel, homey."

Hear me out. I mean, don't get me wrong. The night was long and nerve-wracking. At least this time it was warm, and kind of comfortable. Goil slept in the bed. Me and Seneca Michael Miguel slept on the floor. This time there was blankets. The mice were the same troublesome. And this time every sound made one of us jump, thinking the burglars were trying to get back into the cabin. Seneca Michael Miguel slept with the pistol in his hand. On his chest. Ready for any trouble that may come our way. I had to piss in the middle of the night, but I dared not get up, so the last few hours of sleep were restless. I think the other two were having the same problem, because I heard a couple of moans here and there. I guess I assumed they were piss moans. Maybe those guys were doin' it, but if they were, they were being real quiet about everything. Some time after the moaning noises, Seneca Michael Miguel got up and put another log in the stove. I looked at where Goil was when the door opened, and the light from the burning logs inside shined out. She looked pretty asleep. Maybe she was faking, but it didn't matter. The cabin stayed warm all through the night.

We got up when light started coming in the windows. I put another log in the stove. Went into my bag and took a drink from the water bottle. I took a piece of meat out of the meat bag. I chewed on it as I stood next to the stove, warming my legs. After that I folded my blankets and put them back on the stack where they came from. Seneca Michael Miguel did the same. Goil made the bed. Nobody really talked, but I think Seneca Michael Miguel was thinking what I was thinking. Namely: should we go follow the burglar tracks? I walked over to the window and looked out. It had snowed all night. Lots. The tracks were gone. That was that. I said out loud, "It snowed, the tracks are gone." Seneca Michael Miguel came over to the window, looked out. Said, "I guess so, homey." He went over to the cooler and opened the lid. He dug around for a while, and came out with three tubes of something wrapped in tin foil. He threw one to me. Handed one to Goil. Started unwrapping the last one he was holding. I did the same. They were bean burritos, with pork chili. Pinto beans. They were something else. My meat chunk turned into a hockey puck in my mind. By comparison. I wolfed the thing down. Afterwards I wadded the tin foil, and put it in my coat pocket.

After breakfast, Seneca Michael Miguel started looking around the cabin. I think he was trying to figure out what the burglars were looking for. There wasn't many places for things to be hidden. Aside from all the wooden planks that made up the interior, but the burglars didn't look like they were prying up wood slats, well not from the way they were shining their flashlights all over the place. After a while Seneca Michael Miguel gave up. Kind of shrugged his shoulders, and said:

"Yo, I don't know, homey. Maybe they were looking for that paper Chaz had in the glove compartment, ya know, the grave map."

"Yeah, what was that map?"

"It was a grave map, homey."

"Yeah, I understand, but why did Chaz, and Glazer have it, not you?"

"I don't know, homey, you tell me."

"Why would I know?"

"I don't know, why did they bring you with them?"

"Why did you bring me with you?"

"I brought you because they brought you, homey."

"That doesn't make sense, what good am I? And why did you bring Goil this time?"

"Who the hell is Goil, homey?" I pointed to Goil. "Her name ain't Goil, weto, where did you get that?"

"Well, I mean, don't get me wrong, I heard it from you. How you talked to her."

"Man, homey, what is with you naming people you don't know? It is kind of weird, don't you think?"

"Sorry for livin', I just thought..."

"You don't know anything about the grave map?"

"I don't."

"Then why the fuck did I bring you here, homey?"

I didn't answer because I knew he wasn't asking me. He seemed kind of pissed. I thought he might stab me with something. He turned to Goil, and told her the whole conversation in Spanish. She laughed when he got to the Goil part. Then they both looked at me like they might just murder me for fun. Seneca Michael Miguel grabbed the cooler. This time without my help. Lifted it. Looked at me, and said, "Start bringing firewood out to the grave you were digging last time. I will meet you back there."

I started carrying logs to the back. Stacking them next to the grave I had attempted to dig last time we were here. I took maybe five trips before I wondered where Seneca Michael Miguel and Goil were. When I found them, they were sitting in the truck drinking something out of cups that looked like it was steamy. I am not sure how they got a warm drink, but somehow they did, the jerks, and not only that, but they didn't want to give me any. Whatever. At this point I was getting warm, so I took off my coat and lugged about six more armloads of wood back to the grave. Which was pretty much all of it, except for the stuff that made it inside. When I dumped the last armload, Seneca Michael Miguel showed up alone, carrying a shovel. He handed me the shovel. Said, "That stuff you already dug should come out easy, homey." It did not come out easy. Easier than the first time, but the ground was still frozen. When I got to the bottom where I had stopped chipping frozen dirt chunks out, Seneca Michael Miguel said, "Come with me. Bring the shovel."

He led me into the cabin. Opened the stove and told me to get the coals, and put them in that bucket right there. I did it. I carried the coals back to the grave. He had me dump them in the grave. Then we laid logs on top of the coals. It took a little while, but soon we had a fire going. When the fire got good, we added more wood. We kept adding wood until the whole grave was filled with logs. Then we stood there watching it burn. Eventually I started to get cold on my back. My front was really hot. But I had been sweating from all the grave work. I went back to the porch and got my coat. I looked over at Goil, sitting in the truck. She looked cold. The truck was turned off. I gave her the sign to roll down the window. She didn't. I think because the windows were electric. Instead, she opened the door a little. I said, "There is a fire out back. Fuego. Out back. Warm." I felt really stupid. I mean, fuego means fire in Spanish I think. For all I knew she could speak English, and that Goil thing from before was just a ruse. She nodded and shut the door. I went back to the grave.

The fire was really going now. I mean, don't get me wrong, but what was Seneca Michael Miguel thinking? Sure, the fire would heat the ground up, but then what? We were making a furnace in that grave. By the time we could get back into it, it would be frozen again because we would have to wait until tomorrow morning. I don't know. Maybe he had a plan. Maybe I was being stupid for thinking what I was thinking. But this thing that Chaz got me involved in was turning into a clown show. I mean, how the hell did I become the lynchpin to the whole operation? Two days ago I was just a guy thawing some meat out on a counter, do you know what I mean? And today I hold all the clues. Don't get me wrong, but this stinks.

We stood there watching the fire burn for a while. Eventually Goil showed up. She was shaking. She warmed herself by the fire. Looking at Seneca Michael Miguel for a while. Then she would look down at the fire. Then she would look at me. Which made me nervous, so I would look down at the fire. Then she would stop looking at me, look at the fire some more, then look at Seneca Michael Miguel, then the fire, then me. I had no clue what she was up to. Eventually I couldn't take it anymore, so I decided to go explore, and see if I could find some burglar tracks, or some sign of what they were up to. I walked into the woods. Looking for broken branches, or footprints. I found neither. I walked down hill, thinking that is where they might have come from. There was nothing that indicated that that is what happened. I found a clearing, and scanned the surroundings, looking for a road, or a trail. I found neither of these things. I gave up and went back to the fire/grave.

Seneca Michael Miguel was getting impatient. The fire was burning too slow. At one point he took the shovel, and tried to dig some logs out of the grave. The results were not good. The shovel he brought had a handle made out of fiberglass. When he pulled the thing out of the fire it was bent at a horrible angle. Useless now. He got so upset that he threw the thing into the fire and stormed off. He was gone for a long time. Me and Goil just stood there. Staring at the shovel, kind of melting, kind of catching on fire. After some time Seneca Michael Miguel came back. He was carrying a large metal pole, the kind you would use to move large rocks. The kind that farmers carry around in the beds of their trucks. Also, people who do a lot of driving on shitty dirt roads. Which I guess Seneca Michael Miguel was one of those types of people. He didn't seem like a farmer, but his truck looked like it went "off-road" quite a bit. Or was meant to. Judging by the tires and the sound of the engine. I don't know what his plan was with the prybar, and guessing on the fact that he just collapsed his shoulders when he got to the fire, he didn't either. It was hopeless. Even if we could get the coals out of the grave, there is nothing we could do about it. We either go back to town and get another shovel, or I don't know what, start digging with our hands? Stab our way to the goods with the pry bar? Don't get me wrong, I am not trying to be funny here, there was just nothing doing. Seneca Michael Miguel shouldn't have tried to dig out the burning logs with the shovel.

We stood there looking for thirty minutes at least. Seneca Michael Miguel was dumb with confusion. I mean, we couldn't fill in the hole again, and we couldn't dig when the fire burned out. Not only that, but there was burglars around. I watched him think about this, over and over. Finally he said:

"I hate to say it, homey, I gotta head back to town. We are fucked without a shovel."

"Yeah, okay, let's do it. We can be back in time for dusk. I don't know, maybe we can get some lights or something. That lantern in the cabin."

"No way, weto. You stay here. Guard the grave, homey."

"Oh, fuck that. You can't leave me here, I'll freeze. We burned all the wood. And what if those burglars come back!"

"I don't know what to tell ya. You're staying here. There's woods all over the place. Get some branches or something. I will leave the cooler. You can drink beers."

"I don't think so."

"Oh, but I think so."

Seneca Michael Miguel made a motion that reminded me that he was carrying a gun. Don't think I am being dramatic, because I swear this is how it happened. I mean, don't get me wrong, I was screwed.

I walked him and Goil to the truck. Took the cooler out of the back. Put it on the porch of the cabin. Went back and opened the gate for them. Watched them slowly bump down the road. I closed the gate. I said out loud, "You better come back, you fucker."

Part 3

Like an idiot, I immediately started looking for branches in the woods to bring back to the cabin. Don't get me wrong, I wasn't an idiot for getting branches, I was an idiot for blindly following Seneca Michael Miguel's suggestion without insisting that they don't leave me behind. I mean, what was I doing here? And now I was trapped. It was getting dark already, and who knew what the burglars were up to. Before long I had a pretty good stack of branches piled on the porch. I supposed I had enough to get me through the night — that is, if I had to stay through the night. I guess I was hoping they would be back in a few hours, but something told me I would have a lot longer than a few hours to wait.

For some reason I went and checked on the fire in the grave. It was a nice bed of red-hot coals now. Two feet deep, I supposed. Don't get me wrong, but I was curious about what was down there. I stood there looking for some time, warming my hands. I took a piss on the coals, thinking it would be funny. A bunch of steam came up. This gave me the great idea of taking the bucket I used to carry the coals over, and filling it with snow to dampen the fire. After about twenty trips to the woods, I successfully put the fire out. But now the bottom was just a big wet mess of coal and ashes. What good did that do? Now it was dark out. And there was no way to dig any deeper. Not only that, I had made it so instead of having some ashes to dig through when they got back with another shovel, I think I just added about six inches of ice we would have to chop through when the water froze overnight. I was beginning to think this thing that I got tied up in was forcing me to me make some pretty idiotic decisions.

I mean, things were starting to fall apart. It took a while for me to stop feeling embarrassed for dousing the fire with a bunch of snow. I was feeling like a teenager that did something stupid, waiting for Dad to get home and be pissed about it. I quit standing there and went back inside the cabin. I was getting pretty cold.

I dragged some of the branches I had gathered into the cabin thinking I would light a fire. Now I felt almost more dumb. All the branches I gathered were large branches. Too big to break. There was no ax that I could find. So instead of making a fire like normal, I had to stick the ends of the branches in the stove and burn them by their tips. With the door open. Which was not what the stove was designed to do. The branches burned badly, and the cabin didn't get very hot. Plus it was smoky. Plus there were like four feet of branches sticking out, that kept tripping me up whenever I tried to move around.

I lit the lantern. Which was nice for light, but then it burned out about five minutes later, and I couldn't find any more fuel. I went to get a beer from the cooler, but there wasn't any. Just empty cans and melted ice. There wasn't any more food, either. I remembered I had packed some beer in my bag, so I took one out. It was warm, and foamed all over my hands when I opened it. I took a meat chunk from the meat bag, and chewed on it. Drinking my warm beer. Straddling the branches sticking out of the stove. This was really turning into a nightmare.

Not to be dramatic, but the wind started blowing. At one point the door flew open because of it. I got so freaked out I dropped my beer. By the time I found it, under the branches sticking out of the stove, it was empty. I threw it into the stove, and went and closed the door, locking it. I went and straddled the branches again, slowly chewing my piece of meat. Staring at the lousy fire barely doing anything in the stove but smoke. I couldn't believe it. Three nights I was spending in this cabin. For what? And now I was stranded here. What if they didn't come back? What if the burglars came back? I mean, was I going to have to walk back to town in the morning? I would be lucky to make it to the highway by nightfall if I left first thing.

In a fit of nerves I ate the rest of my meat from the meat sack. This caused my stomach to rebel. Suddenly I was in a panic. I looked around for some paper, and grabbed a newspaper that was lying next to the stove, and ran out the front door. I got a few feet, and dropped my pants. The results were explosive. And gross. The newspaper was not very absorbent. More like smearing. Unpleasant. I did my best, don't get me wrong. But my best wasn't very good. I stood up; my ass hurt. I pulled my long johns and pants up. I sighed.

In my panic I hadn't noticed how much snow was coming down. Giant flakes. They were sticking to my eyebrows. I turned into the wind and got a mouthful. It was really coming down. I made my way back inside. A sinking feeling overwhelmed me. This was not good. I took the headlamp out of my backpack, and tried to get the fire going better. I dragged all the branches in from outside. Trying to find small sticks to burn. I did get the fire going better, but not for long. The branches were pretty wet, it turned out. I made more smoke than fire. Not to be dramatic, but don't get me wrong, I had to open the door to let the smoke out. Which just made it cold in the cabin. And because why not, my headlamp stopped working. I have no idea when I had last changed the batteries in it. I had to make a choice: the smoke or the door. I chose the door. I took the smoking branches out of the stove and threw them outside. I closed the door. Locked it. Any embers that fell on the wooden floor I stomped out. And that was that. No fire. I went over to the stack of blankets, and gathered as many of them as I could in my arms. I stumbled my way to where I thought the bed was. I found it with my shin. I laid all the blankets on top of the mattress, or so I thought. I got into the bed. Boots and coat on. As well as my stocking cap. I layered the blankets on top of me, and stared into the darkness, listening to the wind, and the silence of the snow falling. I could smell Goil's hair on the pillow. This made me feel like a pervert. I tried to avoid it, so I turned on my side. Now I smelled something gross, like sweat and saliva. I turned back, deciding that a good smell was better than a bad smell, even if it made me have thoughts.

The mice came out in force. I could hear them rummaging through the meat bag. I tried to throw something at them, but it didn't change anything. I spent the night half asleep, half awake. Dreaming of meat, and snow, Goil doing that thing where she stared at stuff. But she would turn into Bronzer too, the way that he stared at me in the mirror. In the morning I was exhausted. But at first light, I jumped out of bed and ran to the window. I couldn't believe what I saw. There must have been three feet of new snow. The fence was gone. I opened the door. Snow was piled halfway up the threshold. I said "Fuck," and shut the door. A large amount of snow fell off the roof.

Landing with a thud on the porch. Heavy snow on snow. This was not good.

Don't get me wrong, but this was a disaster. I mean, I don't mean to be dramatic, but this sucked. Even if Seneca Michael Miguel and Goil were coming back, they couldn't get up the road. And even if I left now, there was no way I was getting down. The cabin was freezing. I decided to try my luck with the fire again. Now that there was light, I was able to navigate it a little bit better. I got something a little less smoky going. There was this thing on the pipe going up that I yanked, that made more air leave the stove, so that helped. I mean, it helped so much, that eventually the cabin got hot. And the smoke went away. Which was good. But now my pile of branches looked pretty measly. Even if it burned slow because it was wet, it wouldn't last very long. And the branches I dragged out in the night were under three feet of snow.

Not to be dramatic, but I was really at a loss here. I was hungry, so I looked in the cooler again. Still nothing but empty beer cans and melted ice. My meat bag was chewed to bits by mice. There was nothing in my back pack except a bottle of water, and one beer. My lighter worked. My head lamp didn't. The cabin really had nothing in it. Except blankets, and a bed, and a stove. I didn't panic though. For whatever reason. There was really nothing I could do. I mean, I guess I could start walking, but where? Down the road? I couldn't even see the road. And trudging through three feet of snow for what? Twelve hours, by my calculation, that was based on nothing but the fact that it took like two hours to drive up here? I mean, I was going to die, not to be dramatic, but there was no other option. There was nowhere to go, and there was nothing to do. My only hope was that someone would show up at some point with food, and hot cocoa, and a ride back to town. Don't get me wrong, but I wasn't holding my breath.

During the morning I was pretty optimistic, for some reason. By midday, it started snowing again, and I had burned through half my branches. I decided it was in my best interest to try and go out, and get some more wood. I pushed through the snow, which was up to my waist. I found the fence. I tried to get over it, but I couldn't. There was a pine tree within reach. I was able to peel off a few tiny branches, but that was it. I went back to the cabin, holding the branches in my hands like they were worth something. I had somehow locked the door behind me. I tried to kick it in. I couldn't. I just couldn't get the leverage. I kicked enough snow out of the way to make my way to the window. I was able to break the window, but not in a good way. I could climb through, but in the process, I would have cut a hole in my guts because the glass broke in a bad way. I spent twenty minutes digging through the snow, looking for the branches I had thrown out the night before. When I finally found them, I was able to knock all the glass shards loose so I could crawl in. Now I had an open window, and my branch supply was the same as before. Well, I guess I had the new branch from the night before. And after I got back inside, I went back outside and dug around for the other branches. I found a few. But because I was digging around in snow for so long, I was beginning to shake. My hands were frozen, and my gloves clanked when I finally stood next to the fire to warm up.

Don't get me wrong, I was able to put a blanket over the broken window. It kind of helped. There was less wind coming in, but it didn't really help with the heat. I stood there with a blanket on my shoulders staring at the fire. The cabin getting colder and colder. I took my boots off and put my extra pair of socks on. I put my boots back on. This helped my feet. But not much else. I was now very hungry. Sad that I had eaten all my meat chunks. I looked in the cooler again, hoping for new results. I got the same results. I looked in my backpack, hoping for a peanut, or something. I found nothing. I didn't know what to do. I pushed the branches sticking out of the stove further into the stove and got into bed. Covering myself in as many blankets that I could find. Not to be dramatic, but I started to cry. I was in a pickle. A cold, hungry pickle. With no end in sight. I cried with no end to the depths of how sorry I felt for myself. How bad my luck was, how I could never catch a break. How I would die here, all alone with nobody caring about me at all. Just a guy, trying to make ends meet when the economy really let me down. A pipe donkey, woe betide.

Don't get me wrong, I was feeling pretty spooked. There was no way out of this mess I was in. Not to be dramatic, but there wasn't. I drank the last beer that was in my backpack. A pork chop in a can, they called it. They, meaning my friends, when I was younger and would get hungry when we were out in the hills drinking beer. I'm hungry, I would say. Have a pork chop in a can, someone would always say. This happened enough times that I started filling my pockets with jerky, or peanuts. There was always something annoying about being told to drink a beer when I was hungry. But if I did bring snacks, I would have to share them because my friends were hungry too, they just didn't want to admit it. People are jerks. Eventually, I would just sneak a peanut into my mouth now and again, when no one was looking. The jerky was harder to conceal. The smell and the chewing. Eventually, also, I just gave up on the idea that I would have something to eat when drinking beer in the hills. It was just easier that way.

The beer made me drunk. It tasted really good. It warmed me from the inside. The good feelings didn't last very long. The drunk wore off, and I had to piss.

I opened the door and just started peeing on the snow. Still standing inside the cabin. I heard a noise. At first, I thought it was just my urine melting snow, then I stopped pissing. What sounded like a hum was actually an engine running, way off in the distance. I didn't know what to do. Was this a good noise? Was it coming this way? I stood there looking in the direction it was coming from. Not the road, but down and out towards the meadow I had seen earlier the day before. I saw a flash of light, then darkness. Light again. The noise got louder. It sounded like a motorcycle, but stronger. Part of me knew it was a snowmobile, but for some reason I couldn't think about that, I could only picture somebody on a motorcycle, driving through three feet of snow. I guess maybe because there was such a delay in noise. Loud, kind of, with lights, then a kind of chunk noise, and the lights would disappear, then silence, then the engine noise again. I thought about hiding, but there was nowhere to go. I guess I could go bury myself in the snow somewhere, hope whoever it was wouldn't come looking for me, but maybe it was Seneca Michael Miguel and Goil coming back to save me. This seemed unlikely, but what did that mean at this point? The whole thing was unlikely. Just being here was unlikely. Being part of this scheme was unlikely. Being trapped like this was unlikely. I went back into the cabin, and shut the door, to wait. Hoping that whoever it was that was coming had some food.

It was a good ten minutes before the snowmobile was on top of the cabin. It had stopped near the fence, or it sounded like that's where it stopped. The engine turned off. I could hear two male voices talking to each other. They must have been wearing helmets because their voices were quite muddled. I mean, don't get me wrong, I don't know how clearly I could have heard them in normal times. I mean, I was inside the cabin, but the amount of silence going around at that moment, I think I would have heard them pretty clear if they were speaking in normal voices. They weren't that far away, and I had broken the window, so I could hear outside pretty good, even if there was a blanket covering the hole.

They talked for a while. The engine on the snowmobile started up again. Instead of them driving to the door, they turned around. I breathed a sigh. Relieved. But then the engine turned off again. Followed by absolute silence. Then the sound of someone pushing through three feet of snow. Like swishing horses. I don't know what swishing horses sound like, but that is what it sounded like. Like a horse, but with swishing. The sound got closer and closer. I went to the blanket-covered window and peeked out. I could see light, but I couldn't see what was coming. The window was at the wrong angle. I panicked and yelled, "Seneca! Is that you?" The horse swishing stopped for a second. Then it started up again. Now I was really trapped. I didn't have a plan. I grabbed one of the branches out of the stove, and stood there pointing the smoking end at the door, waiting. The noise got closer. Still closer. It was just outside the door. Then it stopped. I was about to yell something again, something that maybe would do a trick, like pretend that there were more people in the cabin than just me, but the door opened slowly. I was too terrified to make any noise. A flashlight shined at me. Directly into my eyes. Before I was blinded I saw two forms, both wearing black coveralls, and black shielded helmets. I don't know if it was fear, or the lack of food, or what, a warm beer on an empty stomach, but everything around me got really far away. I remember giggling, then I don't remember anything else.

I woke up on the floor of the cabin. Alone. The branch was still in my hands. Smoking. The door was open. A horrible breeze was blowing in. I used the branch to push the door closed. I stood up and put the branch back in the stove. I could see puddles of water all over the cabin. The light from the stove really brought them into contrast with the floor. I guessed that these guys were the burglars from before. Still looking for whatever they were looking for. Maybe they found it this time. I don't know. The cabin was dark. Not that I would know any better if the cabin wasn't dark, but it did look like they had had a look around. The bed was turned over. I could see that. It looked macerated. I could see that too. Which meant that they must have sliced up the mattress with knifes, or something. They didn't leave me a sandwich, which was poor form on their part. Don't get me wrong, I know I'm a card, but I wish they would have left me a sandwich.

I really had no idea what to do. I crammed as many branches that were left into the stove, made the bed right, put the mattress back on it, draped all the blankets on top, and got under them. I decided to try and sleep until morning came. Maybe I would follow the snowmobile tracks to get out of here. I seemed to remember from being younger that you could walk on snowmobile tracks. But then again, I was about a hundred pounds lighter if I remember the memory right. But whatever, what else could I do? If I stayed in the cabin, I would starve. And unless tomorrow was a spring day, full of sunshine and heat, there was no other option but to pull myself up by my bootstraps, and attempt to do the impossible.

The rest of the night came in a fever. Dreams of food and scary men in black suits. Scratching noises with toes with long nails reaching under the door. An old man pacing back and forth on concrete. My parents in another room that I couldn't get to. I kept trying to cut a bowl of hay into pieces big enough to fit into my mouth, but when I finally could get mouth full, I couldn't chew it because my teeth were getting in the way. I would try and chew through my teeth, but they were too hard, and because I was taking too long to eat the hay, it would rot, and I couldn't eat it because I would get sick. Then I would give up, and try and get some business done, but I would get distracted by the old man pacing back and forth on concrete, sticking his long toenails under the door. It was a nightmare that I was glad to be done with when light finally came through the one window that wasn't covered with a blanket.

I got out of bed. Looked around. I was cold. I could see my breath. I draped a blanket over my shoulders. The puddles of water from the burglars were frozen into ice. There were a few branches left that I was able to use to make a fire again. The fire was pretty lousy. But it made me feel better for a second. I warmed up a little bit. The sun was out. Not that it was warm.

Just kind of mocking me. I went outside to look at the burglars' tracks. They had gone around to the back and spent some time at the grave that I had dug up. It was obvious they didn't have a shovel. It looked like they had dug snow out with their hands before giving up. This must have been the last thing they did, because their tracks led to the place where their snowmobile had been. I followed the tracks all the way there. Maybe tracks isn't the word, maybe it is trenches. Trench. I could see that they got back onto the snowmobile and cruised off into the distance with it. Following the trail that they came in on. I found out, to my great pleasure, that I could in fact walk on their snowmobile tracks. I don't know why I didn't just start walking at that moment, but I didn't. The lure of the grave was too much. I think. What the fuck was down there?

By accident I found a cache of branches that was off to the side of the snowmobile tracks. By accident, I mean, I saw that there was a cache of branches off to the side of the snowmobile tracks that I could drag back to the cabin. I spent a good hour dragging branches back to the cabin.

After I dragged all the branches back, I took a break and drank some water from the water bottle in my backpack. I was hungry, but there was nothing I could do about that. I went around the back of the cabin and looked at the grave some more. There was something down there, I swear. There must be, right? I tried to figure out how to get down to the bottom of the grave, and get the goods. At first I just kicked at the snow that the burglars had tried to dig out. Then I really got into it. The next thing I knew, I was waist deep, shoveling handfuls of snow out. Kicking things into balls, and packing them into chunks. I got so sweaty that I took off my gloves and my coat. This immediately backfired when I got so shivery that I couldn't zip my coat back up, or put my gloves back on. I panicked and went back into the cabin. Luckily the fire was still coals, and I was able to get a few new branches burning. I slung a blanket around my shoulders and stood there shaking. I felt pretty stupid for a while. But then I got hot again. I added some more branches. Suddenly the cabin was warm. The burglars' frozen footprints started to melt. I started to pull myself up by my bootstraps again. Next thing I knew, I was waist deep in the grave again.

This time I got all the way to the bottom. I found the ice I had made the day before. Why was I so stupid yesterday? I didn't know what to do. I was cold again. The sun was going down and I was in the same exact position that I was eight hours ago. My stomach was rebelling, but there was nothing I could do about it. I dragged myself out of the grave. Thinking I would go warm myself, and think about how to move forward.

The cabin was dark and frosty. The fire was a whisper. I added some branches— luckily they caught fire. The sun was going down. I had just burned through another day. As much as I wanted to, I couldn't leave now. What the fuck? I thought to myself. I even said it out loud, "What the fuck!" Why did I just waste another day on this bullshit? Now I was truly starving, and there was no way to get out of here.

Don't get me wrong, I mean, I stood next to the stove with a fog hanging around my head. I was stupid to be involved in this scheme, but somehow I now wanted to be involved in this scheme.

❄

The night flew by. Kind of. I slept like a goon. There were all sorts of dreams I couldn't keep track of. Mostly about food. Or people showing up. Or people showing up with food. Or people showing up with better, warmer fires. Shovels. I dreamed I made it down the mountain. I dreamed I made it down the mountain, then somebody gave me a ride back up. I dreamed it snowed to the moon. Then I dreamed all the snow melted, and it was spring. I dreamed I was able to dig down, and discovered the goods in the grave. Then I dreamed I was trying to dig through concrete. Then the sex dreams with Goil involved. Then dreams about Bronzer looking me in the eye from the rearview mirror. The most lucid dream was where I dreamed I was still at home, asleep on my couch with an alarm going off in the background. That dream woke me up in a cold sweat. I guessed the mice caused that one, because they were really going to town when I was awake enough to know where I was. Eventually I wore myself out with dreaming, and fell into a deep sleep until light came through the window.

I got up and got the fire going again. For some reason I looked in my backpack. I was so hungry. I just wished for something. Anything. Not to be dramatic, but to my surprise, I had missed the chunk of cheese I had packed in the backpack — I don't even know at this point, two days ago? That was the tastiest piece of cheese I had ever eaten. I tried my hardest to ration it, but it was just so tasty. It wasn't that much cheese, but it filled me with energy I hadn't felt in years. I became optimistic and focused. I ran outside to check the weather. More snow. Still snowing. I turned around. Went back inside. Shut the door. Still optimistic. I spent an hour sorting branches. I poked around in the mess the burglars left. Some of the bedding could be burned or shoved back into the mattress. They had left their knife behind for some reason. I put it with the stack of useful stuff I was compiling. My headlamp that needed batteries. My backpack. My bottle of water. Matches. Papers. I guess that was it. I opened the cooler, hoping to find food. Nothing. The empty beer cans seemed like they might be useful, so I put them in the pile. Or near it. They were wet. I dumped the water in the cooler out the door, and left the lid open to dry the inside out. I searched the cabin up and down for things of use. I was getting confused about the cabin. It was useless. Usually cabins like this are used for temporary shelter during the winter or fall, like for hunting, and longer use in the summer when people wanted to get away, or whatever. But this one really had nothing in it. Just the stove and the bed. Normally there would be some food, or dishes, or a chair, or anything, really. Not even an ax. But whoever's cabin it was, they did cut wood for it, at some point. I mean, we burned all that wood, but somebody did that, for some reason. And there was the lantern, but I couldn't remember if Seneca Michael Miguel had brought that, or if it was here to begin with, but there was no fuel for it, which would suggest that Seneca Michael Miguel brought it, but by that logic, he must have brought the logs that we burned in the grave, and I know that he did not bring those because I personally hauled all of them to the grave from the porch of the cabin. So there is that.

Don't get me wrong, the day was starting to drag on. The cheese energy was gone, and I was hungrier than ever. I had that knife, and I was racking my brain as how that would help me get some food. Maybe I could stab a mouse or something. Go cut down some berries from the pine trees. I couldn't remember if pine trees had berries. I think some of them did. Could I eat pine cones? I mean, pinyon nuts, right? This made me think of junipers — those are the pines with berries, I think. I decided to go outside, and try and chop down some pine cones, and eat the nuts. I mean, the snow was just getting higher, I thought this maybe would help me reach higher in the trees.

I put the knife in my pocket. I mean, I wasn't stupid, I wrapped some paper around the blade first, so it wouldn't cut a hole. I trudged through the snow until I came to the fence. With some snow rearrangement I was able to get over the fence. I pushed on. I found a tree that looked like I might be able to get some pine cones from. I couldn't reach then though. I shook the tree. Nothing came down. I tried to climb the tree, but I got nowhere. After a bunch of trying a pine cone finally fell down. I stared at it for a while. It was not the kind of pine cone I was expecting now that I think about it. I took it back to the cabin. My hands were frozen, as was my entire outfit. I sat the pine cone on top of the stove. I took off my gloves, and put them on some sticks near the fire to dry off and heat up. I took the knife out of my pocket. I took the paper off. I held the now-warm pine cone in my hand. It looked more like a pine stuffed grape leaf than it did one of those big dry pine cones I was hoping to find. It was green as much as it was brown. I stabbed at it with the knife for a while. Peeling things back. I chewed on it as well — my fingers were useless with the sticky delicate leaves, I guess you would call them.

The further I dug in, the less I found. There were no nuts in this pine cone. There wasn't even a seed, as far as I could tell. I had just wasted an hour of sunlight on this bonehead idea. I was mad at myself for a second, but then I thought, What the hell else would I be doing right now? I chewed on some of the pine cone leaves thinking they might have some nutrition, but they tasted so bitter, I thought I might be poisoning myself, so I spit them out. I gave up on that idea, and tried to think of something else.

Don't get me wrong, there was nothing else to think of. I could stab a mouse, but for some reason I never saw any mice in the day time. I could hear them at night, scampering around, and I could feel them crawling on the blankets I was under, but I never saw them running around. I crawled around on the cabin floor, looking for holes, or droppings, or places they would be living, but I didn't find anything promising. Eventually I gave up, and just kind of stood there, hoping one would come out of hiding, and let me stab it. No mouse ever showed up.

Some time went by, and I looked out the window. Still snowing. The window with the blanket over it was letting snow in, so I spent some time trying to cram the blanket in the gaps of the wood of the cabin walls. This became fruitless and irritating, so I gave up. I sat on the edge of the bed for a while. The sound of the fire crackling was making me anxious, so I got up and paced around. Then the sound of my footsteps on the wooden cabin floors was making me anxious, so I just stood there as far from the fire as I could get. The sound of silence was making me anxious, so I went back to the bed, and sat down again. Then the sound of the fire started to make me anxious again. So I stood up and started pacing. I did this cycle over and over again. Until I literally felt insane. I needed to get out of here. I packed everything of use into the backpack. The empty beer cans included. I left the lantern behind, and folded a blanket, and stuffed it in, careful not to crush the beer cans. When I was unsuccessful with not crushing the cans, I had to take everything out, put the blanket in first, then put everything else back inside. There was the knife, wrapped in paper, so it wouldn't slice everything up. The bottle of water. The matches. The papers. The empty beer cans. A few of them would fit. The head lamp that needed a battery. I put the backpack on. I threw a blanket over my shoulders, and over the backpack. I walked out of the cabin and towards the snowmobile tracks that the burglars had left behind.

The trench the burglars had left was filled with snow now. Fresh snow, but I could see where it went. I followed it. I found the snowmobile tracks. They were hard under the new snow, but not solid. I could take a step, pray my foot wouldn't drop down, my foot would drop down, then I would take another step, pray my foot wouldn't drop down, my foot would drop down. I did this for about a hundred yards, or so, or so I assume, because I took about 100 steps before I gave up. This was pointless. I was both sweating and freezing at the same time. My gloves were rock hard. I couldn't feel my toes. I knew better than to take my coat off, but I got confused as to whether I should leave it on or unzip the front. I kind of spun around and looked at the sky. Falling down into the snow. Snow falling faster now than before. I thought about just staying there and giving up. I mean, not to be dramatic, but what was the point? I was getting nowhere fast, and nobody was coming back to get me. Even yesterday when I spent the whole day trying to dig out the grave, where was that going to get me? Suddenly, like a bolt of inspiration, I realized something, I had the knife! I could cut down into the grave with the knife! How stupid was I being this whole day? And now, by the time I got back to the cabin it would be too dark to do anything. What a fucking idiot I had been!

I stood up with new inspiration and focus. Optimistic even. I followed my foot holes all the way back to the cabin with ease. I dropped the backpack on the floor, threw my gloves off. Sat down on the bed. I took off my boots. My socks. It was quite difficult, because my fingers were nearly useless, but I did it. I stood by the stove in agony as my body regained circulation. But I was okay with it, because of this idea about the knife. Just one more day, I thought. Just one more day, I can get down into that grave, get the goods, it will change everything. Then they will have to come get me, right? If I have the goods? They will need me. Right? Yes, I know I am right. If I have the goods, they will have to treat me right.

That night I held the knife in my hand while I slept. I was determined to stab a mouse. I mean, don't get me wrong, the idea of eating a mouse was repugnant, but I was really hungry. And I remembered that book about that guy in Canada that ate all those mice when he was watching wolves or something, and that is what they ate, so he ate them too, just to prove that you could eat mice as a staple in your diet. Or whatever, I was sure I could eat a mouse if I had to. And, not to be dramatic, but I was at the point that I had to.

I fell asleep thinking about the first job I ever did with Chaz. We were working over by Otto on the Lundgren line making sure the pipe ditch could maintain integrity. He had been working for Wyoming Gas about a week, I think I had been there a little over a month. But it was hot as shit, mid-July. We both had shovels in our hands, a gallon jug of ice that was melting, next to us, on the ground. The dirt was dust. He kept coughing. It was late morning.

The idea was to put the dirt/dust under the pipe we had just laid, in a way that would allow for any runoff water from flash floods not to create craters. I mean. I guess this was the idea. The only thing I ever heard about what was being done and for what was this guy, White, yelling at me to "Cram the dirt, you jack-ass, that pipe can't bend!"

We spent the morning together. Shoveling dust under pipes. Burning. Getting yelled at. He kept saying stuff under his breath that I was sure would get him fired. But I learned later on that nobody can hear shit on the pipeline. Chaz included. But I think he came that way. Maybe he had wax in his ears? It doesn't matter, I am just sayin'. Had White heard the shit he was saying, he would have been canned, first thing. Shit, they probably would have come to punches even. I mean, White was an asshole, for sure, but Chaz was out of line. Money-wise. I mean, he was hired to take the abuse, I guess. I mean, that is the way that I saw it. Take the abuse for the check. Work, as it is. What kind of job do you do where some asshole ain't spewing shit at you all day for a few measly bucks? I know I ain't had one.

Don't get me wrong, I wear muffs. On my ears. I can't stand the loud noises. But you can't not hear shit when you are working the line, it's like war times out there, so I always had the one ear off, which sadly means I got this one bad ear, but shit, it is better than two bad ears like the rest of these assholes. But that is not my point, my point is that Chaz kept talking shit. And it wasn't good shit, it was just shit. Like White would come over and say something like:

"You missed that divot."

Then Chaz would say something like:

"I got a divot for you."

And that would be that. White wouldn't hear him. I would though. Then we would smile at each other. Shake our heads, go back to work.

The work would start very early in the morning, and we would be done by three. At which point the whole crew would head to the bar in Greybull, the Branding Iron, get drunk for hours, and then go crash at the Antler Hotel. Wake up hungover as shit, around four in the morning, and do it all over again.

We did this all of July, and most of August. Chaz and I became friends. Cramming dust in the day, playing darts after work. Shooting stick whenever someone else on the crew had an inkling. Hoping some of the local tail would take a liking to us. Not to brag, but I got lucky a couple of times. Kind of. I passed out both times before anything could happen, but I was able to bring them back to the hotel room with me.

Sadly, I ended up with an empty wallet both times. When I woke up, alone, my alarm blaring three-thirty in the morning, I never told anyone. But something told me this happened a lot. We were easy marks. For some reason they paid us in cash. I think it was for this reason. They knew we would lose the money, which would force us back to work. The guys that didn't get drunk every night were the guys in charge, and I don't think it was because they didn't drink. I think they just drank in their hotel rooms, alone, watching television or something. Knowing there was Oil Bunnies pick-pocketing all of us suckers who had nothing else going in their lives. But, whatever. I didn't really mind. I still remember the two girls naked in my hotel room, even if we never did it, I still have that memory. I mean, I maybe had two hundred dollars in cash that they stole. Peanuts. And frankly, they were always nicer to me afterwards than beforehand. So what? Win some, lose some. Right?

That summer, me and Chaz became friends. By the end of it, he would come over to my room after the bar and drink whiskey and beer, smoking out the windows, or chewing tobacco. Spitting into empty bottles of Mountain Dew. Listening to music on the hotel television. Getting so hungover that we would puke in the morning. Then all day, cramming dust under the pipes. Getting sunburned. Frozen gallon jugs of water slowly melting in the blaring sun.

I mean, that was one thing nice about the hotel, they would freeze our gallon jugs of water for us, have them waiting on the check-out counter at four in the morning. The names written on them in marker. You were fucked if you forgot to drop the jug on your way to the room. On your way up. After getting drunk. It was serious enough that there was a guy, Humphreys, that you could pay to remember to do that for you. 20 dollars a pop, if you thought you might get too drunk to remember. Which kind of happened a lot. But it was worth it. But whatever, I digress. I wanted to tell you what I was thinking about when I fell asleep that night. With the knife in my hand, waiting to stab a mouse. I was thinking about how me and Chaz ended up in Casper.

Donkey

Part 4

Don't get me wrong, there wasn't much to the story. I had been living in a town called, Buffalo, just over the mountain from Greybull. Chaz was from a town in Montana called Livingston. Both of us were sick of having to travel all the way to Casper every time there was a job to do. My car was a hunk of junk that I always expected to break down on the interstate. His commute was grueling. Like six hours. Neither of us had any reason to live where we were living. And since we became quick friends on this Greybull job, we decided we would be okay roommates. One night when we were drinking Red Bull and Jäger in my hotel room, Chaz, as drunk as I have ever seen him, spitting chewing tobacco into a Mountain Dew bottle, most of the spit ending up on his chin, had said:

"Fuck it. Let's just get a place together in Casper. The money we would save on gas alone would make it worth it."

He passed out on my floor that night. Nearly got fired the next day for being so hungover. I think the only reason he didn't get fired is because White thought it was hilarious how many times he threw up during the day. I wasn't doing much better, but compared to him, I was in tip-top shape. Plus, I was never much of a puker. I wished I was. Just purge and get it over with. Sadly, no dice. They called me Iron Gut for a long time before they called me Donkey. I mean, they started calling me Donkey when I switched crews, but for some reason my nickname didn't come with me. Even though it was mostly the same people. I mean, not the same people from the one crew, but the same people that called me Iron Gut, like at the bar, and at the shop, or wherever, were the same people that started calling me Donkey when I became a pipe donkey. I could never figure out why this was, if maybe they hated me, or liked me. I mean, Iron Gut lacked the simplicity of Donkey, so maybe they were all just lazy, and sick of having to make any effort to say my name in the first place. Donkey was much easier. I guess. Don't get me wrong, I have no idea. The thing you have to understand about an oil crew is that there is no real loyalty. Just money and work. You could work for six months with the same five guys and know absolutely nothing about them. Then one day, the work was over, and you never see a single one of them again. I mean, that, or you move to Casper with Chaz, and get a two-bedroom apartment on the outskirts of town so you can save some travel and gas money.

The thing though, don't get me wrong, I mean, I was in fact, not, Iron Gut. I might not have puked on the job site like everyone else, but my guts were not as solid as the nickname would suggest. I just had a different exit strategy. Which involved some complicated maneuverings and some very close calls. Especially after a heavy night of chewing tobacco and Red Bull and Jägers.

We got an apartment, though. Chaz and me. Two-bedroom. On the outskirts of Casper. It had a yard and brown carpet. We scored a couch and some other junk from driving around in Chaz's pickup truck. Drinking Icehouse and listening to classic rock on our days off. Everything kind of smelled, but we never cared. You could smoke in the apartment, so the smells never really made a difference. Chaz felt really rich once and bought an entertainment system that took up much of the living room. Television included. I had a few things that

I brought from my old place. Like a microwave. I slept on a mattress on the floor in my room. Chaz spent his money on a giant water bed. Which I think he thought would lure in the ladies. But I don't think it worked. I mean, I know it didn't work. Every time I saw him tell some girl that he had a water bed, they either didn't care, or were grossed out by the idea. He was clueless about it, though. He would tell them it was heated. It was like sleeping on the ocean. Very sensual. The girls would either ignore him or just walk away. I liked Chaz, so I wouldn't give him shit about it, but it was hard to watch.

We hung up some posters in the living room. Bob Marley. 311. We would work when there was work. Days off we would drink all day. Try and start parties. Which usually meant going to the bar, and dragging people back with us. This didn't usually work. Not at first. Then crystal meth came to town. Then all we needed to do was buy a couple bags, and suddenly half the bar was begging to come over. That got old pretty fast when things started to disappear. Luckily neither of us really had much taste for the stuff, so instead of going out to the bars, we just started hanging out alone at home. Watching movies on the giant entertainment system and getting drunk. Sometimes there would be a couple guys from work that would come over, but for the most part, we became low key. Working around the state on the same crews, when there was work, and hanging out at home in the off times.

Don't get me wrong. We did this for a year. Things were fine. Then I got transferred to another crew and started hauling pipe, and Chaz started dating this girl, Lorinda, who was this redhead that was nothing but trouble, and things started going downhill from there.

Lorinda was a maniac. Half Native American, half Irish. She must have been bipolar. Half the time she was walking around the apartment naked, trying to start some shit, then the other half of the time, she was screaming at Chaz, throwing bottles at the wall, pacing back and forth. Chain smoking cigarettes. Then they would go into his room and fuck as loud as possible. I mean, don't get me wrong, he finally found someone that loved his water bed as much as he did, but as a couple they were a pain in the ass.

It didn't help that we now had different schedules. I would go away for a week, and when I came back, he would be out on a different job. Lorinda would be there. No way to blow off her steam. Take it out on me. I would get up in the morning. Or whenever. Making some breakfast, or whatever. She would come out naked. Do some weird squat at the fridge. Look at me. Take a cucumber out. Then, whatever. It was too much. I would have to stop cooking, or doing whatever. Go into my bedroom. Do whatever. Then she would be standing in the hallway saying, I just watched you whack off, you sicko. I'm gonna tell Chaz. Then Chaz would come home. She would tell him. Chaz would get pissed off at me. I wouldn't know what to say. Lorinda would be standing there, smiling. I mean, don't get me wrong, I couldn't deny it. But it drove a wedge in our relationship. He requested to change crews so he could be on the same crew as me, so he could keep an eye on me, so I didn't try and bone his gal. I don't know how many times I had to tell him I had no plans to bone his gal. He never believed me.

About a month after Lorinda had moved in, I found myself moving out. I took my mattress and my microwave and moved across the tracks, to the apartment I was living in now. I don't know what to say. Don't get me wrong, but I couldn't be more happy about it. Lorinda is a menace. I don't think me moving out solved that. But that is what happened. And that was about eight months ago. Chaz didn't bring it up when he was standing there eating a hot dog behind Glazer's truck a few days ago. Thank god. But as far as I can tell, they are still together. More power to them.

Don't get me wrong, I had a reason for thinking about this relationship with Chaz while I laid there in that macerated bed, holding a knife, waiting to stab a mouse. It occurred to me that maybe Chaz was fucking with me. This whole thing, the frozen grave, Glazer, Seneca Michael Miguel, Goil, the useless cabin, like maybe this whole thing was a ruse as payback for Lorinda catching me beating my meat after she did that thing with the cucumber crouched naked in the kitchen while I was making breakfast. I mean, Chaz could be an asshole pretty good. And he was very passive aggressive, I mean. He was the kind of guy that would put my dirty dishes under my blankets if I didn't do them in his timeframe. This caused a couple near-miss fist fights. And there was that time I ate one of his slices of pizza without asking. He didn't flush the toilet for a month. Huge greasy shits included. Don't get me wrong, this ruse would be pretty elaborate for him. He really didn't use his brain that way, ya know, there were a lot of moving parts to consider. But who knows? Revenge can make virtuosos of us all.

I mean, it wouldn't be that hard of a trick though. To pay Glazer some money. Seneca Michael Miguel and Goil could easily be paid off. It wouldn't be hard to borrow somebody's cabin. The only two things that seemed hard, or hard to manufacture, was getting me to go along with it, which, it turns out, was not very hard at all, but the two burglars. How did they fit into the mix? Kind of a crazy detail. Maybe the thing was real. Maybe there was some goods in the bottom of the frozen grave marked Miguel? I didn't really think this all the way through before I fell asleep. It was a fitful sleep. I kept waking up whenever I heard a mouse scamper around. I would stab into the blackness and bring nothing back. I got up a couple of times to stoke the lousy fire. Add a branch or two. Then get back under the covers. Knife in hand. Shivering. I really needed to get some more wood. But more important was food. I really needed some food.

Don't get me wrong, the night went on forever. Around what seemed like the middle of the night I heard the sound of an engine. This time it didn't take me very long to understand that it was a snowmobile. I got very nervous. At first I was brave, I guess, I mean, my plan was to get the hell out of here, so I hatched some plan to attack the burglars with the knife, demand the coveralls and helmet of one of the guys, and get the hell out of there on their snowmobile. I stood there ready by the front door for what seemed like hours. The snowmobile came closer and closer. It stopped where it stopped before. But the burglars never came in. I could see lights out the back window. What sounded like a shovel digging. I thought about sneaking around to try and ambush them, but that idea was too far-fetched, even for me, in my desperate state. I waited for some sort of sign to let me know what to do. From god, or whatever. Then the lights went out. Silence. I was suddenly so scared I was shaking violently. I heard a creak. I couldn't turn around. It felt like tiny spiders climbing up my legs and then my back. My tongue was swollen and I wanted to scream. Then a flash of light. Then darkness.

I woke up in a pool of blood. The fire was out. The floor had puddles of ice everywhere. Like the burglars had been poking around again. I peeled my stocking cap off my head to see how much blood there was. There was a lot. I touched the wound. It wasn't as bad as I thought. I had a headache. It must have been late morning because the light seemed like the light you would get late morning in mid-January. I mean, don't get me wrong, this is just what I was thinking. I don't think I was using any real logic. It was late morning.

Don't get me wrong, I was confused. I looked around to see what signs the burglars left after they brained me. Nothing seemed out of place. But, here's the thing. One thing was out of place. I had a fit of genius the day before, or was it two days now? I left the lid to the cooler open so that maybe a mouse would smell the food that was once inside, those tasty burritos that Seneca Michael Miguel had brought. The mouse would jump inside to find the food, and then wouldn't be able to get out. I knew it was stupid, but at the time I was convinced it would work. Whatever. The lid to the cooler was now closed. I opened it slowly, thinking that maybe a mouse jumped in, and upset the cooler, and the lid fell down, and I would get a tasty furry treat. Instead, what I found was two zip lock bags with sandwiches in them. Someone had written Donkey on them. In marker. Now I was positive that Chaz was fucking with me.

I stared at the sandwiches for a while. Trying to decide if they were poisoned or not. Eventually I ran the thoughts through my head that led me to the conclusion that, they were either poisoned or not, but I was starving, and until I could think of a way to get down from this cabin, I would starve to death before I would figure it out. Therefore, I should eat the sandwiches, because either way I was a dead man. And the sandwiches increased my chance of survival by fifty percent.

I opened one of the zip-lock bags. Examined the sandwich for poison. Found nothing suspicious. Just turkey, American cheese, iceberg lettuce, mayo, on white bread. I took a bite. Nothing bitter. In fact, the opposite. I don't remember a sandwich tasting so sweet. I stood there chewing, slowly. Savoring every flavor. I ate two more bites. Zipped the bag back closed. Put it back into the cooler and shut the lid. Suddenly I was Popeye, with his spinach. I got the fire going again. My branches pile was not nearly as decimated as I thought it was. I got pretty warm. Pretty fast. I then went out back to look to see if the burglars had dug up the goods or not. The grave had about four inches of new snow inside of it. I jumped down, into the grave, and felt around. It seemed like there was some sort of chipping away at the ice on the bottom, but not much. I got out of the grave, and went to look at the snowmobile tracks. They were covered in snow as well. I tried to walk on them, hoping they would hold me. This time was there was a little more resistance, but I still fell through. Defeated by this, I looked around for a couple hours. Finding random branches that I could reach. Dragging them back to the cabin. There was a point when I noticed that some of the fence posts were sticking out. I don't know why I thought I could do it, but don't get me wrong, I was able to pluck a few of them out of the snow, like grey rotten teeth. All I had to do was wriggle them back and forth a few times, and they came right out. I don't know, I guess the u-nails that were holding the barbed wire had either rusted out, or the wood was so rotten, that they didn't stick into it anymore. Either way, I had plenty of wood to last me for the near future now. And I still had that sandwich and the other half-sandwich to eat.

By the time I was done with all of this, it started snowing again. I went back into the cabin. Stood by the fire, looking. Trying not to think about the sandwiches. I did, however, rack my brains about what the fuck was going on. Why the fuck was Chaz fucking with me? I mean, don't get me wrong, but this was torture. Am I wrong? Who does that? I mean, I didn't really do anything wrong. It's not like I tried to hump Lorinda. All I did was get turned on, and privately rub one out. I mean, she was the one that watched me do it. Without consent, mind you. She was the pervert, not me. Any normal dude would have taken her actions as an invitation to get freaky. I didn't get freaky, I just took care of business, and tried to get back to making my breakfast. But I said this before, and I am saying it now, if you know what motivates someone, you know their soul. I was having trouble knowing either of those things with Chaz.

I decided I could eat the other half of the first sandwich when the sun went down. Then I would cut the second sandwich into four parts. Eat two of the parts tomorrow, and if needed, the other two parts the next day. I mean, don't get me wrong, but the jig would have to be up at some point. Am I right? I mean, Chaz and Glazer would show up at some point, tell me I had learned my lesson, we would all have a good laugh, and then that would be that. They would ferry me down the mountain on the snowmobile, and I would be lying on my couch again, eating a chunk of meat, falling asleep with the television on. A cold beer getting warmer by the minute. No cares in the world.

Don't get me wrong, I tried to be okay with this logic. But something snuck in. I was suddenly inundated with inertia. My legs and arms felt like sandbags. I felt trapped. I screamed out. Why! I don't know how to describe it. But it felt like pure panic. I felt trapped, claustrophobic. I mean, this was on one side of my thinking. On the other side, I was still very interested in the frozen grave, with goods down below the ice. If only I had a shovel, I could dig myself into fresh air, glory! Boot straps! There was something down at the bottom of that grave! I just knew it!

I waited for the sun to go down the way a dog waits for his bowl to be filled. Starving, uncertain. That maybe this bowl of food would be my last. When it got dark enough I couldn't stand it anymore, I went over to the cooler, and got the leftover half of the first sandwich. I opened the zip lock bag, and just smelled it for a while. The smell reminded me of a job that me and Chaz did for Wiliston Basin. After we moved to Casper, but before the incident with Lorinda and the cucumber.

Don't think I am being dramatic, but that summer was the hottest summer ever. I must have spent a fortune on sunblock, and I still got sunburned almost every day. All of us did. I mean, it was kind of gross, but every night, after work, we would congregate at the work trucks. White would show up with a cooler full of beer. We would stand around, with our shirts off, peeling dead skin off each other's backs. Mortified. And in the morning, the opposite ritual, we would stand around, drinking coffee slathering sunblock on each other's back. That part was a little erotic. More than once I noticed a few boners bulging out of the greasers. One guy in particular, I won't name names, but his bulge was something special, and during these rubdown sessions, he would make everyone nervous with it. I think because of the vastness of the gourd nobody gave him shit. But I do wonder about how close we all came to having a good ol' fashioned gang bang. I mean, the cool lotion on our tender backs, combined with the manly hands rubbing them down, and that damn summer sausage busting at the seams of the guy's greasers, I don't know. Don't get me wrong, I don't think anything would have happened, there was some dumb hetero code that everyone followed, but I don't think it would have taken much to set some spark off that would send us all down into an erotic explosion. A circle jerk, at least. I mean, everyone wanted to see the thing, but nobody had the balls to ask.

I guess what I am getting at is, I got really tan that summer. Don't get me wrong, that is not my point, but I guess I was just trying to explain how hot it was. We were staying at the Wheels Inn. Which was a motel. There was one bar in town. Stockman's. Which we could walk to from the motel. Most nights it would be just us in there, and the bartender. Loretta. Who was not very attractive. I mean, this wasn't a beauty contest, but the amount of attention she got from all of us, well, it was a lot. But she had no trouble fending us off. I think it was some sort of game. Both to her and to us. To see who could sleep with her. Not a single one of us even came close. Well, that is not true, one of us did in fact sleep with her. I will give you one guess who it was. Don't get me wrong, but what's the saying? If everything is a game, go for the trophy? Something like that.

I guess what I am getting at is: that's not my point. We drank there every night after work. There were seven of us on the crew. White was the boss. Me, and Chaz, and four other goons. They were calling me Donkey at this point. I had just been promoted. Chaz was still cramming dirt. That kid Humphreys replaced me on the line. Which pissed Chaz off because the kid would never shut up. Even when it was so hot you could puke, he would say stuff like: Hot enough for ya? I thought for sure that Humphreys would end up dead, but I think because it was so hot, Chaz didn't have the energy.

Don't get me wrong, the Wheels Inn didn't have a large freezer like a lot of the hotels we stayed in, which meant that we couldn't get our gallon jugs of water frozen, but it did have three ice machines that we would all use to fill our coolers to the brim with every day. Saving space for lunch and bottles of sports drink. And bottles of water. And sun block. That was kind of the best. An ice-cold bottle of sun block was a game changer. Whenever you were feeling sick, just slather on some of the good stuff, and suddenly you could think straight again. It never lasted long, but for a moment, everything was alright.

Normally I would make myself turkey sandwiches for lunch. White bread. Turkey. American cheese. Mayo. I would make two of them every night after work, before I would get in the shower. Put them in zip-lock baggies. That way when I got too drunk to do it later, I wouldn't forget. I would put them in the fridge. Then I would take a shower. Usually a cold shower, at first, but then I would need to turn the heat up on the water to get the grime off. The hotter water always sent my loins into overdrive. Because my back and arms were so raw from the sun. Half the time I would spank it. Thinking about the only girl in town, Loretta. I mean, I feel like I shouldn't have mentioned her looks before, but I was trying to illustrate a point that she wasn't as attractive as it would seem, judging by how much she got hit on, but she wasn't unattractive. Don't get me wrong, that just makes me seem even more crass by saying that, but my point is, I don't even know. When you spend every waking moment with a bunch of gross dudes, there is usually one thing you think about when you are whacking off in the shower. And in this instance, that one thing was the bartender, Loretta. Who wanted nothing to do with you.

I mean, I am no looker myself. I doubt that Loretta was going home every night, and tickling the bean to the thought of me. I think she was married. I know she lived the next town over. But whatever. That is not my point. I mean, don't get me wrong, I just feel like I am not explaining something correctly. My point is, I would rub one out in the shower, and then put on a different pair of pants. I would leave my greasers on the floor of the bathroom. Gathering creases. Smelling like oil and leg sweat. I would put sunblock on all the places I could reach above my belt. Put on some fresh socks. A fresh t-shirt. Crack open a beer that I had in the fridge. Turn on the television. Find nothing to watch. Turn the television off. Mess around with the clock radio until I found a song I liked. Either throw in a chew or step outside for a cigarette. I would usually avoid the cigarette because there would be at least one or two other people standing outside their rooms smoking. Meaning Humphreys or Earl. Both of whom were lousy talkers, that would try and lure you back to their rooms for a drink before going to the bar. And if you fell for it, you would regret it. Humphreys would always have terrible drugs that for some reason you would do, and then spend the night high as shit, and would wake up the next day totally useless, because you could drink like a horse. Or if Earl sucked you in, you were stuck listening to his new rap records that were uncomfortable to listen to in a motel room in Wyoming. Both out of place and somehow racist.

I mean, sometimes I didn't mind going into Humphreys' room to do drugs, but Earl's room was always too much. He was the kind of guy that saved his money to go to Vegas and buy a pick-up truck that had bullet holes in it. Because supposedly someone did a drive-by to it.

Don't get me wrong, I don't even know. I would put my boots on at some point. Check the time. Decide it was a good time to hit the bar. Make sure I had my wallet, and my smokes, and my room key. Walk over to Chaz's room. Knock on his door. Yell: You ready? He would come out. Wearing cowboy boots, and a button-up shirt. Clean pants. Shiny belt buckle. Clean hair. Fresh teeth. I would shake my head. Every time. Then for some reason I would say: Looking good, Hollywood. He would smile. Then we would walk over to the Stockman's together.

Don't get me wrong, the place would be the same every time we walked in. White would be sitting at the bar. Half-drunk, drinking Seven and Sevens. Chain-smoking cigarettes. Humphreys would be shooting pool, talking shit. Earl shaking his head at the ball he just missed. Hind-Dog and Saggy would be playing darts. Hind-Dog clearly winning. Saggy claiming Hind-Dog was cheating somehow. Someone would yell: Donkey! Loretta, behind the bar, would look up. Some lousy rock and roll tune would be coming out of the juke box. Me and Chaz would go sit down at the bar, close to White, but not next to him. Loretta would come over. Say: Hey huns, what'll it be? I would order two Coors. Pay the five dollars. Leave two dollars in tips. And just like that, the night would start.

Don't get me wrong, we did this every night for five weeks. All of July and one week into August. I mean, on Fridays we would all go to work with all of our shit, clothes, coolers, and stuff, then head back to Casper right after work. Stopping in Shoshone to get a twelve pack of beer for the last hour and a half of the ride. Which was not permitted in the company trucks, but we did it anyway. The road at that point was so straight, and so boring, that it was worth the risk. There were two trucks. White drove one. Hind-Dog drove the other. Neither of them drank beer, so it wasn't really that big of a scandal. But then we would get to the shop. Move our shit into our own cars. Trucks. Head home. Spend the weekend doing whatever. Then come Monday, four in the morning, we were back in the parking lot. Cranky and tired.

I don't know what to say. I was trying to talk about a sandwich, but this other stuff keeps getting in the way. I mean, don't get me wrong, I was standing by the stove smelling a sandwich, and then it made me think about this other sandwich I was eating this one summer outside Basin, Wyoming. What can you do? Am I right?

It was lunch time. The middle of July, I think. But lunch time didn't mean noon or anything, it just meant when we ate lunch that day. That day, lunch was about 10a. I was sitting in the shade of one of the work trucks. Shirtless. Chaz was sitting next to me. Shirtless. I was eating a turkey sandwich. Chaz was eating a peanut butter and jelly sandwich. He was upset because the ice in his cooler had melted, and the water had crept into his sandwich baggie, making his sandwich soggy. I mean, Chaz was prone to fits, but this one seemed kind of extreme. I think he was on the verge of tears. He kept saying: Why is my luck so bad? I can't catch a break. Then I would say: C'mon man, it ain't that bad. Then he would take a bite of sandwich and spit it out. Shake his head, then say: Why is my luck so bad? I can't catch a break. I felt sorry for him. In a way. I also was annoyed that he was so upset. I took my pocket knife out of my pocket, and cut my sandwich in half. I gave him one half. He looked at me with doe eyes. Half smiled. Said thanks. Slowly chewed on it. I then realized he wasn't upset with the sandwich at all. The dirt we were sitting on was dry dust. Both of us were wearing baseball caps. Sunglasses that fit snug around our faces. It was hot enough that we both felt gross in our bones. Well, I assume that he felt the way I did. The badlands spread out in front of us for all the miles between where we were and to where the mountains started.

There was a storm brewing about 100 miles away. I was hoping it would hit us, and we could stop working for the day. We were friends enough at this point that I asked him what was up:

"What the hell dude, you alright?"

"Yeah, I'm fine."

"Like hell, you're acting like that pb and j was going to be the end of you. Your grandma die or something?"

"Oh, bullshit. Why you gotta be analyzing shit all the time, Donk? Ya know that shit is annoying, right. Ask anyone."

"I'm annoying? You get all waterworks about a sandy, and I am the annoying one? And since when do you call me Donkey?"

"Oh, I don't know, if the shoe fits."

"Are you pissed that I got promoted? I mean, shit. You want the job, take it, I don't need the extra headache. Fuck it. I mean, I give you half my Tasty Turkey Surprise, and you treat me like an asshole? I may not know exactly where to tell you to get off, but I think I have an idea of where you can start."

"Fuck your sandwich. I didn't ask for it. So don't give me that shit."

"It's not about the sandwich, dude, I don't give two shits about the sandwich, dude."

At this point I was pissed off. And now, frankly, I was pissed about the sandwich.

"Well, leave me alone. Who asked you anyway?"

"Yeah, well. Enjoy. I'm gonna go twist tread. You can have your crybaby time alone."

"Don't let the door hit your ass."

Don't get me wrong, but I have no idea why this conversation went through my head when I stood there smelling the sandwich. I will tell you that it made me feel hot. Like all around me hot. Not my body hot. But like everything around me was hot. From the outside. I decided it was time to eat the sandwich. I decided to eat it slowly. To not buck the system. I was afraid I would either shit myself if I ate it too fast, or I would get a huge surge of energy that I wouldn't know what to do with. I knew I had the other sandwich for tomorrow, and I knew that in the morning I would have another opportunity to find a way out of this dilemma I was in. I guess, I mean, I was feeling pretty helpless. I mean, I had zero chance of walking down the mountain, and I had a pretty good chance of starving to death. But now that I knew that Chaz was probably fucking with me, I might not die. I guess. I mean, now I had two reasons that he was pissed at me. One, the whole thing with Lorinda and the cucumber, and then this new memory of giving him shit about having emotions. I mean, I don't know what to say. I mean, I thought we were friends. Don't get me wrong. And I always thought he was a reasonable guy. But maybe in the end I didn't know anything. I mean, he obviously had some inner workings that I didn't know about. That he never told me about. And then when I asked him about it, he acts like a big baby about it? But then for him to be such a big baby that he does this whole ruse to strand me up in the mountains to starve to death just because he is pissed at me because I asked him how he was feeling on day when we were working? It really didn't make any sense. But whatever. I don't know what to say.

Don't get me wrong, I mean, what can you do? I mean, I don't know what to say. I mean, I'm not trying to be dramatic, but after I finished the sandwich, my body went crazy. I ran outside. Shooting rope. The newspaper that I wiped my ass with came back bloody. Not because I was sick from the inside, but because I had cut my asshole with the pages. I only got this information when I went back inside and was warming my hands by the stove. The door was open. My hands were covered in blood. I sighed. Went back outside, and washed my hands with snow. I felt like Chaz all the sudden. Why is my luck so bad? I can't catch a break.

I stood there staring at the stove for a while. I guess I was thinking, but there was nothing to think about. I was waiting to be tired enough to give up on standing up. Then I could get back in bed and wait for the morning. I checked the cooler to make sure that the other sandwich was still there. It was. I smelled my fingers. Shit, and blood. The idea of stabbing a mouse seemed stupid. Now that I had a sandwich to look forward to. I stood by the stove for quite some time. Then I decided to go to bed. I went over to the door, to lock it. I decided to open it up, and see what was going on outside. Snow was coming down in giant flakes. I panicked a little. Thinking that maybe it would snow so much that the cabin would become an igloo, and I would be killed by the smoke choking me. I had that feeling of heat all around me again because of this thought. But then I felt like maybe that would be all right. This predicament was overwhelming. I was a trapped spider in a glass jar, or something. Confused but still alive. Going about my daily business. I mean, don't get me wrong, I knew I was trapped, but there was nothing that was stopping me from working. I mean, I could maybe still get to the bottom of that grave, if I wanted. I suppose. I mean, even the burglars still wanted to get down there. And if they wanted to get down there, why wouldn't I? I mean, if somebody needed to get down there, right? Isn't that the way things work? If I don't get the goods, somebody else will. Right?

I got into bed thinking about the nature of things. All I needed to do tomorrow was to work harder. Make a big splash on the scene. Really draw attention to myself. Then I could finally get ahead. Right? I made a plan for morning. Eat half the other sandwich. Go outside, and get more branches. Climb the pine trees, and light them on fire. That way somebody would know I was here. Come get me. Right? They would think it was a forest fire. Then they would send some help. Then Chaz could go fuck himself. What, with all his hurt feelings. I could meet him back in Casper, at our old place, and punch that fucker in the nose.

I won't lie, I slept pretty good that night. Thinking about revenge. The mice scampering around sounded like they were screaming, which woke me up a couple of times. I mean, I don't know why they were in duress, and I thought about trying to stab them again, but I was so bone-tired, that I just ignored the clatter. But then again, the noise made me feel hot, and I would wake up to find the door to the stove had swung open. So I would get up and close it. There was a stick in the way that I needed to deal with in the morning. But then, I don't know, I would get thirsty, and have to go over to the window with the blanket over it, grab a handful of snow, put it in my mouth. Feel better. Hop back in bed. Immediately fall asleep. Hear the clacking of the mice again. Feel hot. Get thirsty. Get some snow. This went on for a while. But eventually it stopped happening, and I ended up asleep like a baby until the first light came through the other window.

Part 5

First thing I did when I got up in the morning was to check the cooler and make sure the sandwich was still there. It was. I closed the lid and tended to the fire. When it was going again, I went back to the cooler. I took the sandwich out. I don't know how, or if maybe it was like this all along, but the sandwich was soggy. Like really soggy. I tried to cut it in half, but it just kind of melted into a mush of turkey, mayo, and wet bread. I made two mounds of it. I left one mound in the baggy, and I wadded the other mound into a ball in the palm of my hand. I ate at it like a meatball. Trying not to scarf it down all at once. I racked my brain trying to figure out if it was soggy the whole time, and because I was so excited when I found the sandwiches to begin with, I just didn't notice. I checked the bottom of the cooler for water. It was dry. The only conclusion I could come to was that Chaz was, in fact, fucking with me. This dude was getting on my nerves. Don't get me wrong, but that is some petty shit to give a starving guy a soggy sandwich just to make a point.

I went outside after eating half of the sandwich. To piss. I heard an airplane flying over. The sky was cloudy so I couldn't see it. And it seemed like it was pretty high in the sky, but it gave me an idea. I could start a huge fire and send up some signals to whoever might be able to see them. Then maybe someone would come check out what was happening. Like the fire department, or forest service, or something.

Don't get me wrong, but I had no idea how to make a big enough fire. Not with the branches I had piled up next to the stove inside the cabin. The only thing I could think of was to burn some standing trees as they were. I knew pine needles were pretty flammable. I picked a few trees that I could get to, and went inside the cabin to make a torch. I got the longest branch I could find. I decided to sacrifice some bedding to make a burning end. It took me a while to decide to cut up some of the mattress. I figured cutting up one of the blankets would be idiotic. Plus, the burglars had already macerated the mattress. I was able to find some pieces of cloth that didn't seem like they were doing much. I wrapped them around the end of the branch. I stuck the end into the stove until it caught fire. I ran to the door. At this point I realized I was being stupid because I forgot to open the door, so I had to turn around with the burning stick, which was like six feet long, in order to reach the doorknob. Luckily, I was able to do this without catching the cabin on fire, but it was close. I was in a hurry because the cloth was burning fast. But I did it. I got out the door. I ran through the snow. Trudged, I guess. Not to be dramatic, but I fell a few times. Holding the stick straight up in the air. I pushed ahead though. Trudged, I guess. I reached the first tree I thought was a good one to burn. I was impressed by how quickly it caught fire. Suddenly there were sparks a hundred feet in the air. Smoke and fire. I did this to two other trees. The scene was glorious. And hot. Coals were raining down on my head. I had to get away. From under the trees. I ran back towards the cabin. I looked up. Coals were landing on top of the cabin now. Which didn't concern me at first, but then the heat got really intense. The snow started falling off in huge chunks. Sheets. The door was covered in a mound of snow now. And the exposed roof had embers falling on it at a horrible rate.

Not to be dramatic, but I was starting to freak out. The fire was really hot, and the roof exposed itself as cedar shakes. I stood there helpless, in danger. I pushed through the snow to the back of the cabin. The three trees I started on fire started catching trees around them on fire. My plan was working, but with terrible results. Before I knew what to do, the whole cabin was naked on the roof, the snow having melted off in huge chunks. Sheets. Making a mound of snow about ten feet high completely covering the cabin. It looked like a snow mound with a roof poking out, the chimney spitting smoke. I watched the chimney for a while. Not knowing why. Then the smoke stopped spitting out, and I knew there was no air in the cabin anymore. This made me worry about the half a mound of sandwich in the cooler. I don't know why. I didn't expect the cabin to collapse, but I did think there was a possibility it would catch fire and I wouldn't be able to get back inside. Which would be a tragedy. I tried to climb up on top of the cabin, with the idea I could put any fires out. But the snow was too soft, and I just fell into it, up to my neck. I was able to get myself out, but now I was covered in snow, and as it melted, I could feel the water soaking into my clothing.

What happened next was kind of amazing. The wall of burning trees started melting all the snow around the cabin. On the ground. First there was sagebrush I could see. Their branches popping out. Then other things that had been left around on the ground. Mostly trash, like cans and plastic buckets. Then there a wheelbarrow exposed itself. Then the wheel started melting. Then the handles caught fire. Then it was just a weird-looking melted bucket. All the plastic buckets melted. The sagebrush caught fire. I stood far enough away that I was out of danger, but it was gruesome to watch. Luckily the fire moved away from the cabin because there were no closer trees to catch fire. All the snow in the front melted away leaving the door exposed. The broken window was full of snow that went into the cabin. That stayed frozen. But everything else in front of the cabin was now a sopping mess. Mud, and burned grass, and sagebrush. As unlikely as it seems, the fire exposed a shovel and an ax, leaning against the cabin, in a previously unexposed corner. Like an idiot, I tried to run over and get them. But it was still too hot, so I had to retreat. I stood there helpless, praying that they didn't catch fire. They didn't not catch fire. I mean, by the time I was able to finally get to them, their handles were black, but not burned through. But hold on, I am getting ahead of myself.

The fire burned on for quite some time. Slowly snaking away from the cabin, and down the mountain. The smoke was pretty good. I could only hope that somebody saw it. I mean, don't get me wrong, I should have thought about this more, and tried to do it when there was maybe a clearing in the weather. I mean, I don't know if smoke can go through clouds, but the way the sky was overcast, and how the fire probably only burned for like an hour, I didn't have too much hope that somebody saw what happened, and was sending out some reconnaissance. I mean, I don't think there are that many fire watchers in January in the mountains. Not like the summer. And since the huge fire I started on purpose didn't really get very far, there is probably a good reason for that. But I still had some hope that something happened, and somebody saw the smoke, and was coming to my rescue.

After the fire burned itself out, with the trunks of the trees still smoldering, I took a look around at the damage it had wrought. It wasn't very pretty. The fence was burned down. Just barbed wire lying listless in the mud. Black mangled teeth of fence posts jutting out at weird angles. I could see the road now. For about twenty feet. The cabin was steaming. Small little puffs of smoke were coming off of the roof. Which I hoped would burn themselves out. Like I said before, the ax and the shovel had black handles. I grabbed them both, but they burned my hands. I put my gloves on, and grabbed them again, throwing them in a pile of snow out back. I went into the cabin. The cooler was okay. I checked on the half-sandwich wad. It was still doing okay. The snow that came in through the broken window was annoying, and I would have to deal with that. The fire was out. But I was able to get it going pretty quick. I went back outside, and saw that it had started snowing again. I ran around finding any branches that hadn't burned. There were quite a few. Luckily. They were all wet, is why. I brought them back into the cabin. This took some time. I retrieved the ax and the shovel. Which were cool now. I brought them inside too. It had been quite the morning. I was exhausted. I looked at the mound of snow that was coming through the broken window. I sighed, but I ignored it. I needed a break. I sat down on the bed. That turned into me lying on the bed. That turned into me asleep on the bed.

Don't get me wrong, this all seems pretty implausible, but all I can do is tell you what happened, so don't hold it against me. I was asleep for some time. I am not sure how long, but the mice came back out, and their scampering screams woke me up again. The cabin was really hot, and snow coming in from the broken window was melting. I grumbled. Like literally grumbled, and used the shovel to shovel snow out the front door. This took a while, but I decided it was better than a huge puddle on the floor. This annoying task gave me another flashback to when I was working with Chaz in that summer of heat. Another reason he was probably pissed at me.

It was well past lunch one day, and nearing the end of the work day. Don't get me wrong, I was in a bad mood. The sun had been relentless, and my shoulders were on fire. I could just feel the cancer coming in. I had run out of sunblock. My job that day was to carry two-foot manifold pipes from the supply wagon to the lode junction. They were heavy and greasy, but the work was easier than the work Chaz and Humphreys were doing. Which was essentially shoveling sand under gaps in the long pipe. I did not envy them. I walked over to Chaz to ask if he had any sunblock to spare. He was in a mood. Humphreys asked me, Hot enough for ya? I said, I suppose. Hey Chaz, you got any block to borrow? He was annoyed with the job, and Humphreys, and I guess me too, he said:

"Oh! His highness needs some block?"

"Ah, c'mon man, just give it a break. My shoulders are toast."

"Yeah? Maybe you should have thought about that before. A man like you, high on the hog."

"Dude, I just want some block, you got any?"

"I got some." Humphreys shoved his shovel in the dirt. Started to walk over to his cooler.

"Knock it off, Hump, I got it." Chaz handed me his shovel. "Do me a favor, keep crammin' this dirt for me, I need to go get it." I took the shovel, and sighed.

"What's that?" Chaz seemed pissed.

"What's what?"

"You too good to cram dirt now?"

"Nah man, I just want some block, back off."

"Back off? Dick like you, just donkey pipe these days, and suddenly I am the loser?"

"What the hell, man?"

"I don't know, what the fuck. Cram some dust, and I'll get you the block."

"Fuck it, I don't need your block, Hump, hand me some block."

"You touch that block, Hump, I'll make you drink it."

"Ahh, c'mon Chaz, he just needs some block, it's hot as shit out here."

"Fuck you, Humphreys, what the fuck do you know about heat?"

"Ah man, Chaz, c'mon." I said.

"C'mon? You want me to c'mon? Cram dirt, and I'll c'mon."

"Alright, fuck this shit." I threw the shovel to the ground. "I don't need your shit, and fuck your block."

I stormed off.

Chaz and I didn't talk for a week after that. In fact, things were never the same after that. I mean, I knew he had a chip on his shoulder at this point. But this was ridiculous. Don't get me wrong, I did feel bad for Chaz: shoveling this wet, watery snow was like cramming dirt. A very thankless job. You could barely get a shovelful with each pass. The work was endless, and very unsatisfying. But that is no reason to be an asshole to your best friend. As much as I could understand where he was coming from, I found it hard to forgive him for being an asshole. Maybe I was just as petty as he was? I mean, I was doubting that now. Being stuck in this cabin like this. By his design. But whatever. You win some, you lose some, am I right?

I shoveled as much of the snow out as I could. The rest would have to find its own way out. Either by soaking into the floorboards, or evaporating, or whatever. There wasn't much else I could do. I stood by the stove for a while when I was finished. Looking at the shovel. Thinking about the goods in the grave. But I was also thinking about the rest of the food I had. That mound of half-sandwich still left in the cooler. In the zip-lock baggy. Once I ate that, I would be out of food again. I did not like that feeling. But what can you do? When life gives you soft avocados, you make guacamole, right? I was definitely feeling like a ripe avocado. A rotten one to be precise. Hollowed out and molding. My skin was stiff, but my insides were nothing but dust at this point. A wet, slimy seed of a soul, waiting around for nothing. Nothing but the garbage heap of existence. Or something. That is a terrible analogy, but that is what I felt like. I mean, avocado seeds take forever to germinate. If they ever germinate at all. And then, unless you have the perfect conditions, you will never see a fruit produced. Don't get me wrong, I am just digging myself in here, but, I mean, this is how it felt. Take it or leave it. Or whatever. Cry me a river. Get your own analogy if mine sucks so much.

Don't get me wrong, but my lousy mood improved pretty fast when I realized the thing I was overlooking. I had a shovel now! And an ax! I debated with myself for a moment about what to do. The day was almost over, but there was still some daylight left. I could go out and try and dig up the goods for a while, then come back in, and eat the rest of the half-sandwich wad, or I could wait for the morning, and eat the half-sandwich wad and spend the day trying to dig up the goods. My hunger got the best of me, so I decided to go out and see what I could get done by nightfall. I put my gloves on and grabbed the shovel. I walked around to the back of the cabin. There was still snow back there where the fire's heat didn't reach. I trudged through the snow until I got within eye sight of the grave with the goods in it. My heart sank. Not only had the snow melted on the side of the cabin that the grave was closest to, but it had melted into a little river. And that river had emptied directly into the grave with the goods in it. I had made a swimming pool out of the grave. Don't get me wrong, I didn't need a shovel, I needed a lifeguard and some floaties.

I stood there, looking. At the grave. At the swimming hole. The ice I had created before was now floating on top. Water underneath. I stabbed at it with the shovel. It was too thick to break up. And when I stabbed at it, it just went under water. Giving no pushback. I made a couple attempts to shovel some water out, but this was futile. I tried to dig around the grave, to make a ditch, but the ground was frozen solid. I was somehow even worse off than before. My mind played back the bucket melting during the fire. That would have been more useful than the shovel at the moment. I thought about getting the ax and breaking up the ice floating on the top, but that seemed stupid. But was it? I remembered the metal bucket that held the newspapers. I went back into the cabin and grabbed it. Dumping the newspapers and kindling out. I also grabbed the ax. I ran back to the grave/ swimming hole. I put the bucket down and took the ax up above my head, and slammed it down. The handle broke in half. Typical, I thought. I screamed. The sun was setting, I was running out of time. I took the bucket and started to bail water. This was nearly impossible. I had to push the piece of floating ice down before I could get a bucketful of water, which meant that I had to take my gloves off, which turned my fingers useless in seconds. I was able to get out two buckets full of water before I had to give up. I was starting to think I would never get those goods. I stood there for a while. Blowing into my hands, trying to get my fingers to work again. My fingers started to hurt, and I was afraid I had just given myself frostbite. I decided to abandon the grave until morning. Thinking that the water in the swimming hole would probably freeze overnight. And, don't get me wrong, at that point I wouldn't need a bucket, I would need an icepick.

Dejected, I made my way back to the inside of the cabin. Leaving everything there, next to the grave/swimming hole.

The only thing to look forward to was a wad of half-sandwich, and a long fitful night of bad dreams, and hunger, and frustration. I mean, not to be dramatic, but this sucked.

I stood by the stove warming my fingers. Trying to decide if I had frostbite or not. I decided that my fingers were fine. They hurt like hell. Which was a good sign, I think. Eventually I stopped thinking about them at all, so I think that indeed, I didn't have frost bite. I waited for as long as I could to eat the wad of half-sandwich. Which was about the same amount of time that my worry about my fingers turned into my worry about starving to death. It is funny how the hierarchy of danger works. I mean, losing my fingers would be bad, but starving to death is worse. But because I thought I was in real danger with my fingers, I totally forgot about my hunger. But when that danger was gone, the real danger kicked back in again. I went over to the cooler, opened it, stared at my last morsel of food for a moment, bent over, and picked it up. I can't tell you how depressing it was eating that wad of half-sandwich. I want to tell you it was delicious, but it wasn't. It was like a wet slug in my mouth. A hot wet slug. Sliding down my throat. Sliding down my esophagus. And dropping into a pit of bubbling acid. Foaming for a minute, and then disappearing into nothing. To send a few tiny particles of life racing through my veins to keep me alive for just a few minutes more. I wish I could say that I suddenly felt better. That I was energized and focused. Pacing around, thinking of my next move. But that didn't happen. I became lethargic. Broken. I mean, I guess I panicked a little with what small amount of energy I had left, but the panic did me no good. I just got shaky, and had to sit down. And much like the last time I sat down, my sitting down led to me lying down, and my lying down led to me falling asleep.

Don't get me wrong, I know that hearing about dreams is pretty boring, unless the person telling the dream had a dream about the person that is listening to dream being told by the person having the dream. I mean, I won't bore you with the details. But, my god, the dreams I had that night. None of them made sense, but if you can imagine a mouse head as large as a pumpkin screaming in your face for hours on end, then you can understand how disturbing they were. I would wake up, and try to punch the mouse head. There would be nothing there. The fire either burning, or needing to be tended. Then I would fall back asleep. Then I would be going along, dreaming about this thing or that, then the mouse head would appear again, screaming. I would wake up, and punch it. Punching nothing. I would sigh. Look around. See what was up. Either get up, and tend the fire, or go back to sleep.

This went on for most of the night. Then it stopped. Followed by silence. Some moments of peace. But then, I mean, I know you will think that I can't get any more dramatic, but I started to hear the sound of a snowmobile again. I know I am starting to sound like a broken wheel, but a broken wheel is right two times a day. Right? I know, it's jokes, but a broken coo-coo clock is right two times a day, I suppose, too. Right? But this time I had no fear. I would confront the burglars. What did I have to lose? They already brained me, twice. I mean, they would probably brain me again, but maybe this time I would get some answers.

I did my best to listen for them exactly. My plan was to meet them at the front door. Not with an aggressive stance, but with a pleading stance. To maybe get some answers. I must have fallen asleep because I woke up to the sound of splashing. Splashing and muffled shouting. I regretted that I had left all the tools out by the grave/swimming hole. My bravado from before was gone. I looked around for a weapon. The knife was somewhere that I couldn't find. It was too dark and I had no idea where I put it. The best I could do was a small log. I carried it out the front door. Trying to be as quiet as possible. That idea was immediately thrown out when I got around the corner, and stepped into the snow. There was just a big crunch, and a pause from the burglars. They shined their flashlights at me. I couldn't see anything. I dropped the log. I held my hands in the air. I walked a little bit closer. One of them ran away. I could hear it. Because of the snow. The other one didn't move. I twisted a little and got a glimpse of what he was holding. It was the metal bucket. But then the light from the flashlight blinded me again. I couldn't be certain but I heard the sound of a gun. Whatever that means. He didn't cock it or something. I just heard some movement that sounded like he now had a gun. I mean, this all sounds pretty dramatic, but don't get me wrong, I only have my experience to go on here.

I mean, I wasn't scared. I half expected the other guy to come up and brain me at any moment, from behind, but I wasn't scared. I was getting tired of this. I just wanted some answers. Or at least, that is what I was telling myself. I tried to get out of the flashlight glare, but the burglar wouldn't let me. I stopped trying. After a few seconds he spoke. I don't know if it was because he was wearing a helmet or what, but his words came out clear, yet they had this noise at the end that sounded a little like somebody cocking a shotgun or something. But not exactly that, more like with a bunch of reverb on the end. Like he was talking through a microphone with an effect on it. He said:

"What are you doing here?" [chunk-chunk]

"What do you mean? What are you doing here? Where's Chaz?"

"You're gonna die if you stay here." [chunk-chunk]

"Yeah, I know! Get me out of here!"

"That's not up to us." [chunk-chunk] "It's nothing personal." [chunk-chunk]

"What do you mean? I'm going to die if you leave me here!"

"That's not up to us." [chunk-chunk] "You gotta get cool, man." [chunk-chunk] "Get the right vibes." [chunk-chunk]

"What the fuck are you talking about? Take me with you!"

"Yeah, I don't know, dog." [chunk-chunk]

"Wait, is that you, Glazer?"

That was the moment I got brained from behind. I didn't even hear the other burglar sneaking up on me. It was either really late at night, or very early in the morning, because I woke up lying in snow, in a pool of my own blood, not dead, with the sun doing its best to push through the clouds. I was so cold that I puked when I pushed myself to my knees. Luckily it was just bile, and not the half-sandwich that was keeping me alive. But I was able to get up and stumble back into the cabin. I noticed wet foot prints all around the floor before I fell into the bed. Shaking like a maniac. Licking the bedding, while also being stiff as a log. Flopping like a snagged fish. My eyes bloodshot, and trying to catch my breath. I kept opening, and closing my mouth. Looking up, and then down. The heat from the stove making long strings of needles everywhere my body was. But there wasn't enough of them to make a blanket. I rolled around, and around, and around, until I was tangled in the bedding. I kept biting at the air. For what seemed like hours. But was probably minutes. Eventually my body normalized, and I was able to make a regular face. But now my feet hurt, and my fingers hurt, and my ears hurt. The door to the cabin was open. The fire in the stove was going out. I could feel it. Dissipating. I jerked myself out of the bed. The blankets falling to the floor. I was able to close the door with my foot, while at the same time cramming some branches into the stove. I don't know how, but I got the blankets off the floor, and wrapped around my body again. I flopped like a fish on the bed again. Kicking out into oblivion. My mouth making oxygen motions. Something tripped, and I was finally equal to the comfort of room temperature instead of what ice feels like. But all that did was trigger a reflex that made the next hour feel like pink fiberglass racing through my blood. Then I got shaky. Really shaky. Like I wasn't even on this earth anymore. Somehow outside. Like a hummingbird heart. Then something snapped, and I was warm again. Just enough heat for my eyes to stop seizing and blinking. I could have sworn I heard the snowmobile drive away, but that didn't make sense in the timeline I was experiencing. My body made one last fit of total madness, and I blacked out. Thinking of armless, legless babies.

Don't get me wrong, but I woke up in a lot of pain. I was logy. My body ached all over. My head hurt. What woke me up was those damned mice screaming in my ears. Clacking, I guess is the way to describe it. I managed to get out of bed and stoke the fire. Adding a couple of branches to the stove. There were puddles of water around the cabin. Like every time the burglars come around. I really wish I knew what they were looking for. Absent-minded, I looked inside the cooler. To my delight, and also to my annoyance, there was more food. This time it was peanuts and cheese. Two bags of 99-cent peanuts, and a block of yellow cheddar. What was annoying about it was that I knew what it meant. That specific food had meaning, meaning that I would have no choice but to think about when I ate the food. As hungry as I was, I shut the lid. I was in no mood to go down memory lane at the moment. I went over to the stove, and stood there, looking. This charade had gone on too long. I was feeling sick and fading. Faded. I put my gloves on and went outside. To see what kind of clues the burglars left. There wasn't much to see. It had been snowing since I fell asleep, and all the tracks were covered. I went out back to the grave, that was also a swimming hole the last time I saw it. Now it was a skating rink. I stood on it gingerly. With one foot. Nothing happened. I put my weight onto my leg. Still nothing happened. I stood on it with my other leg. Still nothing happened. I jumped up and down. Nothing. Rock solid. Rock solid ice.

I gathered the shovel, the broken ax, and the metal bucket. They were still visible, but covered in snow. If I left them there longer, they would surely disappear. I walked around to the side of the cabin where they had parked the snowmobile. No tracks. I didn't even bother trying to find the tracks under the snow. My emotions were bunk. I was tired and alone. I walked back to the front of the cabin, and went back inside. I put the things down. I mean, I guess I threw them. Out of anger. Frustration. I looked at the cooler. That damned cooler. Fucking Chaz. Why was he fucking with me this way? Was I really that bad of a person? Had I hurt him that much? I was overcome with depression. I mean, was this it? Was I doomed to stay here until the snow melted in a couple months? Getting some food every couple days? Getting brained each time? My mind was starting to get foggy. I can only assume that it was the multiple whacks to the skull that I took. I mean, I must have a concussion, right? I mean, I was feeling sleepy, but suddenly I thought twice about taking a nap. I mean, you shouldn't take a nap if you are concussed, right? Won't that kill you? I mean, why is that? Is it like that old chestnut about dying in a dream? But like, maybe when you fall asleep with a concussion, your brain doesn't know how to get back to Earth? Like all the wires are crossed, and you end up somewhere else in the Universe? Don't get me wrong, but I guess I just didn't know. I mean, I am not a doctor, or nothing, I was just wondering. Like, what is the logic there?

I managed to give myself a little panic with these thoughts. I paced around for a few moments. Had to go outside to get some fresh air. Panicked even harder when the silence of the wilderness made me feel absolutely alone. I went back inside.

Spent my nervous energy breaking branches into smaller branches. Then pacing back and forth. Then sitting on the bed, which led to me lying on the bed, and then I would get scared that I would fall asleep and die, so I would get up and pace some more. I had really worked myself into a state. I had nothing but my own brain to keep me distracted, and my brain was panicking. I dropped to the floor, and started doing push-ups, hoping the exercise would sweat out the anxiety. I was always bad at push-ups so I didn't get very far. I rolled over and started doing sit-ups. This lasted long enough for me to realize I was wasting energy. That I didn't have much energy to waste. I was starving. I knew it. I mean, in theory. I mean, I hadn't had to shit since that time I ate all that meat, and I gave myself diarrhea, I think. I stood up. Had the thought that I couldn't prevent the inevitable. Went over to the cooler. Opened the lid and took out a bag of 99-cent peanuts. Don't get me wrong, I know this sounds dramatic, but I tore open the peanuts. Took one peanut out. Put it in mouth. Suddenly, I was transported back to Basin, in the middle of July, in the hottest summer I had ever experienced.

Me and Chaz were sitting in my motel room. There was a twelve pack of IceHouse on the bed. The air conditioner was on full-blast, but the room was still hot. It was after work. We hadn't opened the twelve pack of IceHouse. Instead we were drinking Red Bull and vodka. Out of the little plastic cups that come with your motel room. The ice bucket was full. I was sitting in a chair by the telephone, next to the bed. Chaz was sitting in a chair by the windows. He was spitting into a Mountain Dew bottle. There were two bags of 99-cent peanuts on the bed next to the IceHouse. A block of yellow cheddar cheese. Dinner. I wasn't hungry. I don't think Chaz was either. Or at least he had no plans to eat the 99-cent peanuts or any of the cheese because he didn't even look at them when I threw them on the bed, and said, Dinner. He just took out his can of Copenhagen, snapped it twice with his finger, and put a dip in. His lower lip. Made a weird face. Opened the lid to the empty Mountain Dew bottle he was holding. Then spit into it. I don't know why I watched him do this so closely. He noticed. Looked at me. Offered the can of Copenhagen. I shook my head. Took a sip of my drink and felt embarrassed.

We sat there in silence. Listening to the air conditioner. Every now and again one of us would get up and make another drink. Neither one offering to make a drink for the other. I knew he was pissed at me. I knew he had something to tell me, but he was working himself up about it, I guess. Or not. I mean, lately he had been pretty silent. I mean, after the sandwich incident. I think he was embarrassed about that. But what could I do? It wasn't my fault that I got promoted, and he didn't. There was no reason to be angry with me about it. Not only that, but I think he was jealous, which was even more insane. I mean, I have no idea why I was promoted from cramming dust to pipe donkey. I don't think I was any better at that than he was, but I got promoted, and he didn't. So what? I mean, he would get promoted soon enough. Half the time someone wouldn't show up to work, and suddenly you would be doing a job that was way above your skill set. Just to keep things going. Not only that, but people tended to burn out pretty quick on this job. The money was good, but the work sucked, and was dangerous. Maybe not the dirt work, or the donkey work, but the further along you went, the more dangerous it got. And anyone that wanted that work was rewarded for it. I mean, in a certain sense, you could pull yourself up by your bootstraps, given you had the gumption, and the stick-to-it-iveness. But who knows? Maybe Chaz was right. White did like me better. Maybe he had chosen me over Chaz just based on my shining personality. I mean, I did smoke more, so I did find myself hanging out with White more than Chaz. But whatever. I mean, shit, none of this made sense to me.

We sat in silence for over an hour. I mean, aside from the air conditioner. I put an end to this. I was feeling loose. Drunk even. I said:

"What's up, dog? You been broody for days. You got something to say to me?" Chaz sat there. Spitting every now, and then into his now half-full Mountain Dew bottle. The green bottle black with chewing tobacco spit well past the bottom of the label. He said nothing. I tried again. "You're killing me, Homes." This worked, because he made a face, and then his eyes changed. He looked over at me.

"Oh, Homes is it, Dog? You sound like one of them. I don't get it with you uppity types. You think you are like my buddy or something. You think you can just steal my money, and take food from my family, and all the sudden I am your friend? It makes me sick. I don't owe you nothing, Donkey. You're just as bad as they are."

"What the hell are you talking about? I ain't taking shit from you. Your family? What family? You're the same loser I am. We don't got no family. Not only that, but shit, you just called me Donkey, what the fuck is that about?"

"You're a donkey, Donkey. You know that as well as me. That job should be mine, and you know it."

"Ah, c'mon, Chaz. I give it two weeks, and you got the same job I do. Shit, even less than that. It ain't no fucking walk in the park. Not only that, but what? I make an extra buck or two an hour. Fucking peanuts, Homes."

"There you go again calling me Homes. I ain't your Homes, and I ain't your dog."

Chaz held up his Mountain Dew bottle. He looked directly at me. Slowly, he turned it on its side.

"Don't you fucking do it."

Chaz smiled. He dumped the spitter on the carpet. I don't know what came over me, but the next thing I knew Chaz and I were on the floor wrestling.

I managed to punch him. Then he rolled over. I grabbed his head and mashed it into the spit puddle on the carpet. He screamed out, and pushed me up. Threw me across the bed. My back landed on the unopened twelve pack of IceHouse. I made a weird noise, because it hurt. He tried to jump on top of me, but I rolled out of the way. I gave him a swift elbow to the ribs, which made him make a wheezing noise. He grabbed me by the belt. Threw me to the floor. Kicked me in the ass, which somehow just hit my butthole. I screamed, and did a running turn-around, which knocked a lamp over. My face ended up in the puddle of chew spit. I pulled up from the carpet. A string of spit stuck to my face. I dry-heaved. Chaz grabbed the twelve pack of IceHouse off the bed. Slammed it down on my back. Cans went in all directions. I reared back like a bronco. Chaz grabbed my face from behind. Pulling at the edges of my mouth, forcing it to smile. I could taste his fingers. Salt and Copenhagen. I tried to duck around, but I ran my head into the wall on accident. I tasted sparks. That was the end of the fight. I don't know what he did after that, but I was knocked out.

I won't lie, I woke up staring at a can of IceHouse. I was confused. I sat up, trying to remember what happened. The door to my motel room was open. The two bags of 99-cent peanuts were still on top of the bed. Next to the chunk of yellow cheddar cheese. I was still a little drunk. The memory of the fight came back to me. I cracked open the IceHouse. Took a drink. The beer was warm now. It tasted pretty gross. I took another drink. My back hurt, as well as my butthole. My elbow was covered in chewing tobacco spit. My face as well. The smell was overwhelming. Spearmint. I got up and stumbled to the door. I shut the door. I went into the bathroom and washed my face. My elbow. I drank the rest of the IceHouse while looking in the mirror. Don't get me wrong, but I don't know how I felt. I wasn't pissed, but I wasn't not pissed. I didn't know what to do. I mean, I guess I kind of knew what to do. I brushed my teeth. There was a bruise on my forehead. Nothing else. I got my wallet, my room key, and I walked over to the bar.

When I got inside, two or three people yelled, Donkey! Chaz was sitting next to White. He smiled, and waved at me. I waved back. Loretta asked me what I wanted to drink. I ordered a Jager and Red Bull. I tipped her two dollars. Then, just like that, the night went on like nothing happened at all. The next day I would find out that Chaz got promoted to pipe donkey as well. Leaving only poor Humphreys as the lone dust-crammer. But, to be honest, that job only needed one person, and working with Humphreys was a job in itself.

I don't know what to say. I mean, one peanut, and this is the reaction? Don't get me wrong, but what do you do with that information? It doesn't make sense. I mean, Chaz isn't that vindictive, is he? I mean, that night we arm wrestled when the bar was closing. He told me no hard feelings. I don't think we ever spoke about it again. I mean, a couple times I did say, What are you going to do, pour spit on my carpet? Like a joke when we were giving each other shit. But for him to get the two burglars to drop off that memory mind-fuck? I just don't get it. Don't get me wrong, my fears about my memories went away pretty fast after that first initial punch. I ate about half the bag of 99-cent peanuts without thinking anything aside from how tasty the peanuts were. I forced myself to stop. I could have eaten the whole bag. I allowed myself to eat a slice of the cheese. I let the cheese melt on my tongue before I chewed it. I don't remember getting the knife, or what I did with it afterwards. I was not sane anymore. Things were starting to come in and out of focus. I was certain that I had a fever. I couldn't tell, because everything seemed hot. After eating the slice of cheese I put everything back into the cooler. I got into bed. Convinced I would feel better in the morning. I forced myself to get back up and put some more branches in the stove. I tried to close the stove door all the way, but there was that chunk of branch that was keeping me from doing so. I would need to deal with this soon. My exact thoughts as I drifted off to sleep. My breath was shallow now. I just needed some rest. I could deal with everything in the morning.

Part 6

That night I dreamed I got the goods. I built an engine hoist over the grave. With an electric auger I was able to drill a hole into the ice and insert an anchor. Using the chains on the hoist, I was able to pull the block of ice out. With the chunk of ice dangling in the air above the grave, I jumped down into the hole. The dirt on the bottom was warm and loose. I was able to dig with my hands. When I got the goods I stood up and put them on the side of the grave. Suddenly I couldn't get out. I didn't have the strength. I tried jumping up and pulling myself out, but the dirt on the sides of the hole's walls would crumble down. I tried over, and over, and over again. The same results. I got really upset. I looked down into the hole where the goods had been. I could see something shiny. I got onto my knees and started digging. It was a ladder. I dug it up as fast as I could. It was big. Hard to maneuver. I swung it up and around; the top of it went above the top of the hole. I stumbled a little. The ladder knocked into the engine hoist. Switching the direction of the sprocket engagement. Suddenly the block of ice came crashing down on top of me. Now I was trapped in the grave, and the goods were outside. I started to claw at the ice, trying to get free. The air got less and less. Suddenly I was panicked. I was trapped, and there was no way out. I tried to scream but my voice wouldn't work. Then I woke up.

Don't get me wrong, I was shaking. The dream was hypnotic until the very last minute when I realized I was trapped. That part seemed quite real. The feeling of being trapped didn't really go away, even when I was awake. I tried to do some experiments to prove I was awake. I got up and stoked the fire, adding a few branches. This didn't change the feeling.

Had there been a light switch, I would have tested it. I mean, that is how you know if a dream is real or not, right? If when you switch a light switch on, and off, the lights go on, or off. The other thing I did was eat some peanuts. I mean, I feel like whenever I eat things in my dreams, I never actually taste the food I am eating. But the peanuts tasted just fine, and real. I mean, really fine, and really real. I had to stop myself from eating them all. I put the peanuts back, and went over to the stove. I touched it. It burned my finger. I mean, I was awake, there was no way around it, but why did I have that feeling of being trapped without actually being trapped? I mean, don't get me wrong, I was trapped. I was trapped in this cabin, on top of this mountain. With no way out. Aside from death. But this was different. Like my body was trying to make me think of something. Like there was a clue in the dream.

I stood there dissecting the dream. I mean, the details. The engine hoist was fantastic. There was no way I could have built that by myself, so that seemed a little like a bad place to start. The ice and the ladder. I mean, those things seemed meaningless. The soft dirt and goods seemed like something, but in the end they were just wishful thinking in dream logic. I don't know, don't get me wrong, but all the thinking I did got me nowhere. I guess in the end, it was just a feeling I was having. Like I was old before my time, or that feeling that nothing you do actually matters. I mean, maybe I crossed some wires in my brain since I had taken so many bonks to the noggin since I got up here? Like maybe because I fell asleep with a concussion my brain was now broken, like forever. Like I would always be trapped inside my body with a useless brain. You know, smart enough to know that you are dumb kind of thing? Like if I could just break my bad habits I would be successful kind of thinking. But every time you make a move, something else shows up to gum up the works? I don't know. Maybe I wasn't trapped, maybe I was just a loser, and I needed to accept my lot in life?

All this thinking was bumming me out. I decided to get some more sleep, and hopefully feel better in the morning. I got back in bed and fell back to sleep. The only dream this time was just the screaming of the mice. Clattering. In my ears. I was really getting sick of the mice. I wished there was something to do about them. In the morning I woke up slowly. I had hatched some plan in my subconscious that I would catch the mice off guard when I woke up. So when I woke up, instead of just getting up I slowly opened my eyes. Not moving my body. I peeped around the cabin. The part of the cabin in front of my field of vision. Trying not to make a move. I saw a little movement just out of the corner of my eye. Underneath a piece of fabric. I pounced on it. Hoping to catch a mouse. I got nothing. It must have run out before I got there. Sensing my moving body. I was frustrated, but not surprised. I mean, I don't even know what to say. The mice would be fine if they wouldn't just scream in my ear all night. Clattering around.

The feeling of being trapped was still there. Don't get me wrong, there was nowhere for it to go. Like me, the feeling itself was trapped. I kind of got the impression it wanted to leave too, but had no choice but to stick around until something good came along so it could ruin that thing's fun. But for now, it was stuck with me. Which, I guess, meant that we were buddies now. Which was a funny thought to have at first. But before I knew it, I started talking to it. And not in the way that your brain narrates your actions sort of way, but more like, actually talking to it. I mean, not to be dramatic, but I guess I was feeling pretty lonely at this point. Or alone, or whatever. I mean, I wasn't seeing things, like a ghost of bad feelings, or whatever, but by the time I had decided what I was planning to do for the day I was talking out loud. And at first I was kind of freaked out about it, but before long, everything was all the same.

"What do you think, Tracy?"

Those were the first words I said out loud. To myself. Don't get me wrong, what led to this was the song, Give Me One Reason, by Tracy Chapman, which had become an earworm when I woke up that morning. And because I was apparently in some state of shock, or something, I thought it was hilarious to call this extra feeling I was having of being trapped, which was now my companion, Tracy Trapman. I mean, I was kind of giddy when I thought of it. And I laughed, and laughed, and laughed until I spoke those words.

"What do you think, Tracy? I mean, don't get me wrong, but I think I could do it."

I was thinking up an idea for a mouse trap. I would use the metal bucket. Fill it with snow. Melt the snow into water. Put a stick on top of it. Put a tiny piece of peanut on the stick. Which would lure the mouse out, and then the mouse would drown in the water. I had heard this would work. Although I think you were supposed to use a paper towel roll and some string, or something. But I had an idea that I could whittle a stick down with tapered ends, and this would make a real slippery bridge for the mouse to walk on. Right? Plus, I figured that I could sacrifice a little bit of peanut for this, if it meant that I would catch a mouse. Which I could eat. As gross as that sounded.

Tracy thought it was a good idea. I took the metal bucket outside and filled it with snow. I looked around. It was snowing again. All the snow that had melted from the fire was back again. Not as high as it was before, but by this point, a couple of feet of snow had fallen. Did it always snow this much in the mountains? I honestly had no idea. You look at the mountains enough, and you just assume that the snow that you see is always there. I guess you never really think about how it gets there. But man, it had been snowing for days now. I mean, I guess this is why rivers are so busy all the time. I mean, where does the water come from? I mean, I guess it is this. From here. Up on the mountains. But still, this seemed ludicrous. But whatever. Nothing I could do about that now. Nor ever, I suppose.

I went back inside and put the bucket on top of the stove to melt. I poked around in the piles of branches until I found a branch that I thought would work. I said:

"Tracy? Yeah, I think so too."

It took a while to find the knife because I couldn't remember where I put it. I found it under the pillow on the bed. I guess the last time I had used it was when I was trying to stab mice during the night, or I guess when I was slicing the cheese. I thought I should keep it on me from now on.

I mean, I suppose that the burglars would be back. I mean, I should probably stab them next time. Steal their snowmobile, and be done with this. The problem with that, though, is that the knife was dumb. And I didn't have a way to carry it. Don't get me wrong, it was an open knife. I mean, it wasn't a folding knife. It was just a knife. I mean, what? You can't carry a knife around in your pocket, you'll cut a hole in your pocket, right? Whatever.

I found the knife, and I went to work whittling a stick to make a slippery bridge for the mice. I made a good one, I think. I cut a divot in the middle for the small piece of peanut to go. I tested it on the metal bucket that was melting snow on top of the stove. It seemed good. Length-wise. I stood there waiting for the snow to finish melting. I was surprised it was taking so long. The air in the cabin was hot. The stove was hot. But the snow was taking forever. Maybe I had got some extra cold snow? Was that a thing? I stood there watching for a while. Nothing. I got bored and decided to go check out the grave site. To see if anything had changed. I pushed through all the new snow. Got to the grave. It was just the same as always, impenetrable. I went back to the cabin, my feet and half of my legs covered in snow. I stood by the stove as it melted off. The snow in the metal bucket still hadn't melted. I grabbed the handle. Which was just a piece of thick wire bent into a U shape. Don't get me wrong, because the snow hadn't melted, I thought it would be cold. It was not cold. It burned my fingers. I put a glove on, and grabbed it again. I lifted up the metal bucket. I looked under the bottom. I saw dirt. Lots of dirt, crammed inside the edges of the metal bucket. I must have crammed that dirt in when I put the bucket down after I had tried to bale the grave out. The dirt was keeping the snow from melting. Don't get me wrong, but this was annoying. I threw the bucket to the corner of the cabin. Snow and dirt went everywhere. I sighed. I said:

"Tracy, that was stupid."

I walked over and picked the metal bucket up. The metal bucket was fine. For the most part. Slightly oblong now, and the bottom had a dent that made it sit wrong when I took it outside. I filled it with snow again and put it back on top of the stove. This time the snow melted fast. It was not enough water, so I went back outside, and gathered a ball of snow, and brought it back. Put it in the metal bucket. It melted. There was still not enough water. I went back outside two more times before there was enough water for the trap. I put a glove on and took the metal bucket off of the stove. I placed it somewhere that seemed good for catching mice. Although they did seem to be everywhere — even though I never saw them, but they did seem to be everywhere.

Don't get me wrong, it took forever to set the trap. My whittling skills were not very good. The divot I dug out for the piece of peanut kept ending up on the bottom. I assumed the thing needed to be precarious for the mouse to fall into the water, but in the end I had no choice but to cut another divot on the other side. Otherwise there was no way for the trap to be baited. And as much as I wished a mouse to just come and take a walk on this slippery bridge, I knew that unless there was a reason for it to do so, it would not.

I went over to the cooler and opened the lid. I took the open bag of 99 cent peanuts out. Poured six in my hand. Ate five of them. Said, Five for me, and munch munch munch, one little chunk for you, you slippery bastard. I put the 99 cent peanuts back. Walked over to the trap. Crouched. Whittled down a peanut with my teeth until it was just the right size. I baited the trap. Don't get me wrong, it took some doing. But in the end, I was successful. I stood up. The trap was set. I was feeling triumphant. I said:

"Tracy, I did a good job." Tracy answered this time.
"You did a great job, Donkey."

Even my emotions were calling me Donkey at this point. I let it roll off my back, as they say.

"Ah, shucks, thank you."

I stood there staring at the trap. I felt proud and empty. My whole day was now over. I mean, I was out of projects. And not only that, but I was afraid of disturbing the trap. I didn't dare walk around. I stood there looking at the trap until there was no reason to look at the trap anymore. I slowly backed away. Making sure I didn't knock the whittled peanut into the water. Don't get me wrong, but that was it. I stood there next to the stove now, staring. Getting hot. There was nothing to do. It was like noon now. Or something. I had plans to eat some cheese around sunset. I guessed I could go out and try and get some more branches, but my supply was good. Plus it was snowing. I could take a nap, but I wasn't tired. I could go light some more trees on fire, but it was overcast. I was trapped, and now I was bored. Don't get me wrong, but I hadn't been bored since I got here. There was always something happening. But now there was nothing. The cabin was starting to feel like a desert island. Without sun. And instead of an ocean, there was snow. And instead of turtles, there were mice. Or crabs, or whatever. There was nothing to do. Nothing to read. The only song to listen to was the earworm with the lyrics, Why… I should stay.

I stood there thinking about those song lyrics. Don't get me wrong, but the lyrics didn't make any sense. I mean, she was leaving, I guess, but she was asking for a reason to stick around? I mean, I understood the meaning, but the details were troubling. Like was she just walking out the door? Like, was she walking to the door, and then she was saying over her shoulder, I am leaving, unless you tell me to stay? I mean, it kind of sounds like she was looking for a reason to leave, more than she was looking for a reason to stay. Just give me a reason to stay here, and I'll turn right back around. But, I mean, if you are saying that, you have already turned around. Am I right? I don't know. I thought about asking Tracy, but she didn't know this. Not because she didn't understand, but because she didn't write the song. The person that wrote the song was a pop star. Somebody that actually pulled themselves up by her boot-straps. With talent. But my Tracy was just a bad feeling that wouldn't leave me. So instead of talking about the song, I asked her a question about math.

"Tracy, how come work isn't fun anymore? I mean, I go to work, but I never get anywhere. It just all seems so stupid."

"You're looking at it wrong, Donkey, work is its own reward."

"Yeah, okay, haha."

"I'm serious. You work hard, you will get somewhere."

"How is that?"

"Oh, I don't know. I mean, have you ever tried it? I know lots of people that worked real hard, and got places."

"Everyone I know works hard, and none of them get places. Hard work is a load of beans. I mean, it seems like you are work-shaming me. How hard do you work? Seems like to me that you just sit around, and make me feel bad. How is that hard work?"

"I don't have to work hard, I got idiots like you to do it for me."

"What, me sitting around feeling sorry for myself is doing your work? That's pretty rich."

"Society, man."

I don't know why this conversation with Tracy made me so upset, but I stormed out of the cabin because of it. I got outside, and pushed through the snow until I reached the burned down pine trees. At that point I sobered up. Realizing that, I stormed out of the cabin because I got into an argument with myself. I went back inside. Took the block of cheese out of the cooler, and bit a chunk off. Put it back. Slammed the lid back down on the cooler. I was angry. But I didn't know who I was angry at. Don't get me wrong, it was myself, but it was a different version of myself. I mean, it seemed like Chaz was teaching me a lesson, but the lesson sucked.

I mean, I feel like I need to explain some things. Because, don't get me wrong, I mean, things were starting to feel pretty dramatic. But I need you to know that I know that. Like with Tracy and whatever. I mean, none of this happened in some concrete way, like I was the master of all my thoughts in this time of crisis. I mean, thinking about Tracy was giving me some weird feelings of longing, but that longing was starting to meld into one big nebulous ball. Like Tracy in my mind was starting to take on Goil's appearance. And this feeling of malaise that I was having, this mid-life thing itself, its own crisis, was starting to feel like Seneca Michael Miguel. I don't know how to explain it. But I was feeling like they were there with me. I mean, I'm not crazy, but every now and then I would catch something out of the corner of my eye. Or reflected in the one good window. I would find myself startled. Then I would get goose bumps, but then there was really nothing, and never was anything to begin with. But this would happen. At first it was a mind-fuck, but as time went by, I don't know, I mean. Tracy was starting to get kind of sexy. And the malaise that was Seneca Michael Miguel, was really grinding on my nerves. I couldn't ditch him. He was always there. But Tracy, or the Goil Tracy, she was always somewhere off in the distance. Like it was summer, and she was down at the creek washing herself in the nude. Sunshine glistening through her hair. Et cetera. But also, who knows? Am I right? Maybe Seneca Michael Miguel was right, I really did have a weird notion to name things I didn't know the name of.

But it all worked itself out in a weird way. And in order to be honest, I guess I just need you to know this. I mean, don't get me wrong, but whenever I did anything stupid, I would suddenly be talking to Seneca Michael Miguel, saying shit like, Yo homey, you think that's right, weto? Or if I did something that I was unsure of, suddenly Goil Tracy would come to mind, and I would say, What do you think, Trace? And she would always respond, I think you are doing a great job, Donkey. Then I would smell vanilla. Like for instance. The little peanut disappeared from the middle of mouse trap I built. But there was no mouse. I bit off a chunk of peanut, and reset the trap. I would think, Is that good, Tracy? And she would tell me I did a good job, but then the peanut would disappear, and there would be no mouse, and Seneca Michael Miguel would suddenly be there saying, Oh homey, why you feeding the mice, pinche weto? It was confusing, but not confusing. You know what I mean? I mean, I understood them both, but they were really riding my jock. Both of them. One good, one bad. But whatever, I feel like I did a good job explaining that. What do you think, Trace?

"I think you are doing really great work these days, Donkey."

The next day it snowed, and snowed, and snowed. I was thinking about it, and I decided it was February by now. I thought about marking the passage of time. But then I didn't really have a reason to. I mean, I would either starve to death, or Spring would come. There was no other option. I mean, there was still the idea of burning trees when the sky was clear, and trying to get some attention from an airplane, but for now, it was just snow and clouds. I had no reason to think that the burglars would not be back. In fact I expected them tonight. So, I had that going for me. But I was pretty resigned to my destiny at this point. My branch supply was good. I was warm enough. I got enough to drink if I was thirsty. I had the mouse trap to keep me occupied. I had Seneca Michael Miguel and the Goil Tracy to keep me company. In some ways I was doing okay. I mean, I didn't have to go to work. I did have a brief panic when I realized my rent was due, but so what, I don't think they could come get me to make sure I paid it. I mean, I wished that they would. Save me from my troubles. I still had some peanuts and cheese. I mean, I kind of wished that somebody was longing for me, and maybe looking for me, but the only friend I had was Chaz, and he knew exactly where I was. My mom was still around, but I rarely even talked to her, there was no reason for her to even think I was in trouble. I mean, my lifetime of isolation was kind of giving me what I deserved at the moment. Although, I mean, I would argue that I did not deserve this at all, but I guess that wasn't for me to decide.

I mean, don't get me wrong, one problem I was having was a physical problem. Aside from being logy, I really didn't like getting brained every time the burglars showed up. I don't think it was doing me any good, mentally speaking. And my head always hurt the next day. I wished that I could tell the guys that I didn't need the braining. That I would just hang out and mind my own business until they were done doing whatever the hell they did every time they came around. I mean, I couldn't think of a solution aside from just asking them. So when I heard the snowmobile in the distance that night, I decided to just confront them out by the fence, and hope that everything turned out alright. I mean, I did have one thought, don't get me wrong, Seneca Michael Miguel thought the idea completely idiotic, but Goil Tracy thought it was smart.

When the snowmobile got closer, I took the piece of wood from the mouse trap and put it safely on the window sill of the good window. I took the metal bucket outside, and dumped the water out. I put the metal bucket on top of the stove for a moment. To burn any water off. Then I took it off. Let it cool. I put the metal bucket on top of my head. Like a helmet. I asked:

"How do I look? Think it will work?"

"You look like a jack-ass, homey. That is some weto-ass shit." Seneca Michael Miguel said.

"I think you look great, Donkey. You are doing a really good job lately." Goil Tracy said.

"Why thank you, Trace, I think so too. Seneca, see? Tracy thinks I am doing a great job." I said.

"You look like a jack-ass, homey." Seneca Michael Miguel said.

"Well, opinions are like assholes. Maybe you should keep yours to yourself." I said.

"Okay, you look like an asshole, homey." Seneca Michael Miguel said.

I took the knife and went to wait for the burglars. The metal bucket got pretty cold pretty fast. I had to put a glove in between the top of my head and the metal bucket. To keep my head warm. That meant that my one gloved hand held the bucket on, while the other was in my coat pocket. Holding the knife. Trying not to stab a hole in my pocket.

I trudged through the snow. It was really deep. My legs were freezing. Immediately. I got to the point where the burglars usually stopped. I waited. The waiting was taking forever. And the burglars seemed so close, but never got as close as I thought. I stood there for quite some time. I couldn't take it anymore. My head was now really cold. My hand too, holding the metal bucket. My feet were frozen. And the burglars didn't seem to be getting any closer, even though I could hear them approaching. I went back inside.

Don't get me wrong, I mean, I took the metal bucket off when I got inside. Put it on the floor next to me, as I stood by the stove. My gloves back in my coat pockets. The knife got placed next to the piece of wood for the mouse trap on the window sill. It was very painful warming up. My teeth were chattering. My jaw was tight. I stomped my feet. Eventually I warmed up. I mean, I thought about this. I mean, what would have happened if the burglars had just brained me outright? I mean, the last time they brained me I nearly died from freezing, and that was like late in the night. I mean, if they brained me first thing, I might just die out there in the snow. I mean, I guess it was smart that I came back inside.

I stood there looking at the stove for what seemed like forever. Listening to the snowmobile approach. When the burglars finally got here, I suddenly got giddy with fear. I put the metal bucket back on my head. Like a helmet. I grabbed the knife. Pointed it the door, ready to stab. One hand holding the bucket on my head. The other one holding the knife. I could kind of see light coming through the broken window. Through the blanket. The door opened. A flashlight shone in my eyes. I held strong. I mean, I held the knife out, like I would use it. But it was apparent I was shaking. One of the burglars was there. I could hear noises in the back. The other burglar I decided. I did my best to state my case. Hoping for good results. The burglar in the cabin, holding the flashlight, held it like a police man. Pointing the light at me, but kind of over his shoulder. In a way that I knew that policemen did, so they could brain people they were shining the light on. Like, for ease. I gathered my courage, and said:

"Hey man, I don't mean you no harm! Just don't knock me out this time, I'll let you be, I swear!" My voice was echoing inside the metal bucket. Shaky.

"Oh, Donkey, you really don't get it. [chunk-chunk]" That sound that they made when they talked. It really was disturbing.

"Oh, c'mon, man! You nearly killed me last time!"

"Well, sometimes you win, sometimes you lose. I don't make the choices, man. [chunk-chunk]"

"Okay then! Get ready for some pain!"

Like an idiot I stabbed at the burglar. I could hear Seneca Michael Miguel say, Oh homey, that was a weto-ass move. The flashlight came down on top of the metal bucket with a ring. I think it hurt my ears more than it hurt my head. But the whiteness that followed didn't feel like anything at all. I remember seeing snow boots, and then the floor. Then nothing.

I dreamed of murdering dolphins. In a grid. There was a guy holding a clipboard. Calling out grid numbers. Eighteen! Then I would throw a grenade into the water. Three dolphins blasted out of the water. Grid eighteen! Three dolphins! I would yell. Then he would say, Nine! Then I would throw a grenade into grid nine. Eight dolphins would explode out of the water. Grid nine! Eight dolphins! Et cetera, and so on. This went on until the dolphin pool was empty. There was a point when I thought I should take the remaining dolphins and run away, but then I realized that they could only swim, and were destined to their fate. Which made me sad.

I woke up on the floor. My ears ringing. The earworm running through my head. The metal bucket was ruined. But there was no blood. I reached out toward the bucket, and pushed it over. I guess my mouse trap experiment was over. I could hear the sounds of chopping ice in the back, behind the cabin. The burglars were still there. My head hurt. I tried to stand up. I couldn't. I looked around. There were puddles of water everywhere. I really had no idea what they were looking for. I got excited, thinking that there would be more food in the cooler. I was able to roll over and push myself up enough to open the cooler lid. I looked inside. I couldn't believe what I saw. It was a ten-pack carton of cigarettes lying on top of the remaining 99 cent peanuts and cheddar cheese. I said, Shit. Seneca Michael Miguel said, Oh, homey, that's some real bad news. I knew. I said, I know. And instead of trying to get up and go to the bed, I just curled my way around the bottom of the stove, and went to sleep.

Don't get me wrong. There are times in your life when cigarettes are better than food. But not when you are starving. And not only that, but these cigarettes were loaded. I mean, loaded with meaning, not with those things that blow your cigarettes up when the Fourth of July comes around. It must have registered in my brain that all that the burglars brought was cigarettes, because that is all I thought about as I slept there, next to the stove. At some point the burglars left. I kind of remember them leaving. Not that that did me any good. But I noticed. I kind of got up, or woke up, or whatever after they left, and had a good laugh. Not a funny laugh, more like a You can't live on cigarettes alone kind of laugh. Everything was doom and despair at this point. And this was a curvy twist the knife kind of thing.

I dragged myself over to the bed, and got into it. With hope. I mean, I guess the word is hope. I don't even know. I was sleepy, and I kind of wanted to sleep until I could think that things would improve. I mean, cigarettes, really? You can't eat cigarettes. And I didn't even smoke. I mean, not really. Not enough that I would be happy that a ten-pack carton of cigarettes would show up instead of food. I mean it kind of made me angry. Like why would you give someone something they didn't need when you had complete control over them? I mean, it kind of felt like when the oil company offered me a 401k. I mean, sure, but how about you just pay me right, and let me save some money first. I mean, that shit is meaningless when half the time I don't even know if I will be working for you next week. I mean, I guess, the future is nice for you, and you are trying to share your knowledge, but are you? It seems like a tax scam that will ultimately leave me broke, and will make you tons of money in the meantime. Am I wrong?

But whatever. I knew what the ten-pack carton of cigarettes meant. I would have to deal with that later. I just wished that the burglars would have left me a juicy steak, with some potatoes, and a cup of queso. And Seneca Michael Miguel would leave me alone. And the Goil Tracy would come lie naked in the bed with me, and touch my erection. If wishes were kisses, am I right?

Now, don't get me wrong, the cold hard facts were that things were getting desperate. A man can't just live off of 99 cent peanuts and cheese and cigarettes for very long. I mean, I didn't even smoke anymore. I had a chaw every now and again. I burned myself out on cigarettes one night when I went over to Humphreys' motel room and did meth with him until four in the morning, talking conspiracy theories and chugging vodka. That hangover lasted the entire week. I mean, the thing happened on a Monday night. I was burned out already from Chaz being such a baby all the time that I had no desire to hang out with him. I think the feeling was mutual because he didn't come over to my room after work. So, I just sat there in my room, drinking Ice House, and listening to the air conditioner, alone. Eventually I got bored and went and knocked on Humphreys' door. He answered the door wild-eyed and shirtless. His skin bright red. He had a screwdriver in his hand. I looked past him; his bed was covered in the electronics from his room. Well, the alarm clock for sure, I couldn't tell what the other stuff was. There were just pieces of it. I counted three electrical cords. He said, Hurry up, Donkey, get your ass in here. He handed me a cd case. With three big lines on it. And a rolled-up dollar bill. Then he locked the door. Went over to the bed, and got back to work. I did a huge line. My eyes watered. I put the cd case down, next to the television. I cracked open the Ice House I was holding.

Sat down in the chair by the windows. The air conditioner was on full blast. There was music coming from something on the bed, but I couldn't understand what. I laughed to myself. The drugs snaked through my veins. I found my focus narrowing. Narrowing. Narrowing. Before I knew it, I was right there with him. Trying to get my mind around a circuit board. I snuck back to my room, a little paranoid that I would have to talk to somebody. I grabbed my small bag of tools, and the Ice House from the fridge, and went back. I didn't lock the door, or tell Humphreys that I was leaving. I opened the door to a knife in my face. I jumped back. He said, Oh shit, it's just you, Donk, don't do that to me. Come in. He let me in. Locked the door behind us, and went back to work.

For the next eight hours we chain smoked cigarettes, snorted lines of meth, and drank Ice House, at first, then we switched to Potter's vodka after that. On ice. From plastic motel room cups. I don't remember who got up the courage to get the ice, but one of us did. By four in the morning I was so spun out that I really didn't know what to do. I mean, I knew I should stop doing lines of meth and get some sleep, but we needed to get up in an hour, and get to work. I decided it was best to go back to my room and chill out for a second. Maybe sober up. I guessed. I tried to bring this up with Humphreys. He didn't care. He was in his own world. I mean, I didn't want to lose my job, for whatever reason, I mean, I guess I didn't want to get fired. So I managed to stumble back to my room.

I drank as much water as I could. I drank so much water that I threw up. Then I drank more. An hour later, when it was time to go outside and get in the work truck, I was still very high, still very drunk. I smelled like a cigarette. I mean, I must have smoked two packs of cigarettes that night. I tried to hide my smells, chewing on chewing gum. I wished that I would have taken a shower. Hind-Dog was driving. Chaz was in the back with me. From the front seat Earl said, Damn, Donkey, you smell like a brewery. I tried to act cool. I looked over at Chaz; he just shook his head.

Work was almost impossible. But somehow I managed. Humphreys did just fine. I half-expected him not to show up, but he was shoving dirt, same as usual. No worse the wear. This pissed Chaz off, though. He knew what we had been up to. And even though Humphreys was doing his work like normal, he took offense about it. During lunch time he came over to me, and said:

"Fun times last night? I came by your room. I guess I wasn't invited to your secret party."

I was still drunk. Still high. Chugging water. My cooler had a sandwich in it that I had no plans on eating.

"Yeah, you're better off my friend. I am never smoking ever again."

"Well, thanks for the invite."

"Oh, c'mon, dude. It wasn't nothing special. I was just blowing off some steam."

"Yeah, I will remember that."

Chaz walked off. To go sit by White and Hind-Dog, who were both sitting in the shade of the other truck, smoking cigarettes. I watched him sit down and say something that made them look up at me and laugh.

The rest of the day was brutal. I threw up multiple times. I was so dehydrated when I got back to the motel room that I ran a bath. I drank cup after cup of water. Getting out of the bathtub multiple times to shit piss out of my ass. Around eight someone came and knocked on my door. I didn't answer. My lights were off. Whoever it was didn't persist. I assumed it was Chaz, but whatever. I was in bed at that point. My head pounding. Feeling like a migraine. I spent the night throwing up and drinking water and shooting brown juice out my ass. The brown juice turned to yellow juice by the morning. I felt better than the day before, but only barely. That day at work was brutal. I felt sick and achy. I did a good job, I guess, I didn't get fired, and I didn't shit my pants, or throw up. I could only drink water. That night I did the same thing I did the night before. Just lay around, and drink water, and shit. Once again, around eight, there was a knock on my door. I ignored it. It did not persist. The knocking.

The next morning, I was almost back to normal. I was kind of hungry, but not hungry enough to try and eat. The work sucked, but my body had recovered, and I did a good job. I guess. I mean, I didn't get fired. I didn't eat lunch. In fact, I hadn't eaten anything in three days. I was well enough that when Chaz knocked on my door, around eight, I answered it. He was standing there with a ten-pack carton of cigarettes. A smile on his face. And, don't get me wrong, now that I think about it now, the dude was a sociopath. Because he said, Mind if I come in? I let him in. But that look on his face, it wasn't really a smile, it was more like, he was enjoying my suffering. He said:

"Damn, dog, it smells like a hospital in here, you doin' alright?"

He sat down, throwing the ten-pack carton of cigarettes on the bed.

"I brought you a present."

I looked at the bed. It was tangled mess of sweat and violent sleep. I wished that he wasn't there so I could get back in it. I found the remote, and turned the television off. I sat down on the chair next to the bed. He said:

"How you doin'? The guys are worried about you. You sick or something?" That same smile came across his face.

"I'm okay, I must have eaten something wrong is all. I'll be better by tomorrow. What's up?"

"Oh, nothing, just checking in is all. What? You don't offer me a drink?"

"Oh, I am sorry, where are my manners." I said this ironically, but I walked over to the fridge, and opened it. "I got water, or water. What'll you have?"

"Ah, nah, I'm okay, heading to the bar if you wanna come."

"I'm okay, think I just need another night."

"Suit yourself. You know where to find us."

Chaz stood up and left. I got back in bed, threw the ten-pack carton of cigarettes to the floor, and turned the television back on. Thinking about this now, I realize that he was already fucking with me. I mean, who brings a guy a ten-pack carton of cigarettes as a get-well present? Especially when I had declared that I would never smoke again. I mean, I don't know, but maybe Chaz was just an asshole all along. I just didn't understand that until just now. However, shit. I wish I would have understood that then. Maybe I wouldn't be in the situation I was in now? Like maybe I wouldn't have trusted him with this thing that had led to me being trapped in this cabin, starving to death. I mean, I was thinking about this now, while figuring out how to stay alive. I made a promise to myself not to trust assholes anymore. Not that it would do me any good. I mean, not unless I got myself out of this mess that I was in.

I couldn't get to sleep. This memory was haunting me. I wanted a cigarette. Don't get me wrong, this was a nice distraction from Seneca Michael Miguel, and the Goil Tracy, and my hunger. But it was just a distraction. I got out of bed, and went to the cooler. I took the ten-pack carton of cigarettes out. I shut the lid. I stood by the stove, and opened the carton. I took a package of cigarettes out. I put the rest of the carton on the floor. Next to the bed. I opened the package of cigarettes. Letting the plastic fall to the floor. I smacked the butt-end of the cigarette package on the butt of my hand. I opened it. It was a hard-pack. I tore the paper out. Threw it into the stove. Which was open. I still needed to deal with that piece of wood that kept the door open. I tried to shut the stove door again, but with the same results. I reached around to find my lighter. I couldn't find it. I found a small branch, and lit the end on fire. I lit the cigarette. I threw the branch into the fire. I stood there smoking. The chemicals made me dizzy. It had been months since I had smoked. I dropped ashes on my feet. My boots. Between the cigarette, and my hunger, I was warm all over. But then I got nauseous. I was afraid to puke, because that was where any food would be, in my stomach. I threw the lit cigarette into the stove. Half-smoked. I got back in bed. I wrangled covers around myself. I put my hand in the pocket of my coat, palming the package of cigarettes. I didn't remember putting them there.

Don't get me wrong, that is how I stayed until I fell asleep. And for some reason, I slept really good.

Part 7

I mean, I slept good, but for those goddamn mice screaming in my ear. Clattering. I must have found it disturbing because I dreamed that I was drinking root beer and Mountain Dew, trying to make myself throw up a dead mouse that was in my stomach. I couldn't tell you why my brain thought root beer and Mountain Dew would make me throw-up, but before that, I tried to eat a mouse head, to get the same results. I couldn't throw up though. I woke up with my face in a puddle of drool. Coughing. Almost violent coughing. I thought maybe the stove had got clogged, but there was no smoke in the cabin. I mean, it must have been from the cigarette, the half-cigarette that I had smoked. Strangely instead of just throwing all the cigarettes in the stove, I got up and lit a cigarette. This made me cough so much that I started laughing about it. Don't get me wrong, I had no desire to smoke, but there was some sort of mandate because the burglars had left the 10-pack carton of cigarettes behind. Like it was my duty to smoke them all. I tried another drag. Got the same results, threw the cigarette into the stove.

I couldn't tell if it was morning or not. I looked out the good window. I think it looked like dawn. I guess. It was snowing. Lots. I mean, like a blizzard, lots. I added some branches to the stove and stoked the fire. I tried to shut the door. There was that damn stick in the way. I really needed to deal with that. I went over to the cooler. Treated myself to three peanuts and a sliver of cheddar cheese. I sucked the salt off the peanuts, one by one. Then I nibbled them standing by the stove. When those were gone, I put the sliver of cheddar cheese on my tongue and let it melt away. I had a little burst of energy, followed by a fit of coughing that almost made me throw up. Puke. I went outside to grab a handful of snow and to look at the scene. The snow was really coming down. I looked at the burned down pine trees. That made me sad. A failure on my part. If I just had patience. I thought. Then Seneca Michael Miguel responded. He said:

"Then what, weto? You would have burned down the whole forest?"

"Ah, c'mon, Seneca, don't give me the grief, you know what I mean."

"Yeah, homey, I know what you mean, you're a dumb ol' pinche weto. Big surprise."

"Tracy, tell him I did a good job, please."

"You did a great job, Donkey!"

"No, not me, him."

"You did a great job, Seneca."

This stupid conversation ended as abruptly as it started. I went back inside and stood by the stove, sucking on the ball of snow I had gone outside to get. I stood there looking. Sucking. Not sure why the Goil Tracy was so robotic in my imagination, and Seneca Michael Miguel was so developed. I mean, if the Goil Tracy was supposed to be encouraging me to move forward, and if Seneca Michael Miguel was supposed to be holding me back, then what was it inside myself that gave him more power? I mean, I wanted to get out of here. I also wanted to find the goods at the bottom of the grave. It was like I wanted Seneca Michael Miguel to win out. To force me to suffer for the goods. The thing down inside that grave that couldn't be breached. But that was stupid. And I understood that. At least I thought I did. But why wasn't I thinking of a way to actually get out of the cabin? I mean, don't get me wrong. I don't think I am a stupid guy, I mean, I must be kind of resourceful, right? I have stayed alive this long. No thanks to nobody else, am I right? I mean, I feel like I should be making some homemade snowshoes, or something. A sled? I mean, I feel like I was giving up. That I gave up the second I decided that I wanted to get to the bottom of that icy grave. Where the goods were. And maybe all along Chaz knew this about me? I mean, I mentioned this at the beginning, that if you know a man's motivation, you will know his soul. I mean, did Chaz figure out my soul long ago, and is that why he was torturing me? Or more precisely, how he was torturing me? Like he knew that I would abandon my own self-interest for the sake of a supposed treasure, even though there was no real indication that I would ever get it? I mean, if anything, being trapped in the cabin felt more like a shitty job than it did anything else. Had I not quit shitty jobs in the past? I mean, I don't think I have. Now that I think about it, every job I have lost I lost because I got fired. What the fuck does that mean?

I mean, if that is what Seneca Michael Miguel was up to, what did the mean about the Goil Tracy? I mean, she was mostly silent, but complicit. Egging me on for no reason. A little hope on the horizon. Just enough nice energy to keep me going. A carrot to my Donkey, as it was. But even that was ridiculous. What was it that I would ever get from her? A nice word every now and then. Something unattainable. A vapid desire? Leading me to destruction? Like one of those Sirens on the rocks? I mean, don't get me wrong, but all the dumb choices in my life leading to this one moment, this moment that required all of my heart, and body to overcome, and all I had inside me was a desire to see what under a huge slab of ice in a grave, where the goods were, and a nice word from a pretty girl? Was that all that I amounted to?

I won't lie: this thought process created a panic attack. I had sucked all the water out of the ball of snow in my hand, and as a way to make myself stop thinking, I put the piece of ice in my mouth and bit down, hoping that my teeth would rebel, and wake me from my stupor. It kind of worked, but then the pain was so acute that I had to pick up a stick and start chewing on it. The taste of the stick was disgusting. Like dog shit or something. I spat it out and rubbed my tongue. With my fingers. I lit a cigarette. This made me sick, and dizzy. I started coughing. Violently. I might have stopped the panic attack, but by doing so, I felt like I might actually die from my actions. I ran outside into the snow. And for some reason I dove into a snow drift. And, funny enough, this stopped it all. All the thoughts. All the panic. It was peaceful, and kind of warm under all that snow. And dark. Pitch black. I lay crammed inside the snow for a few moments. Knowing I needed to get out, but not wanting to. What if I just stayed here? Let everything go? Just be done with it? I was happy to do so, until I got really cold. Or I supposed I was really cold. I mean, in a way I felt warm. And the idea of being really cold is what got me to get out of the snow bank. I thought back to the time the burglars brained me outside that one time, and I woke up freezing to death. That feeling was awful. I guess the desire to not have that feeling again was what motivated me. To get up. To get out. To go back inside.

Don't get me wrong, Seneca Michael Miguel was waiting for me when I got inside. I slammed the door, and stood by the stove. Shivering. The snow melting off of every inch of me. My hands out. Grabbing warmth. He said:

"Smooth move, Ex-lax."

"You didn't call me weto, Seneca."

"Why should I? You're the one who names things, homey."

"I don't know, I just, what does weto even mean?"

"I don't know, white guy, or something?"

"You don't know?"

"I know as much Spanish as you do, what do you think it means, homey?"

"I don't know, I guess, white guy."

"Well, there you have it, weto. What the hell was that? Jumping in the snow like that, homey."

"Oh, I don't know, I guess I just panicked is all. It was like a reset button, or something."

"Well, it was pretty stupid. You look cold, homey."

"I am cold."

"Are you? You seemed to have lost your mind, it looks like to me your weto-ass is impervious to reality. Maybe you should try another cigarette, just to prove me wrong."

"You don't think I will?"

"Oh, I know you will, homey."

"Oh, yeah? Just watch me."

I lit another cigarette, and coughed, and coughed, and coughed. Seneca Michael Miguel dispersed into the ether. I couldn't believe that I tricked myself into smoking another cigarette. Or, I guess it wasn't smoking a cigarette, just tricked myself into lighting another cigarette. I threw the thing into the stove. I was shivering and wet now. Steam was coming off my body. I wanted to lay down, but I didn't want to get my bed wet. I forced myself to stand there, drying off. I treated myself to a peanut as a reward for not getting into bed. The peanut was super tasty. I sucked the salt off of it first. Then nibbled on it for as long as I could. Which wasn't very long. I was so hungry. So tired. I had another bout of coughing. Then the earworm came back. And then I must have passed out standing up, but the mice started screaming in my ears again. Clattering. I woke up standing up. I was really losing my mind, and, I think, dying. I really had to pull my shit together. I mean, there was no help on the way. What was Chaz going to bring next? A twelve pack of Ice House? A bag of dirt? Some sunblock? Ice? I mean, how much further could he rub my nose into my own shit? It wasn't funny. There was no end to his cruelty. I guess. I mean, what the hell did I know what the future held?

For all I knew, the burglars would show up with an icepick tomorrow, and bag of sand, or salt, and a shovel that worked. A blow torch, and a plate of hot grilled cheese, and a bowl of tomato soup. Or whatever, they would take off their helmets, and declare this was all just a great big ruse. And I could go home, and eat hot dogs, and go to sleep in my own bed, and maybe get Seneca Michael Miguel, the actual Seneca Michael

Miguel to give me Goil's number, and her real name. I mean, I guess a guy can dream. Right?

So what, is what I say to that. I mean, there was no hope. I tried to make a plan to get out of the cabin, but I didn't get very far. I decided I should count all the 99-cent peanuts left, and slice the cheddar cheese into as many tongue-melts as possible. That way I could divvy up the remaining food for as long as possible. I didn't actually do it. I just thought of it. Instead of doing anything, I declared myself dry enough, and got into bed.

Don't get me wrong, the bed felt really nice. I mean, it was really cozy. I mean, don't get me wrong, but it felt dangerous. The malaise and inertia of what felt like a mid-life crisis, combined with the heat from the stove, the brow beating I kept getting from Seneca Michael Miguel, the sweet whisperings from the Goil Tracy, the snow gently falling outside, burying the landscape, I mean, I was hungry, but content. Not in the content with my life kind of way, more like, resigned to my fate kind of contentment. I don't know how to explain it. You know what I mean? I mean, I was depressed, but it was okay, because I was beaten down. And because I was beaten down, I could relax. Does that make any sense? Whatever, why am I asking you? I am telling you how it was, and that is how it was.

I mean, remember when I told you before that I was getting bored? Like the whole time I was stuck in the cabin it never occurred to me to be bored, there was too much to do? I realize I should clarify that statement. I don't mean to imply that I was actually bored. It's just, when you run out of things to do sometimes, you find yourself at a loss as to what meaning there is in life. You know? Like when you work 15 hours a day for six days straight, and suddenly you are done with the work, and you find yourself at home, having slept for like 12 hours straight, and you wake up hungry, so you eat something, but then there is nothing to do, so you start drinking at like ten in the morning? That is what I meant by bored. Like you know that there will be more work in the future, and not only that, but soon, but having too much freedom is a version of boredom. Like, I imagine that being rich feels like that. All dressed up with nothing to do but wait for lunch.

Don't get me wrong, the reason I bring this up is because I don't know how to explain things sometimes. So I just say stuff. Like when I named Seneca Michael Miguel, Kevin. Or Tracy, Goil. You know? Just spit it out, and hope for the best. And when somebody calls you out on it, backtrack. It has always been a problem of mine, and it seems it is just getting worse as I get older. Whatever.

I hung out in bed for a while, and then I got hot, so I stood up. I paced around, trying to think, but then I thought that I should count the 99-cent peanuts, and slice the cheese. But that just made me tired, so I got back into bed. Then I would just hang out. Drifting in and out of sleep. Getting hot. Hoping something would change, and I would get some new perspective. Then I would get too hot, stand up, pace around a bit, trying to think, think of a way to get out of the cabin, but this would make me think about how I should divvy up the 99-cent peanuts, and slice the cheddar cheese, and I would get tired again, and get back in bed. I did this all day. Eventually I gave up. I went to the cooler. Looked inside. Saw the cigarettes and remembered I should try and smoke. I lit a cigarette. I coughed, and coughed, and coughed. I threw the full cigarette into the stove. Too nauseous to eat suddenly, I got back in bed. I coughed some more. I felt achy and clogged up. I was hot. Really hot. This alarmed me. I put my hand on my forehead. My hand was just as hot as my forehead. I felt like I might have a fever, but who knows. I mean, I don't think trying to smoke was doing me any good. I was thirsty, but I didn't get up to get any snow. I just stayed very still. Trying to dodge the obvious signs that I was in fact getting sick. Or was sick. That I had a fever, and the coughing was not just from the cigarettes. Something else was going on. Something I should probably be worried about.

Now don't get me wrong. I know this sounds dramatic that I would be getting sick on top of all this other shit that was happening, but I didn't want to believe it either. I tried to test my body to prove I was doing okay still. I held my breath and counted to thirty. I don't know what this proved, but I could do it. I did a couple sit-ups. In the bed. To prove that I could do that too. I played with my genitals until I got an erection. That was good news, I supposed. I thought about masturbating, to prove something else, but I didn't have it in me. Not sure if that meant that I failed that test or whatever, but I guess I failed that test. I tried to fart, thinking that that would prove my insides were still working, but I had no gas to let go. I did a big stretch, thinking that that would help my blood flow. All that did was make me aware of a weird pain in my side that I hadn't noticed before, which made me even more anxious that I was sicker than I thought I was. I got kind of scared and started shaking. Then I got dizzy. Then I realized I was working myself into a tizzy. So I just laid there. Arms at my side. Looking straight up. Waiting for something to change.

I fell asleep like this. Dreaming of disembodied heads flying around me. Laughing. Like some dumb cartoon from my youth. Scrooge Duck or something. Or I guess that is Dickens or whatever. But I woke up thinking about those heads floating around. Laughing at me. I poked them with a pin, and they would explode. They didn't mean anything to me. I mean, it's not like they were Chaz, or Glazer, or Seneca Michael Miguel, or Humphreys, or whatever. They were just scary heads that made me self-conscious. That I would poke with a pin and then they'd explode. Then I would fall back to sleep, and they would haunt my dreams, and I would wake up, and poke them with a pin. This went on into the night. Every time I woke up, I would be very hot and sweaty. At some point I managed to take my coat off. Which was good for a while, until I woke up shivering. Then I had to put it back on, but this was too complicated, so I just wrapped it around myself. Then my legs got hot. I unzipped my coveralls. I tried to pull everything down. I was too confused, and just ended up wadding my pants into my coveralls. Then my butt got cold, and I tried to pull everything back up, but everything was too confusing, so I just ended up uncomfortable, with some of my body parts exposed, and cold, and some of them extra-covered, and very hot. The whole scenario was just a wadded-up mess. In the end, everything kind of balanced everything else out, but I felt like I was lying on the bathroom floor, after a hot, and very wet shower, naked but half-covered in a semi-rolled-up towel, using the bath mat as a blanket. Things scratchy. Things wet. Things cold, touching linoleum. Things hot and humid. Plus the laughing, disembodied heads.

Don't get me wrong, this is going to sound stupid, but I thought the solution to what I can only describe as my fever, was to fumble around through my wadded-up clothing, and find the cigarettes, and the lighter, and smoke a cigarette. I was convinced that Chaz was fucking with me in a way that only if I got hooked on smokes again, he would let the burglars take me home. I lit a cigarette, and immediately felt like throwing up. That escalated into me having a coughing fit that pushed a fart out. I guess I finally passed that body test. I mean, I say that because I laughed about it at the time. I was able to stab the cigarette out, and fell back into the bed. Trying to get the covers over my body. Suddenly very hot and very cold at the same time. I needed some water. I just needed some water. And then, against all of my wishes, I threw up on the floor. Right on top of the cigarette butt. It was yellow bile, with small chunks of 99-cent peanuts in it. My hot red fingers picked through the mess, picking up the chunks of peanut, putting them back in my mouth. I was confused as to how I could see them. Then I realized that in my fever adventures, I had managed to turn myself around on the bed, and was now facing the stove. The light from the fire was peeking out. I really needed to get that piece of wood out of way so the door could close properly. I mean, I guess. I was glad I could see the little chunks of peanut floating in the puke. Also, I knew what I was doing was gross, but something in me didn't care. I couldn't lose that food. I just couldn't. What stopped me from eating all of the peanuts chunks was that the heat from the stove reduced the bile to some sticky, slimy goo, that acted like long boogers when I pulled it from the floor. Like there was now chunks of dirt, and branches, and whatever else stuck in it. I couldn't tell what I was picking up, and putting in my mouth. I played around with the cigarette butt after I gave up trying to eat the peanuts. This was relaxing, I guess, because I fell back asleep.

Don't get me wrong, I am sorry to bore you with all these details, but there was something funny about this when it was happening. I mean, I was in dire straits, I guess, I mean, isn't that what you say? Dire straits? Where does that come from? England? I say that, and the earworm comes right back into my mind. Damn it! But all of this was funny at the time. Not because it was actually funny, just because I was having this moment of: Can anything get any worse? Eating peanuts out of my own puke? Who does that? But it's not like I had a choice. I was thirsty too, and that was funny to me. It would take all my energy to get up, and get some snow to eat. I mean, who has that kind of energy? Not only that, but my hands were so hot, I imagined that I would try and grab some snow, and my hand would just make a hand-shaped silhouette in the snow bank. Like some dumb cartoon. Like I was cursed to die of dehydration. Like I had made a deal with the devil that I could be as hot as a fire in the land of ice and snow, but my curse would be that I would always be thirsty because I couldn't touch water, or something. I could breathe steam, but my thirst would never be slaked. Doomed forever, to be denied the one thing I desired in life. I mean, that is what I thought was funny. Because there was no way around it. All my poor choices led to all my poor results.

I spent the night asleep with my head at the foot of the bed. The light from the stove adding motion to my fever dreams. Thirsty, the taste of puke in my mouth. My body wadded up in pants pulled down and half-covered in coats, twisted blanket. All of it funny. Kind of. Mice, screaming in my ears. Clattering. The ear worm. One nice thing was the Goil Tracy was nice to me. Kept telling me, You are doing a really good job, Donkey. A great job! At some point I begged her to stop calling me Donkey. But she didn't hear me. Or maybe she did, but she didn't stop calling me Donkey. Maybe my voice was too weak. But whatever, what am I talking about? She didn't listen to me anyway, it was all brain stuff. I mean, I told her with my vibes to stop calling me Donkey. She didn't listen. And I was doing a great job. There was no doubt about that. So who am I to nit-pick. Knit-pick? Where does that saying come from?

Nits, and lice. Knits, and knitting. You pick nits with lice, do you pick knits in knitting? You drop a loop, is that the same? No, that's not true, you drop a stitch in needle-point, what the hell am I talking about? All this talk about fever is making me feel like I am having the thing that I am talking about, it doesn't feel healthy. Don't get me wrong, but I was trying to break through this fever. And try to explain it to you. What I mean is, I tried to tell the Goil Tracy to stop calling me Donkey, but she didn't listen. For good reason. If I wasn't going to stop calling myself Donkey, why would she? It really doesn't matter. It was all pretty funny at this point, kind of.

Don't get me wrong, this was the point when things kind of took a dark turn. Not that things were so righteous to begin with. But when I think back on it, I mean, I guess this was the moment things changed. My fever was getting worse. There was no denying it now. I was trapped. I was alone. Sick. My hunger was gone. I wanted out. I just wanted out. But there was no getting out. My guts were starting to rebel. I laid in bed trying to stay as still as possible. I think I had a migraine, or something. There was a place right behind my right eye that bright white with pain. My teeth felt like they were growing. I just knew that if I moved, something would break free, and I would explode. One way or the other. So I just laid there. Trying not to move.

Sleep came a couple times. Usually just long enough for my body to panic and think it was dying. Then I would wake up in pain and paranoia. The stove seemed to be working overtime. I don't remember putting branches in it. But it was hot. White hot. I laid there, trying not to move. Trying to think of anything that was different than the pain I was in. Which, don't get me wrong, was impossible. I tried to go inside my brain, and massage the pain behind my right eye. That didn't work. I tried to stab it. That didn't work. I tried to ignore it. That didn't work. I decided that I needed some water, some ice, something wet and cold. I debated this for some time. Trying to stay still. When I finally decided that getting some snow it was because I had a daydream about molding a chunk of snow into an icicle and licking it. I mean, I thought about for long enough that I decided that I just had to have it. It became the solution to all of my problems.

I stood up from the bed. I moved slowly toward the door. In my daydream I thought about getting snow from the broken window, but I didn't think I would be able to cover it back up again in a good way. Which would mean that I would just have to worry about the window. Which seemed like a dumb thing to worry about. I mean, I decided it was in my best interest to get some snow from outside the front door, instead of the behind the blanket covering the broken window. I took one step, and then that was it. I found myself running for the door. Puke streaming from my mouth. By the time I got to door, I had stopped puking. I stood, bent over, my hand on the handle. Breathing heavy. By sheer force of will I made myself feel better enough to open the door. I got outside, and that was it, again. This time I didn't try to run. I just bent over, and puked on the snow. I mean, the snow was fresh, so the puke just kind of made a hole in the snow, and disappeared. I waited for more to come up. Nothing. I grabbed as much snow as I could, and wadded it into a ball. My hands were so hot that it started melting immediately. I was too sick to lick it. I felt a wave of nausea. But I didn't puke. I waited for a few more seconds. Nothing. I went back inside. The puke on the floor was slippery, and I nearly ate shit, but I was able to get back to the bed without injury.

I got back in bed. I placed the snowball next to my face, and licked on it. It was more like an ice ball at this point. My hands were cold, and I put them between my thighs to warm up. I had to pull my knees up to do this. This made the ice ball roll down towards the bottom of my neck. Instead of moving the ice ball, I just bent my head down. This put me in a fetal position. My tongue was hot, and my breath was hot. I made steam with my short, shallow breaths. I didn't get much water, but I did feel better. The ice tasted very good. It cooled my tongue down. When my hands got warm, I reached up, and pushed the ice ball closer to my face, and I sucked on it. I was able to get some actual water out of the ball. I rolled the ice ball around, and sucked on the other side. This had an unfortunate consequence. It reminded me of a time when me and Chaz were standing outside the shaved ice stand in Basin during the hottest summer that I knew of.

Chaz was licking on a Tiger's Blood. I had got some weird combo that had banana flavor in it. Banana, and root beer, and something else. We had come back to town in the middle of the afternoon to get supplies, and since we were there, we decided to have lunch at the A&W. It was just him and me. I wasn't positive, but I think White had sent us back to town together as some way for us to clear the beef. I mean, we weren't getting along. That was certain. Not since that week of a hangover, and him giving me that 10-pack carton of smokes. I mean, I guess that was a joke, on his part, I just was never really sure. I mean, now I know it was because he was being an asshole, but back then I wasn't sure.

That weekend, the weekend after the hangover, was kind of bad news. I mean, I don't think we said a single word to each other at the apartment. I mean, I knew his feelings were hurt, but I could never figure out why. I mean, I guess I could have asked, but there was that incident with the sandwiches when I tried to understand his feelings, and then that time he knocked me out, and smashed a twelve pack of Ice House on my back because I asked him about his feelings. I mean, in hindsight, Chaz was kind of a big baby. Now that I think about it.

Anyway, we didn't talk all weekend. Not face to face. We avoided each other in the apartment. I mean, I think we had a couple of parties. But that was just drinking beer in the back yard. And it was easy enough to avoid each other's company.

But Monday came, and we still weren't talking. We both drove our own cars to work, even though we didn't need to. I mean, either of us could have driven. No reason to take two cars. Loading the work truck was awkward. The drive to the jobsite was awkward. I mean, I think White had us drive to town together not because he was hoping we would build a better friendship, I think he was just sick of us making things awkward. And, in his defense, I think he had two choices, either fire one of us, so things could go back to normal, or send us into town together so we could patch things up. And if that didn't work, he could still fire one of us. Or at least, move one of us to a different crew.

We didn't talk on the way into town. I don't know how we decided to go to the A&W, although I do remember White saying: You can stop at the A&W for lunch on your way back. Maybe that is all it took. But we stopped there for lunch. Which we ate in silence. Chaz got two corn dogs, a Big Papa Burger, and a large curly fries, as well as a root beer in an iced mug. I was surprised when he squirted ketchup on top of his fries. I didn't know that he did this. Which, in hindsight, I should have kept that information to myself, because it is what really drove a wedge between us.

After lunch we were feeling pretty good. I think I said a thing or two of small talk that led to us kind of talking again, and for Chaz to suggest that we get a shaved ice for the road.

We walked over to the shaved ice stand. He ordered a Tiger's Blood, I ordered something with banana and root beer. A combo thing. It was unbelievably hot out. The sun was relentless. Oh, I forgot to mention, on our way in, I decided to get a newspaper from the machine outside of the A&W. Machine? The newspaper box that takes quarters. Quarter machine? Whatever you call it. I put my quarter in and it didn't work. I pushed the refund button and the quarter got stuck. I could see it. There was a gap in the metal. The only thing I had on me that would fit in the gap was my house key. I took it out of my pocket, and tried to get my quarter to come down. Instead of my quarter coming down, my key went inside. I put another quarter in, thinking that maybe if I opened the box, I would gain access to my other quarter and my house key. That is not what happened. I got my newspaper. But my house key and my quarter were lost in the machine. I was pissed, but also embarrassed. I even asked the cashier. I said: Hey, you got keys to that newspaper machine out there? It ate my quarter. She said: We don't. That guy comes around first thing in the morning, I guess you could come over then, and talk to him then. I said: Oh, okay, no big deal. It's just a quarter. All the while thinking about my house key. I didn't mention that this happened to Chaz, but I think he saw. Or, I know he saw, but at the moment I just thought that he might have seen it go down.

But there we were, eating our shaved ices. Standing in the terrible sun. Burning alive. Chaz was eating his Tiger's Blood with the red spoon straw that they give you. I was licking mine, sucking out the sugar juice. Saying: Damn it's hot. Chaz smiling, in a way at the time that I thought he was my friend again, but maybe already planning to trap me in a cabin, and starve me to death. He said: Hot enough for ya? I smiled back. I said: Humphreys been rubbin' off on ya, eh? He said:

"Oh, Humphreys, fuck that, that dick is a douche. I can't believe you hang out with him."

"E-yeah, Hump is alright. He's just lonely."

"The dude's a junky, Donk."

"Don't call me Donkey please."

"Why not? You call me Chaz, what's the difference?"

"Oh, I don't know, you have always been Chaz, to me at least."

"I wasn't Chaz before I started this stupid job, ever think of that?"

"Yeah, alright, you got a point, but still."

We stood there next to the shaved ice wagon, Chaz, spooning his Dragon's Blood, me, sucking juice out of my weird combo with banana and root beer. I don't know why we didn't get back into the truck, and head back to the work site. I think we were wasting time. I guess. I wasn't driving so it wasn't up to me. And instead of just keeping my mouth shut I said:

"So you put your ketchup on top of your fries, huh?" I thought I was just ribbing him.

"Yeah, and? You feed your house key to the newspaper box, what's your point?"

He stopped eating his shaved ice. He looked up at me with one of the angriest faces I have ever seen.

"No, no point." I said. Trying to play it off.

"Just sayin.'"

"Just sayin'? That's pretty fucking rich."

He squeezed his shaved ice. The Styrofoam held his finger marks for a second before they bounced back. I was afraid he might punch me.

"What about you? What, with your side of ranch? Excuse me for not getting my dipping sauces in containers when I eat my lunch."

I got a Big Papa Burger too. Except with onion rings, and a side of ranch. Not that I could take that back, or that he didn't have a valid point. I said:

"Hey man, I was just ribbing you, just something I noticed is all. I just never noticed you ate your fries that way, is all."

"Sometimes, Donkey, I don't even know what to make of you. Staying out all night with Humphreys, doing meth, hungover all week. I mean, you're not really the same guy as when I met you. I am starting to think you are a bad friend. I mean, you don't even work very hard. You just, I don't know, do your job or whatever, it's like you aren't even trying to get ahead. I mean, I think you might be lazy."

"I'm lazy? You are still pushing dirt, man. If anyone should be hanging out with Humphreys, it's you! You two are like a couple peas in a pod! Humphreys and Chaz, they should write a fucking book about it. Except nobody would, because it would be so boring. And you wouldn't read it because you are too lazy to do shit, and you would probably use the book for a pillow because you can't stay awake for two seconds! Even if you have a chew in your mouth!"

"What the fuck are you talking about? I fall asleep in the truck, and that makes me lazy? What does that mean? You stay awake, and suddenly you should be the king of the world? Dude! All you did last week was your job, and now I should be impressed? You really are a piece of work. I don't even know how to say it."

"Yeah, well, don't bother saying it, because I already know."

"You know what? Fuck this! I'm done."

Chaz threw his shaved ice to the ground. The Tiger's Blood went everywhere. The Styrofoam cracked in half. Bright white. Reflecting the sun. Red syrup dripping down its sides. I looked at the teenager who was in the shaved ice wagon. She seemed horrified. I made a mouth thing that said, I'm sorry. I put my banana and root beer combo on the metal counter outside the sliding window. Chaz stormed off to the work truck. I couldn't bear riding inside with him, so I got into the back. I had started to sit down when he peeled out in reverse. I fell onto everything metal that was there. Slicing my arms and my hands to pieces. I don't think this is what White envisioned when he sent us to town to get supplies. But this is what he would get back.

Part 8

Don't get me wrong, but I could taste the banana and root beer in the ice ball that I was sucking on. I could also taste the chewing tobacco spit in the Mountain Dew bottle that Chaz used when he had a chaw in. I thought that maybe I did actually have a mouse in my guts that I needed to throw up. Like that dream I had was coming true.

I was not feeling well. And I did want to throw up, but I didn't. I stayed curled in the fetal position. Trying not to move my body. The white light behind my right eye was still there. Throbbing now, instead of being an acute source of pain. I visualized cramming ice into it. Then the ice would melt in the center. Then that would fix things. That helped. Briefly. But then I took a bite of ice, and gave myself an ice cream headache that made me writhe in bed thinking I had given myself a stroke. When that pain was gone, I tried to stay as still as possible. Which made my stomach rebel. And I was running towards the door for a second time. Puking the whole way there, but fine by the time I got my hand on the doorknob.

On my way back to the bed, I slipped on the vomit, but I was also able to put some more branches in the stove. I was still very hot, but the stove looked empty. I decided that not freezing to death was probably a good idea. Even if I was as hot as I was.

At one point there was a loud creak from the roof. Then another. Then the sound of water running. Then the creaking sound again. I ignored it as much as I could. I was nervous, but I didn't think something was wrong. I listened as intently as I was able to. In my fever brain I thought that Santa Claus had come. I listened for bells. There was no bells. Only the mice screaming in my ears whenever I fell asleep. Clattering. But the creaking seemed like it was slipping. Then just like that, all the snow that was stacked on the rooftop fell to the ground. I woke with a panic. My heart was racing. I sat up. Not knowing where I was. There was nothing to do about it. I imagined the cabin being snowed in completely. I pictured myself opening the door to a wall of snow. I mean, I guess the fire from the stove was so hot that it melted the bottom of the drifts that were on the roof. I mean, right? Why else would it come down like that? The only other scenario was that there was so much snow coming down outside that it had reached some critical level, and maybe the weight of the snow was too much? I mean, I didn't want to believe the second scenario. Because that would mean that things were pretty fucked. As much as I was ignoring the idea of getting out of this trap, part of me was still trying to figure a way out. And that figuring involved less snow.

Don't get me wrong, I don't know if my fever broke, or it got worse, either way, the same thing happened. And, frankly, I don't know what would have changed things. But as I lay there, licking the ice ball, curled in the fetal position, listening to the snow dropping from the roof, making a fortress out of the cabin, getting freaked out about it, I heard the snowmobile approaching.

Don't get me wrong, this noise was kind of not wanted. Not because I didn't want to get the fuck out of here, and damn-it I would! I mean, I thought this every time the burglars came around, but still, this time I would fuck those assholes up and ride their sleigh back into town like a hungry, rabid, Santa

Claus. But I had this fever, and I didn't want company. I was puking, and soon, I was sure, that things would start coming out Santa's bag.

My point is, I was not in the mood for company. And especially company that would ka-bong me when I wasn't looking, and leave me a 10-pack carton of cigarettes as a door prize. I mean, just talking about this reminds me that I should smoke a cigarette.

I lit a cigarette, hoping it would ward off the burglars. Thinking maybe they would catch my vibe. But they were the same as the Goil Tracy. Not that I made them up in my brain, just that they wouldn't listen to me anyway.

The cigarette backfired. I just coughed for a while, and then I puked. Then I laid back in bed. The ice ball got stuck somewhere that I forgot about. Don't get me wrong, I found it pretty fast when It told me where it was. But it was gone for a long time first. Then it was wet. Then I threw it at the wall because I was angry. Then I looked at the snow melting to the floor, and it made me thirsty. Then I felt like an idiot.

My fever made me feel like shit. I was trying to do some thinking. I mean, I kept having this plan to ambush the burglars. But I couldn't do it because they always outsmarted me. I mean, I guess that is how you would say it. What they did, mostly, is sneak up on me, and wonk my head when I wasn't looking. Which I guess is them outsmarting me. But whatever. They think they are so cool, we will see about that, right, Goil Tracy?

"You are doing a great job, Donkey."

I thought so.

The problem with the burglars is that they were always elusive. Whenever I tried to get them, I would either fall asleep, or they would brain me when I wasn't looking. Which meant, I mean, if you think about it, this meant that I should find a better place to hide. Somewhere they wouldn't find me. Which, if you remember, all the snow fell from the roof, and no thanks to anything, I was thinking that I might have a chance to climb that snow and get myself situated up there. Then they wouldn't have a clue about my whereabouts, and I could either jump down on them and give them the braining they kept giving me. Or, OR, hop on their snowmobile and ride off into freedom.

I made myself get up. Shaky, and hot. Not puking, but nearly. I made it to the door. I opened it. There was a wall of snow. I punched a hole in it. I say that like it was easy, it was not easy. I punched a single punch. Which went through the snow. But then the heavier snow on top collapsed on top of my hole. I punched through again. With the same results. I punched a third time, and the whole thing collapsed. I mean, the top collapsed, and I was able to crawl up out of the cabin, and onto the roof.

I didn't want to leave the door open, but there was no other choice. There was no way to shut it. The roof was slippery, but made of wood. Cedar shakes. I got to the peak and straddled it, like a horse. I could see the light from the stove coming through the door I left open. This made me sad. All the heat was pouring out. But whatever, I had other ideas on my mind. I looked over to where the snowmobile noises were coming from. I could see a light bouncing about the forest. I thought I was being pretty clever. I mean, I was still feverish, but my plan was working out alright.

Time went by. The burglars were taking forever. But I didn't lose focus. This is how they got me every time. Lull me into complacency, and then whammo! a bonk to the noggin. I stayed there riding the cabin horse-style. Waiting. Watching. An hour must have gone by. But I stayed focused. And then, like an ingrown hair being teased out of its puss-filled sack, metaphorically speaking, of course, the burglars showed up. Hauling ass through the clearing next to the cabin. I mean, the one that was up, and away, and ended at the now toothless fence.

I watched the burglars stop the snowmobile. Turn it off. One of them was holding a small cooler. The other one was carrying an ice pick. The one with the cooler went to the right. Towards the door of the cabin. The one with the ice pick went towards the grave with the goods inside. I waited until I heard the one that went into the cabin. I don't know how he got inside, but he did, I mean, I could hear him moving about, but I slid down the side of the roof. As quiet as possible. I could hear the other burglar chopping at the grave with the goods inside. I ran as fast as I could to the snowmobile. I was slow, I mean, because of my fever, but I got there pretty fast. I turned the key. I started yanking on the cord. In order to get the thing started. As I was doing this I looked up. The burglar from the back of the cabin was running towards me, his ice pick held up above his head. Stumbling in the snow. Then I saw the other burglar coming at me. He had managed to get out of the cabin, but he didn't have his tiny cooler with him.

I got the snowmobile started just as the burglar from the grave reached me. I pushed the accelerator, and drove off, towards the other burglar coming from the cabin. Somehow the grave digging burglar had grabbed on, and was tearing at my clothing, and then in another bit of bad news, I ran over the small cooler burglar, but he also was able to get on the snowmobile. All of us dropped down in front of the cabin, and then took a turn around and into the back. I managed to steer the snowmobile into the graveyard. Knocking over three grave stones. Michael. Michael. Michael. Then we hopped the Miguel gravestone. Dropped down, and took a left. One of the burglars grabbed my leg. I went tumbling into the snow. The burglars drove off into the distance. Going away the same way they had come in. I sat there in the snow. Out of breath. I was very excited. I had got pretty close. I mean, I was still feeling pretty lousy, but I had got somewhere. I mean, I guess.

I forced myself to get up. My victory was not what it had seemed. I was still in the same place. And now I was lying in a bed of snow. I was cold, and it took all of my energy to get out of the snow bank I was lying in. I have no idea how I got back inside. But I do kind of remember sliding through the rabbit hole that was now the front door. I mean, I remember suddenly being very warm after sliding down something very cold. I mean, everything was dark, but then everything was light. I mean, all I am saying is that I ended up back in bed, and as insane as the snowmobile ride was, I was safe now, and the burglars were gone.

Don't get me wrong, I mean, I know that I was being dramatic about how things were getting pretty dark, but I won't lie, I mean, I did feel like this was a victory. I mean, nobody brained me, right? But that is the thing. I mean, I realized that I was up against too many odds. There was no future for me. Even if I could get on that snowmobile, I could only ride it around the cabin before a couple goons dragged me off of it. Same too with the goods in the bottom of the grave, I mean, if the same goons that were dragging me off the snowmobile were the same goons that couldn't get down to the bottom of the grave, and find the goods, what chance did I have? Not only that, but what other chance did I have of getting out of here? I mean, now I was sick and my food was replaced by cigarettes? Am I working in a coal mine suddenly? I mean, I was starting to think that death was just the same as life. I mean, at least in death you don't have to worry about shit anymore, I presume.

Don't get me wrong, but a lot of time passed before I was cognizant of my surroundings again. I must have been sleeping like a dead man, because I don't remember any dreams. The mice didn't scream in my ears. Clattering. There was no deep hungering. No Seneca Michael Miguel. No the Goil Tracy. Just heat. Heat, and blackness. I mean, my fever must have broken, or gotten worse. I mean, there was no difference at this point. Completion, I guess you would call it. My cough was getting worse. I mean, I guess this is what woke me from my dead man's stupor. And like the idiot I was, when I woke up, I thought it might make things better to light a cigarette. I did this. I coughed so much because of this that I nearly threw up. I mean, I coughed so much that I convinced myself that my bones had separated from my muscles, like my skeleton was now independent to my insides. And it wanted to get out. My back hurt. My shoulders hurt. My head hurt. My legs hurt. My eyes hurt. My ears hurt. My fingers hurt. Everything hurt. I felt like I had a hangover from drinking too much after a particularly hard day at work the day before. I mean, you know what I mean? Like I went out drinking to forget the day of work, but then the next day I had both a hangover from the booze, plus the hangover from the work. A double whammy of sorts.

After resting from coughing, I looked down at the cigarette I was holding. I tried one more time to take a drag. This gave me the exact same results. But this time it burned my eyes like I had walked into the smoke from a camp-fire. You know, like you think you can hold your breath, and the smoke will go away, but instead the smoke just sticks there, and your eyes burn, and you have to run away from the fire? Like that, but I had nowhere to go, so I threw the cigarette to the ground and coughed a bunch. My eyes watering. I thought for sure that would be the last cigarette I tried to smoke, but something inside me said it was not. Don't get me wrong, but I would cross that bridge when I got to it. Or whatever.

I did manage to get out of bed. To check on the fire. I made sure I stamped the cigarette out when I stood up. I mean, don't get me wrong, at this point I didn't really care if I dropped dead, but the idea of burning to death was appalling. That was no way to go. I looked inside the stove. The branches were coals, and since the fire was low, there was smoke coming into the cabin. This is part of the reason why that cigarette was so brutal. I hadn't noticed how smoky it was until now. I put some branches in. Got the fire going real good. Then tried to shut the door. There was the damned piece of wood that I should remove that was keeping me from shutting the door. I thought I should remove it. But I didn't remove it. I don't know why. I could see it. But now the fire was really hot. Next time, I decided. I stood there looking at the stove. Not really doing anything. Thinking maybe I should get back in bed. Then out of the corner of my eye, I saw something new. I turned my head. The small cooler one of the burglars was carrying. The one I had noticed before my wild snowmobile ride. It was upside down, and kicked up against the wall. I guess he had to ditch it quick when he heard all the commotion outside.

Now don't get me wrong, I already knew what was in the cooler. It was one of those small zip-up coolers, gray, with a strap on it to carry over your shoulder. The kind that fits a six pack of beer real nice like. I walked over to it. Picked it up. I did like a mental hand maneuver next to my head, and said out loud, A bottle of Jager, and an orange. I then said *Voila*! out loud. Unzipped the cooler. Sure as shit, there was a bottle of Jager and an orange inside. Chaz was getting pretty predictable. Don't get me wrong, I mean, I was starting to see the pattern. And I was starting to realize how this would end, but there was still time. I took the orange out, and put the cooler back down on the ground. I walked back to the stove, and held the orange in my hand. Looking. I had no intention of eating it. It wouldn't stay inside me anyway. But I did look at it. Hoping for an answer. I mean, I was starting to think that if all this shit that Chaz was doing to me was meant to torture me for the accidental nature of watching his girlfriend do that thing with the cucumber that one time, and then having her catch me rubbing one out because of it. I mean, maybe there was a secret way out of this conundrum. Like maybe this was meant to be a clue, and not just a torture devise?

I stared at the device for a long time. The orange I mean. And like clockwork, I was thrown into a memory so visceral that I didn't even need to peel the orange to taste it. Nor open the bottle of Jager. I was back inside the motel room in Basin, during the hottest summer ever. I was naked, and lying on top of the bed. The air conditioner was at full blast. I was fresh out of the shower. I was playing with my boner in my right hand, and flipping through the channels on the television with my left hand. Hoping to catch some good-lookin' babe on the news or something. I came to some infomercial that was selling bras for plus-sized women. That was enough for me. I shot a load onto my stomach. Got up, and wiped my stomach down with the dirty shirt on the floor next to the bed. I don't know if I had left the door unlocked, or slightly open, or whatever, but Chaz must have watched this happen because as soon as I put my pants on, he came into the room. Holding a gray soft cooler with a zipper, and a shoulder strap. He said *Damn, dog, that was some load!*

I was startled and kind of creeped out. I did a quick move to try and hide, but then I thought that was useless. I stood there shirtless, and watched him cross the room, and sit in the chair next to the windows. He unzipped the cooler. Put the bottle of Jager on top of the dresser with the television on it. Threw the orange on top of the bed. I reached down and grabbed the remote control. I turned the television off. I stood there looking at him for a while. I didn't want his orange or his Jager. And I was quite annoyed that he had just watched me rub one out without my consent. But he was here now, and aside from yelling at him to get the fuck out, I went and found a clean shirt, and a clean pair of socks. Put them on. The socks, while sitting on the chair next to the bed. The shirt I put on the bed. I was hot, and didn't feel like putting it on. I didn't feel like saying anything. I was waiting for him to say something stupid that would piss me off. We sat in silence.

Chaz had a way of getting me to do things I didn't want to do. And this was kind of the way he did it. By forcing me to sit in my own motel room in silence with an orange on the bed, and a bottle of Jager on the dresser, after watching me masturbate without my permission, like a creep, I mean, in hindsight the dude was a sociopath. But at the time, I just got nervous, put the shirt on, looked at the orange, and said:

"You gonna crack that, or am I?"

"Your room, your rules."

I sighed. He said, "What? Can't a dude offer an olive branch anymore?"

"Chaz, you're a…"

"I'm a what?"

"I don't know, a real piece of work. Let me get some ice."

I took the ice bucket and went outside. The concrete was hot on my socked feet. I ran into Humphreys on the way to the ice machine. He was smoking a cigarette outside his room. He said:

"Yo Donk, nice socks, you run out of boots?"

"Hey, Hump."

"Come over later, you want, I got some primo."

"Yeah, maybe."

"Oh, okay. I saw Chaz peeping your room earlier, what's up with that?"

"Ya got me. I mean, I don't know. Just getting some ice, I guess."

"You or Chaz?"

"Whaddya mean?"

"Who's getting the ice?"

"I'm getting the ice, Hump, I don't like where you're going here."

"Hey, man! Just sayin'."

"Well, say it to yourself."

"Oh, alright, gonna be like that then, come by later, you want."

"Yeah, we'll see."

Humphreys went back inside his room after flicking his cigarette into the parking lot. I went to the ice machine and filled up the ice bucket. I went back to my room.

Chaz was sitting in the chair next to the windows. Peeling the orange. I put the ice bucket next to the bottle of Jager. I found two plastic cups that didn't have cigarette butts or chew spit in them, and went into the bathroom to rinse them. I looked in the mirror; my face was annoyed. I tried to make it less annoyed. I am not sure if I did a good job about it or not. I took the cups back out into the room. I placed them next to Chaz. He put ice in them. Filled them to the brim with Jager.

Put an orange wedge in the cups. Causing the Jager to spill over. Handed me one of them. Held his cup up, and said:

"To the good times!"

"To the good times."

We both took a drink. Then ate the wedge of orange. The drink was nice. It turned into two. Then three. Before long, half the bottle was gone. Then we were drunk. Chaz started smoking in the room. Which was allowed, but gross. It made everything smell like shit. I still wasn't smoking because of the weeklong hangover Humphreys gave me. I did have some snus that I was sucking on. That kept me from smoking. But as time went on, I was getting tired, and didn't feel like getting drunk anymore. The smoke was giving me a headache, and the Jager was making me jittery. It was the middle of the week, and the next two days were going to be brutal. I tried to suggest that we call it a night, but Chaz was not having it. He was funny that way. Sometimes he would go for weeks without drinking, and then suddenly you would go out with him, and he would get so drunk that you would think he might die. I mean. He drank all the time, but never in excess. Not like the rest of us. But when he decided to get drunk, he really got drunk.

"What? You trying to get rid of me? We still got half a bottle!" Chaz said.

"Man, Chaz, the next two days are going to be brutal."

"Yeah, so what? You only live once! Let's ride it out, work is stupid, dog. Work is work. I got a whole pack of smokes burning a hole in my pocket-o. What else you gotta do? Suck Humphreys' dick? Whack one out to the bra channel?"

"Yeah, I don't know, man, it's late already, let's pick this shit up tomorrow."

"Tomorrow? Tomorrow! You think this shit will matter tomorrow? I don't even know what tomorrow, hey! listen! What do you think those fuckers are thinking about you, and tomorrow, I mean, listen! You think those fuckers give two shits about tomorrow? Your tomorrow?"

"I don't know, Chaz. I gotta hit the sack. None of it's fun, but I'm tired."

"Oh, fine! I'll drink this shit on my own, maybe Humphreys is still up, fucking better friend than you are!"

Chaz grabbed the bottle of Jager and stumbled out of the room. He left the lid behind. I locked the door behind him. I could hear him banging on Humphreys' door. Yelling, Humphreys! Humphreys! I got something to tell you! I am not sure if he got in or not, but the banging stopped. I felt bad for kicking him out of my room. I knew it would come back to haunt me. My only hope was that he would get too drunk to remember. Sadly, that wasn't true.

Don't get me wrong, but around midnight there was a banging on my door. Chaz was yelling, *Donkey! You dumb-fuck, open the god-damned door! Donkey! I know you're in there! Donkey!* I got out of bed and put my pants on. I opened the door. Chaz stood there swaying. There were tears in his eyes. He was drunk as a skunk. I said, *Go to bed, Chaz, we got work in the morning.* He said, *You and your fucking work. Is*

that all you think about? Come, let me in, let's have a drink. He looked down at his hands, surprised to see there was no bottle in either one. He held out his left hand, and said, *My hands.* Then he put his right hand up. He said, *Can you see my hands? These are my hands.* I said, *Chaz, you're drunk, go to bed.* He said, *Don't tell me what to do, you faggot-ass loser, I got more friends than you could ever think of.* At this point he kind of stumbled and collapsed like a finger giraffe. I sighed. Looked around. I could see Humphreys peeking out of his curtains, but aside from that, the parking lot and the rest of motel was silent and black. I dragged his body into my room. By his hands. The same hands he was just bragging about. I looked down. His crotch was growing wet. I sighed again. I got him just far enough in the room so I could close the door. I closed the door.

I took off my pants, and got back into bed. Trying to get some sleep. It was hard though. Chaz was snoring like a log, and every now and again he would fart. Which was whatever, but then the smell would hit me, like smelling salts, and I would be wide awake again. I did manage to get some sleep. But it was gross and annoying. When my alarm went off, I got up. Put my pants off, went into the bathroom, took a shit, and brushed my teeth. I drank some water and left the bathroom, leaving the door open. The smell must have woke Chaz up because he grumbled, then got to his knees, then the next thing I heard was him throwing up in the toilet. I got dressed. Not knowing what to do with him. I mean, I guess I should try to get him ready for work, or something, but I wasn't quite sure that that was a good idea. I mean, I asked him if he was okay. Silence. I went into the bathroom. He was passed out on the floor. I kicked him and said his name. He just mumbled. I got my lunch, and my water jug, and tried him one more time. Nothing. I said, Okay, Chaz, I am leaving, come now, or you'll probably get in trouble. He managed to tell me to go fuck myself. I made sure I had my room key, and left him where he was.

When I got to the work truck White asked where Chaz was. I said I didn't think he would be coming in today. He said, *Why not?* I said, *Brown bottle flu*. White got an annoyed look in his eyes. Threw his cigarette to the ground, and said, *Okay, let's go.*

Work was long, and hard, and hot, and unsatisfying. When I got back to the room the door was open, but Chaz was nowhere to be seen. I guess he must have chased the housekeeping away because the room was just as dirty as I had left it ten hours ago. Nothing was missing that I noticed. I didn't think much else about it. I took a shower and laid on the bed naked for a while, drying off, then I turned the television on, and flipped through the channels, looking for something to rub one out to. After that, I took a little nap. Got up, ate some smoked oysters and cheddar cheese on saltine crackers. Drank a couple Ice House. Brushed my teeth, and went over to the bar.

When I walked into the bar, someone yelled, *Donkey!* Humphreys and Earl were playing pool. White was smoking a cigarette at the bar, talking to Chaz. Chaz's face looked fallow. I couldn't tell if it was because of what White was saying, or because he was hungover. I ordered a Coors, and stood there at the bar. Chaz and White finished their conversation. Chaz stood up. Walked over to me. Said, *You're a fucking dick.* Then walked out of the bar. I shrugged, confused. White stubbed his cigarette out, and lit another one. I walked over. I said, *What was that all about? Oh, nothing you should worry about.* I said, *Okay*, and went over to watch the pool game.

A few beers later the rest of the crew was inside the bar, minus Chaz. Music was playing, and things seemed joyful, nearly drunk. I took Humphreys to the side, and said:

"Hey, man, what was that shit with Chaz and White earlier?"

"Shit, Donk, you got him transferred to a different crew."

"How is that?"

"You should have covered for him this morning. Kind of a dick move, man."

"Oh, bullshit! Dude was passed out on my bathroom floor, what, I drag him to work? I'm not his fucking puppet thingy."

"Yeah? You coulda lied. Said he was sick or something."

"Yeah."

I had no desire to argue with Humphreys. I also noticed at this point that the other guys were looking at me different than normal. My body got hot, and I was suddenly very annoyed. I sighed and chugged the rest of my beer. I said, *Fuck it*! and went back to my room. I knew that White was annoyed with the drama that me and Chaz were having, and that he had to make a choice about having us stay together or split us up, but how do you explain that to anyone that doesn't give a shit aside from what they saw? I mean, I guess I was the asshole here, but that wasn't the whole story. But who knows? Maybe I did get Chaz transferred? Maybe it was on purpose. I mean, I was sick of his drama, and I was sick of his bad attitude fucking my shit up. But what could I do? When I got back to my room, I realized I should have stayed at the bar and done some sort of personal relations shit to save my reputation, but I was not really in the mood. Chaz was being a dick, not me. I just wanted to do my job, get the paycheck, and go home on the weekends.

I mean, I guess I was wrong about just letting it go. I mean, here I was getting the treatment from Chaz, low-end torture. Stuck in this cabin with nothing but coolers filled with memories. I decided to try and drink some of the Jager. Maybe the booze would break my fever. I mean, I still couldn't figure out if I actually had a fever. Or if I was just a fever. I mean, in the scheme of what was happening. I mean, opened the bottle of Jager, and took a drink. I mean, it was gross, and warm, and hot on my insides. My stomach didn't like it, but I managed to keep it down. I lit a cigarette, hoping for a different result. I just coughed, and coughed, and coughed. I threw the cigarette to the ground, stomped on it. Felt a little dizzy. Took another drink of Jager. This made me nearly throw up. I put the bottle on the floor, and got back into bed. I was drunk. The room was spinning. The mice were screaming in my ears. Clattering. I thought out loud, to myself:

"That was stupid."

"Smooth move, ex-lax." Seneca Michael Miguel was back.

"Not your finest moment, homey."

"Yeah, well, I do a good job, right Tracy?"

"You do a great job! Donkey." the Goil Tracy said.

"See!" I said to Seneca Michael Miguel.

"You got it, weto. You get your friend fired, and now you are trapped in a cabin, getting drunk on an empty stomach, real classy, homey."

"I didn't get him fired, just transferred, and it wasn't my fault anyway."

"Whatever helps you sleep at night, muchacho."

"Muchacho? Your Spanish is worse than mine, Seneca."

"My Spanish is your Spanish, idioto."

"Oh hell, Tracey! Tell Seneca I am doing a great job."

"You are doing a great job, Donkey."

"Thank you."

Don't get me wrong, I fell asleep at this point. The booze, the fever, the empty stomach, the stagnant cabin, the memories of Chaz, and the drama he made, the burglars, and the goods down in the bottom of the grave, I was tired. Very tired. I think I should have tried to get up, and eat a couple of peanuts, maybe have a slice or two of sucking cheese, but I was too hot, too tired, my cough came back, but this time, instead of it being in my throat, it was getting into my lungs. I remember sleeping and coughing at the same time. Like I was under a blanket of smoke or something. I mean, I really needed to get that piece of branch out of the stove door, the smoke coming in was even worse than the cigarette smoke. Later, later, later. This was kind of how to describe the sleep that came to me. Later, later, later. I would take a nap, get refreshed, get up, eat some 99-cent peanuts, put some sucking cheese on my tongue, and fix the stove door. But for now, I would get a couple winks.

Don't get me wrong, it took a while to figure out where I was when I woke up. I was in a pretty awful state. I was sweaty and hot. I remembered, finally, that I had made a promise to myself to eat something. I couldn't stand the idea of eating the 99-cent peanuts, or putting a slice of sucking cheese on my tongue, but the orange seemed okay. In my weird ubiquitous nature, I was now every part of the cabin, and I somehow willed the orange to be underneath my back. I guess I really wanted it, because soon I was peeling the skin off of it, and slowly chewing on a wedge. The taste was good, but the orange was pithy. And there was seeds that crunched when I chewed. I got mostly juice from the wedges. Then I just spit what was left in my mouth on the floor. I did this until the orange was gone. Then I decided I should try and smoke again. The package of cigarettes I had in my pocket was now empty. I managed to get out of bed, go to the cooler with the 99-cent peanuts and the slices of sucking cheese, and get another pack of smokes. I made my way back to bed. Opened the cigarettes. Took one out. Lit it. And coughed and coughed and coughed. Don't get me wrong, I knew this was stupid, but I don't know, I guess I really thought I could get through to the other side of this horrible reality by doing this same maneuver as many times as was necessary.

I stabbed the cigarette out on the floor, then spit on it. I was tired, and hot, and now I had a headache. I decided it was the middle of the night now. There was nothing left to do but sleep. My stomach burned from the orange juice. I swallowed mouthfuls of saliva. My eyes hurt too, but I guessed it was because I was tired. Even though I was hot, I forced myself to get up, and put a few more branches in the stove. I tried to shut the door, but that damn chunk of wood was keeping me from doing it. Tomorrow. I would remove that chunk of wood tomorrow. For now, I would get some rest. Maybe think about why exactly Chaz was fucking with me, and how I could use that knowledge to save myself. I mean, I could feel myself getting stupider, but I could still solve mysteries, I mean, I guess.

Donkey

Part 9

Don't get me wrong, but I had the worst dream of my life that night. I can't even say what it was. I mean, I can say what it was, but what it was is hard to describe. It was more of a feeling than a dream. A feeling of finality. Like something inside me tipped over. Like this was it, the end of something. Me? The cabin? The mice? The burglars? The goods in the bottom of the grave? The Goil Tracy? Seneca Michael Miguel? Chaz? I mean, I woke up actually really scared. It was like my dream told me I had a brain tumor and everything was suddenly going to be finished for me. I mean, I mean. I mean, it reminded me of getting a migraine back in my younger days, when I would suddenly see flashing lights, and I would have a panic attack and think I was dying. I got out of bed, shaking. I was in a full panic. I thought that the piece of wood had something to do with it, because the smoke coming into the cabin from the stove was starting to overwhelm me. I tried to get the wood out, but the stove was too hot. I picked up a branch and tried to wedge it out. Nothing doing. I mean, anything to focus on. The panic hit again. I did the same thing I did the last time I had a panic attack, and went outside. It was snowing. The air was cold. I was about to jump in a snow bank to shock myself out of my misery, when I heard the snowmobile approaching. I thought, Oh, shit! I went back inside to think.

Don't get me wrong, I know this seems dramatic, but the panic was gone now. I paced around, trying to think up a plan as to what to do about the burglars approaching. My mind was blank. Why was I so stupid? I said it out loud:

"Why am I so stupid?"

"Because you are an idiot weto." Seneca Michael Miguel said.

"Thanks, Seneca." I said.

"Sure thing, homey."

"Tracy? What do you think?"

"I think you are doing a good job, Donkey." the Goil Tracy said.

"Thanks, Trace."

"A great job, in fact."

"Awww. You are too kind."

I paced around some more. I could hear the snowmobile coming closer. It was morning, I think. They were coming early this time. I honestly didn't know what to do. I didn't want to get brained. I was starting to think that the panic dream I had was related to getting brained so many times in a row. Like maybe the burglars knocked something loose up there. I wished that there was a tree I could go climb up, or something. Wait them out. I mean, I had nothing to say to them. And it was apparent that they had nothing to say to me. I mean, I wasn't going to steal their snowmobile, I learned that last time, the hard way. And as far as I could tell, the only reason they came around was to give me a cooler filled with memories and to fuck with my emotions. Like an evil-hearted Santa Claus.

Don't get me wrong, but I had two choices as I saw it. I could hang out in the cabin, and hope for the best, or I could run out into the trees, and maybe freeze to death. I mean, I guess I could get up on the roof again, or try and fight them, but those ideas seemed even stupider than the other two options. I guess, in the end, I did the one smart and inevitable thing: I stood in a corner, facing the wall, and waited for the nightmare to be over. At least I would be warm. Brain bonk or not.

When the burglars showed up, I heard them shut the snowmobile off. Both of them came into the cabin. I stood there motionless. My eyes closed. Arms at my side. I heard them walk in. Shut the door. The cooler lid got opened. I guess, or that's what it sounded like. Then I heard them talk:

"Where is the dude?" [chunk-chunk]

"I don't know, I guess he is outside somewhere?" [chunk-chunk]

"Oh shit!" [chunk-chunk]

"There he is, in the corner!" [chunk-chunk]

"What the fuck!" [chunk-chunk]

"I don't fucking know man!" [chunk-chunk]

"Fucking creepy-ass shit!" [chunk-chunk]

"Let's blow!" [chunk-chunk]

I guess I scared them off, because they left in a hurry. They didn't even brain me. Nor did they go out back and try and chisel the goods out of the grave like usual. They left the door to the cabin open. I heard them drive away on their snowmobile, as fast as they had come in.

Don't get me wrong, but I was glad they were gone. I was glad they didn't brain me. I can't say I was too excited to see what they had left behind in the cooler. I mean, unless it was a pair of snowshoes, or a pistol so I could put an end to this, there was nothing in there that would make any of this any better. I stood in the corner for some time. Not wanting to turn around and face reality. Eventually there wasn't any reason to just stand there looking at the wall anymore. I turned around. Walked over to the bottle of Jager. Picked it up. Took a drink. It was gross and warm. I dry heaved a little. I tried to take another drink, but I just couldn't. I lit a cigarette. This was stupid. I just coughed, and coughed, and coughed. I threw it to the floor, and stamped it out. I walked over to the stove. Tried to get the piece of wood out again. The stove was too hot. The smoke coming out was too much, so I threw some more branches in to get the fire going. This helped. Smoke-wise. I stood there staring at the stove. Then, without really thinking about it, I walked over to the cooler and opened the lid.

A cucumber.

Don't get me wrong, but I had to laugh. I had to laugh because this was all so fucking stupid. I mean, I know you are going to think I am a liar now, but what can I do? I guess I need to come clean. I mean, that cucumber was one of those long ones with the plastic on it. Long and skinny. Dramatic. A very dramatic cucumber. The same cucumber Lorinda had done that thing with, that one time in the kitchen when I was standing there trying to make breakfast. The same cucumber that kind of ended my relationship with Chaz. The same cucumber that made him make me move out of the house we shared, and forced me across the tracks, into the house I was living in now. I stood there looking at the cucumber. Laughing. I mean, don't get me wrong, the laughter wasn't like a hearty, guffaw-style laughing, more like, I can't believe it kind of laughing. Plus, I think that maybe it had the opposite effect of what Chaz has intended. I found myself aroused looking at that dramatic cucumber.

I mean, hear me out. I may have said things earlier that made it seem like I was a choir boy when it came to the events that transpired that day in the kitchen. But I guess I should come clean now, otherwise you won't trust me when I explain a few things later. I mean, don't get me wrong, but here is what went down.

I was standing in the kitchen doing whatever, making breakfast or something. Lorinda came in, naked. This is true. I mean, I was turning some bacon over, or something, flipping an egg. She went to the fridge. Opened the door. Squatted down. Took a cucumber out, the same kind of dramatic cucumber I was looking at. Still in the plastic. I don't even know. I mean, she somehow rubbed the cucumber down below, and kind of licked the tip of it, or whatever, at the same time. This is true. All the time, looking at me, staring, I guess. At this point I turned off the heat under the skillet. I had to double check it was off, even though I was very distracted, because I had a habit of leaving the burner on just a little bit, which had caused a few scares a couple of times over the years. I mean, who is bad at turning off burners? I mean, it usually happened when I was very tired. I mention this because it meant that I stayed a couple extra seconds as Lorinda did that thing with the cucumber.

Don't get me wrong, but I don't remember if I was wearing a bath robe, naked underneath, or boxers, or long johns, or what, but I couldn't hide my excitement. And I know you will hate me, but I didn't try to hide it. In fact, I kind of put it on display. I walked out of the kitchen, and into my bedroom. Now, I know you will hate me even more, because I did not in fact close my door. I left it wide open. And instead of discretely taking care of my business like I led you to believe before, I laid there with all my glory, hoping that Lorinda would come in. And the thing was: she did, in fact, come to the door, and said something like: *Well, aren't we making a show of things?* She shut the door, and what happened next was the violation of a coveted friendship that would not survive.

After we were done, I told her we should never speak of this again. Which, for good reason, made Lorinda very angry. I mean, I wasn't sure she had feelings for me, and there was every indication that she did in fact, not, have feelings for me, but whatever, what happened happened. I tried to explain to her that this was not good. That we should come up with an alternative storyline in case he thought something was fishy. Which, I mean, Chaz was kind of a wildcard, and he would sense something was up. And he knew that Lorinda liked to march around the house in the nude, so his paranoia wasn't that far off, but the lie I came up with was to tell him a half-truth, that she had caught me wanking it, after seeing her doing that cucumber maneuver. But I guess in the end, she told him the complete truth. I mean, I guess that was apparent now, looking down at the cucumber in the cooler.

Don't get me wrong, at this moment, aside from being aroused, thinking about that indiscretion, I kind of had the feeling that Chaz was going to show up pretty soon, and put an end to this farce of an imprisonment that he was subjecting me to. I mean, what else was there to do? What else was the end-game? What other times had we struggled in our relationship? I mean, I'm serious. I didn't mean to lie about what happened with Lorinda, but I had no choice. I mean, you wouldn't even listen to a single word I said if you knew that I slept with my best friend's gal, right? I mean, all this guilt and anguish that I am feeling right now, how can I explain it without putting it into context, right?

Whatever. Hate me all you want. But it still won't compare to what I have coming to me. And if you can just give me one more chance, I won't let you down again. I swear.

Don't get me wrong, seeing that cucumber made me feel better. I mean, not in the way that I felt better seeing it, more like in the way that I knew now that there would be an end to all this madness. Not only that, but probably soon. I mean, in some ways it was better than snowshoes or a pistol. I mean, things would be coming to a head soon enough. Like maybe Chaz would show up on the snowmobile next time, and we could have it out, and he would kill me, or whatever, or we would just get into a fist fight, or he would just say something like *Donkey, you have suffered enough, you are an asshole, but I forgive you, just keep your hands off my hot stuff in the future.* Or something.

In that feeling of relief, I ate the entire cucumber. I also ate the rest of the 99 cent peanuts, and all of the sucking cheese. I felt pretty good afterwards. My anxiety was gone. Like a weight was lifted off of my shoulders, as they say. I had a full stomach. I drank some Jager without feeling ill. I even smoked a cigarette all the way to the butt before it made me cough out a lung. I was feeling so good that I almost got the piece of wood that was keeping the stove door from closing, out. I mean, almost. That thing was really in the most annoying position. I gave up when I burned my fingertip so bad I gave myself a blister. But so what? I celebrated my newfound freedom with another shot of Jager. Then, being warm, and half-drunk, I went outside to make plans about how to get to the bottom of the grave again. To get at the goods waiting for me.

The snow was really coming down now. I mean, I know I was on top of a mountain, but is it always like this? I mean, I felt like I had been here for months now. Was it only weeks? A week? Was it Spring? Was this Spring snow? I mean, I didn't really know. The days were getting longer. I supposed. I mean, I could hardly tell, I mean, with the clouds in the sky all the time. But the days did seem longer. But then again, I could barely tell if it was day or night anyway anymore. Watching the snow fall made me feel like an idiot for eating all my food. I mean, the burglars were coming around every couple of days, but that didn't mean shit. I mean, maybe the idea with Chaz was to lull me into a false comfort, so that I would think that this would all be over, only to leave me starving to death. I mean, how was I to know that that wasn't his plan. I said out loud:

"Man! I am such an idiot!"

"No shit, Sherlock." Seneca Michael Miguel said.

"Okay, smarty-pants, what the fuck would have you done?"

"Oh, I don't know, homey, maybe not eat all my food for one."

"Well, thanks for chiming in when I needed you."

"I'm not your mom, homey."

"Yeah, where's Tracy? Tell me I'm good, Trace!"

"She ditched, dude. She knows you are a liar, and a creep now."

"Oh, fuck that, Tracy!"

"Good luck weto. She's not coming back, not until you make things right."

"You don't know that!"

"Oh, but I do. Look, it's snowing."

Don't get me wrong, but Seneca Michael Miguel without the Goil Tracy was not very pleasant. I left him outside, and went back inside of the cabin. Slamming the door. I mean, I knew I was an asshole, but was I such an asshole that Seneca Michael Miguel had one up on me? I mean, I doubt it. But maybe I did doubt it. I was filled with all sorts of doubt all of a sudden. And as stupid as this sounds, because I ate all the food, I now had a bunch of energy to feel doubtful about lots of things. And the thing I had the most doubt about was: why the hell did I think things would be fine all of a sudden? I mean, I was still stuck in the cabin, with nothing to eat, and only Jager and cigarettes to keep me alive. I mean, a dude can't live on cigarettes and Jager alone. Can he?

Don't get me wrong, but I was feeling sorry for myself again. The dream that gave me all of that anxiety came back into my mind. I was just stupid. Nothing I did would ever amount to anything. I could try all I wanted, but I would never pull myself up by my bootstraps. I was born to be poor. Born to search for goods in an impossible grave, while feeling guilty about all the things I did to get to this point. I mean, was I as bad as I thought? Was I really that big of a liar? If I just changed my ways would that make me a better American? I mean, I should have gone to college. I should have got married. Had kids. Instead I am stuck here in this cabin, starving to death, blaming all of my problems on a guy that doesn't care if I live or die, and the idea of a phantom Mexican filling me with self-doubt. I mean, am I both racist and lazy at the same time? Or did I just fall into some crack that society created when education switched from being useful to a thing that you buy to be in charge of things?

I mean, all I ever wanted to do was go to work, work, go home, and live. I don't know how it got so complicated. I mean, I might be a liar about some things, but those things are not all of the things. I mean, I don't think pitting me against my co-worker is the way to make things better. I mean, I guess I don't know if this is out of left field, Chaz, but I think your problems with me, are actually problems with White, and his inability to address our problems. I mean, the thing with Lorinda and the cucumber is bad news, but that has nothing to do with you getting transferred. I mean, White is the problem, not us.

Don't get me wrong, I can say all I want into the ether, but it won't get to the intended target. Wishful thinking is bunk. You have to live in a magical world for magical thinking to make a difference. I stood there thinking, and looking, the last of my food running through my veins. Feeling stupider by the minute. And hot. And frankly, alone.

I don't know what to say. I mean, don't get me wrong, my grim prospects were both a comfort and a source for great worry. I mean, I was starting to convince myself I had one last chance to get out of here. Out of the cabin and off of the mountain. The trees in the back, behind the graveyard. All I needed was one clear day. Just one. I would start another fire. Just like the first fire. The trees back there were more dense. The fire would be larger. The only problem, though, was that some of the trees were pretty close to the cabin, and I would probably burn the cabin down if I did this, I mean, if the last fire was an indication of how things would go. But whatever, I mean, if it got to that point anyway, I was better off just going out into the snow to freeze to death anyway. I mean, I was pretty close to running out of steam as it was. It wouldn't take that much to push me over the edge. I mean, unless Spring suddenly came, or some heat-wave or something, that would be a game-changer, or if Chaz decided to have mercy on me. Or the burglars brought me a steak and potato dinner, with a pair of snowshoes. That would be cool. But a bottle of Jager and a bunch of lousy cigarettes weren't going to get me anywhere, anytime soon.

I spent some very slow hours poking around the cabin. Thinking. I mean, I guess you could call it thinking. It was more like looking at stuff, and trying to make the stuff a solution to my problems. I mean, it was a little like looking in an empty cupboard with just a couple dried noodles and a box of baking soda. Trying to come up with a meal. There was no meal. Just some dried noodles and a box of baking soda. I mean, I had some tools, kind of. Like maybe I could make a sled or something. But when I thought this through, I mean, the problem was not the making of a sled, or something, but the problem of great big piles of snow, everywhere. I mean, what I needed was some Jesus powers to walk on top of it. You know? Or some Moses powers, to split it. Or like a giant blow torch to burn a channel through it. I mean, I did have the bright idea to try and make some skis. I even tried to pry up some floor boards. But then I snapped the blade off of the knife while doing this, and this made me so morose that I laid down and took a nap.

I mean, there was something about that that really made things hit home. I mean, don't get me wrong, I wasn't suicidal, but even if I was, the knife blade was now underneath the floor boards. And I couldn't get to it. So, I mean, now I had one less option to free myself. What is that, irony? When I woke up from my nap I felt really slimy. Dirty. Depressed. Everything had this film on it. Like dirty dishes that you cleaned, but you had no soap or hot water. You know? Like I tried, but by trying, everything just got worse. I mean, I don't know how to describe it. It was like I had made a decision, weeks, months ago, a small decision, a bad one, that had just led to another bad decision, and then another, and then another, and now all of the bad decisions had collected, collated, into this giant ball of darkness, and helplessness that I couldn't get away from. I mean, it felt so specific, this slimy feeling, that I was actually trying to figure out exactly the day, the minute, the second, everything took a turn for the worse. And because I was in this state, I just laid in bed, trying to find it. The moment when everything went wrong.

I mean, it sounds dramatic, but it was like my life was flashing before my eyes, not in some Hollywood movie way, but in some really depressing, starving to death, and feeling sorry for myself way. You know? Like my childhood. How sad and stupid it was. Free from joy. Just a lonely kid with no friends, and some lousy broken toys from Goodwill. Or like my teenage years. Devastated by acne and an angry father who had reduced my mother to silence with his emotional abuse. My first kiss, that wasn't even a kiss, but just me and Jill sitting on a couch while the sun came directly into the room, as I reached over her shoulder, and tried to get my hand under her bra, as we both were sweating profusely. Or getting tricked into getting drunk for the first time, and realizing my closest friend was a bully who was trying to get me in trouble, on purpose, and then trying to hide it from my parents, but then realizing that they didn't actually care. And then High School, and the terror that that was. And then living on my own, and terrible jobs, that paid shit, and how I just used all the money to buy 18 packs of Ice House, get drunk with other bullies I had found myself attracted to. Not in a sexy way, just in a, this is what I am used to way. And then all the moving around, and the job at the gas company, and Chaz, and Lorinda, and this fucking cabin. I mean, I was in tears by the end of all these thoughts. I mean, I cried. I cried, a lot. What a waste of a life. I mean, what did I ever do to deserve this? I mean, I wasn't a bad person. Or at least, I didn't think so. And not only that, but what would I do if I got out of here? The same old shit?

Go back to work? Pay my rent? Eat meat that I left on the counter for days at a time? I mean, I guess I was lonely. I guess I wanted a girlfriend, or something. Something to look forward to. But at this rate, I was going nowhere. Just a pipe donkey starving to death in a cabin, getting molested by an asshole bully that used to be my best friend. Tricked into finding some mysterious goods at the bottom of an unknown grave. Up in the mountains somewhere. I mean, I cried for quite some time. I mean, I cried myself to sleep again. I mean, it was a pretty brutal couple of moments inside of my mind that were, in the end, very exhausting. I don't think it is sustainable to feel that sorry for yourself for as long as I did. But I did it, and in the end, I was glad I did, because when I woke up from the second nap, I didn't feel nearly as bad about myself as I did before I fell asleep.

I got up from my naps. It was still light out. I put a couple of branches in the stove. I lit a cigarette. I coughed, and coughed, and coughed. Instead of just throwing the cigarette into the fire though, I held onto it. I took a drink of Jager. Then another. Then I took a drag from the cigarette. I coughed even harder. This made me laugh. I don't know what I was trying to prove. Or if I was trying to prove anything, I just felt like maybe if I could get back to smoking cigarettes again, maybe Chaz would know this and take pity on me. But as far as my body was concerned, this just was not working. I took another drink of Jager. My eyes burned. Not from the Jager, the Jager was smooth for the most part. And not from the cigarette, the cigarette ended up in the stove after the second coughing fit. I guess it was from the smoke coming out of the stove. I guess. The fire was really going now, and very hot. I had moved back from it. Like a few feet. Maybe all that crying had a roll. I mean, the last time I had any water was when I was sucking on that ice ball. And I couldn't remember when that was. Maybe my tears had dehydrated my eyes? I took another swig of Jager, hoping that would help. It did. Not because of the liquid going into my body, but because I was starting to get pretty drunk now.

Don't get me wrong, have you ever gotten drunk off of Jager? It's a tough nut to swallow. Like getting drunk off of cough syrup. It sneaks up on you from behind. Not like whiskey, or vodka, those guys come at you face-first. Jager just drags you down like a monster climbing out of a bog, or something. I mean, the reason the crew mixes it with Red Bull is because that way you don't just fall into a stupor. It's the kind of booze that fills your socks first, then your legs, then your torso, and by the time it hits your head, you are a goner. I mean, after taking what I think was about seven hits from the bottle, I was dead on my feet. Swaying back, and forth, talking to anyone that would listen.

"Seneca! Where'd ya go! Where is Tracy? You dick!"

"Oh great, a drunk weto, ain't that a fantastic addition to society."

"Oh, get off my ass. And stop being so negative, man."

"Hey, homey, you should watch who you're talking to."

"I can talk to whoever, however, you dick, where's Tracy?"

"Try that again weto, I think you should check yourself."

"Me? I should check my! Self! I'll punch you right now if you come closer. Coward like you."

I guess Seneca Michael Miguel punched me, because I could taste blood. Then my stomach hurt. Then I found myself on the ground. Then I looked over, the bottle of Jager was sitting on top of the stove. I stood up, thinking I should rescue it from getting too hot, when everything inside my body wanted to get out of my body. But this time it wasn't coming out of my mouth. I ran outside, and had to scurry up a snow bank, which was soft, and didn't support my body. I tried to get some distance from the snow and my naked ass, but there was no way. Suddenly I was shitting on an ice-cube. Or at least, that is how it felt. It was pretty gross. I was surprised that it didn't just go everywhere. I mean, I think it melted the snow, so at least my clothes were still kind of clean. Well, not covered in shit. But my ass, and the back of my legs were. I sighed. I was drunk, and I didn't know what to do about it. I kind of stood up, and dropped my ass into a clean space of snow. My balls shrunk. I wriggled around to clean myself. Then I waddled back inside. Just barely not tripping over my clothing. I was surprised I was able to get my overalls and my pants down so quickly. I don't know how I did it. I also don't know how I didn't just shit my pants. When I got to the stove, the Jager was boiling. I tried to grab the top with my pincer fingers, but it was so hot, the bottle just dropped to the floor and cracked open. The hot Jager spilling into the floor boards. I sighed. I mean, what a fucking day I was having. I scooted away and bent over. I could feel the heat warming my asshole. The shit on my butt cheeks and legs grew crusty and flaked off. When everything seemed dry again, I pulled up my long johns, my pants, and my overalls. I had to take my jacket and my long-sleeved shirt and my coat off before I could re-attach the hourglass hoops to the metal buttons. I put everything back on. I stood there feeling stupid and annoyed. The Jager was now gone. All that was left was cigarettes. I mean, even my dignity was gone now. I smelled like shit. I was still drunk. I thought, I mean, don't get me wrong, but I was pretty emotional, but I thought, Who would love me now? Then I started bawling.

Like a teenager, I ended up on the bed again. My tears draining into the pillow. This didn't last very long, because I fell asleep pretty fast. I mean, it was all pretty funny, how miserable I was, and my sobbing was very dramatic, so dramatic, that my mouth was as wide open as it possibly could be, before I just started shuttering, and weeping, and then I felt warm, and like I said, I passed out. And then that was it. I was done for it. I slept the entire night through. Waking up only when the sound of the mice screaming in my ears became too much. The clattering. The ear worm came back. And I'll turn right back around. Give me one reason. I mean, I guess the Goil Tracy came back. Or Seneca Michael Miguel let the Goil Tracy come back. I forgot how it worked. Or maybe that isn't how anything worked. But the song kept going this time. My youthful heart will love you, if you give it what it needs. But then it pulled back. Switched back. Why...I should stay. Then the mice screaming in my ears. Clattering. I mean, as far as restful nights of sleep are concerned, this was not one of them. But because I was drunk and I could smell shit coming up from the depths of my clothing, I mean, considering, I slept pretty alright.

Don't get me wrong, I mean, between all the waking up, and going to sleep, and waking up, and going to sleep. The worry in the daytime, the worry in the nighttime. The trying to get somewhere I knew I would never get. The hoping and wishing for something better to come along. The bad decision after bad decision. The hunger, and the hangovers, the poor diet, and the embarrassment. I don't even know. Somewhere, deep within me, a light went out. I mean, it wasn't like a big thing. Like an epiphany or something. It was something more common than that, like I was starting to realize that I wasn't much in grand scheme of things. I was inevitable, and expendable. A cog in some shitty machine that didn't care if I lived or died, as long as I was suffering just enough that I didn't have the energy to rebel, but comfortable enough that I would keep trying to get ahead. Even when I knew that the entire machinery was designed to destroy me. I mean, that morning, I knew something was up. Something was over. Something had happened somewhere far off that had sealed my fate. And as much as I wanted to care, I just couldn't. I mean, what was the point? I mean, I knew I would never get the goods at the bottom of the grave, they were never meant for me in the first place. I mean, I was starting to think that the only reason the burglars were trying to get the goods whenever they came around, was to trick me into having hope. And that this last time they came around, they intentionally didn't try to get the goods because they were now trying to destroy that hope. And in a normal world, this would just make me want to get the goods even more, but because I was too stupid, and too poor, I mean, poor in spirit, I didn't care anymore. I mean, I cared enough to still think about it, but not enough to do anything about it. You know what I mean? Not to mention, I was also hungover.

I got out of bed and looked down at the broken Jager bottle. Don't get me wrong, but it filled me with shame. I kicked it under the stove. Out of sight. I mean, I didn't want to look at it. I put a couple branches in the stove. Lit a cigarette, and coughed, and coughed, and coughed. This was bad. This coughing was getting worse now. I mean, it felt like it was coming from deep inside my lungs now. Like I had gone too far. I mean, like I had pushed myself over some edge of no return. I kept thinking about telling Chaz, I am never smoking ever again. Why did I think that making myself smoke now would make him treat me better? You know? I mean, don't get me wrong, but the dude was a bully before, and now he was like a bad boy bully that could make me do stupid shit that I wouldn't normally do, just for his own amusement. The problem was, I mean, I had pushed it too far, even for myself, and now I was feeling quite ill, like I had ruined my lungs for good. I mean, maybe it was because I wasn't drinking enough water, or I wasn't eating enough food, or the stress of being stuck in the cabin with no way out, or maybe just the simple fact that I couldn't get the goddamned piece of wood out, the one that was keeping me from closing stove door, and all the extra smoke that it caused. I mean, I don't even know. I mean, I felt oppressed. And not in the normal way. I mean, I felt oppressed by my own body. I mean, I think I knew the light went out, because I think I knew something was wrong. I was starting to think I was actually dying.

There wasn't much for me to do in the cabin. Anymore, I mean. I kept vigil by the good window hoping to see sunshine,

I mean, that the snow would stop, and the skies would clear and I could set the woods on fire. I mean, the trees. I mean, that was my plan now. My last-ditch effort to get out of here was to start another forest fire, and signal my distress. Don't get me wrong, I knew it was stupid. I mean, I was certain now that it would probably burn the cabin down when I did it, and it would mean I was truly fucked. But as it stood right now, I was truly fucked anyway. I can't tell you how I knew, but I knew I was alone. There would be no further visits from the burglars. No savior. I was my own self-licking ice-cream cone. And the flavor I chose was dirt and cat shit flavor. I mean, I had two, maybe three days left before my body gave out. And I would be too weak to enact my exit plan, even as stupid as it was. I tried to stay busy. I mean, to not think about it. I mean, I would try, and smoke, and then I would cough, and cough, and cough. Just getting to the edge of throwing up. I mean, I didn't want to have to eat my own puke again. So somehow, I was able to always cut it off at just the right moment. And, I mean, don't get me wrong, but this took up a lot of my time.

I paced around as well. A couple times I went outside to get a handful of snow, trying to get rid of the headache that seemed to have taken hold but never got so bad that I was in too much pain. I guess I got in bed a couple times. Hoping to take a nap. But the worry of impending doom wouldn't let my brain relax, so I would get up again, and either pace, or smoke so I could stop thinking, and just cough. I mean, there was something peaceful about it all. Seneca Michael Miguel even seemed to have ditched me. Taking the Goil Tracy with him. The ear worm was gone. Everything was warm. And tight. And cozy. It was like some soft rainbow hat drifted into the cabin.

Like a mood lighting, of sorts. I mean, sometimes you just give up, and the solution presents itself, and sometimes you just give up, and that is the end of it. I mean, things were kind of really scary, thinking about things ending all of a sudden, and the idea of losing all control was a hard truth, but I mean, I don't even know what I mean, how does one explain what it feels like to be dying? I guess that is my point. At the time, I didn't really care. I had done my best with what I was given, and if that meant that I died in a cabin on top of a mountain, I mean, I guess that is how things go. Don't get me wrong, I won't pretend I wasn't angry, but my anger was not going to save me. And not only that, but who the hell was I supposed to be angry at? Chaz? God? Seneca Michael Miguel? Lorinda? I mean, if I was angry at anyone, I was angry at myself for acting the way I did in my life. And because it was me, frankly, I forgave myself. I mean, I did the best I could, with what I was given. So what? Suck it, Society.

Don't get me wrong, but I thought about making a will. But that seemed stupid and impossible. Impossible! What did I own? My stupid crappy car? A few thousand bucks in my bank account? A gallon of milk in the fridge at my apartment? The thought was ridiculous. I also thought about my legacy, don't get me wrong. I mean, like, what was my purpose here on earth? Getting drunk with oilfield assholes? Working for oilfield assholes that were making millions while I just lugged pipe around for them? Sleeping in shitty motel rooms in butthole towns in Wyoming? Doing drugs with Humphreys? Sleeping with Chaz's girlfriend? I mean, it was all just a day-to-day humiliation. What was the point? I had to cut myself off from thinking about it because it was so depressing. I just stood around after these thoughts. Staying comfortable. Looking out the good window hoping for sunshine. Trying not to think. Smoking cigarettes to cough away the time. I mean, when it got too dark to see things, I got into bed. And when my mind would calm down just enough, I would drift off to sleep. Then the mice would come back. Screaming in my ears. Clattering. I would wake up in a sweat. Remember all the things that were happening. Try and calm myself down. Then drift off to sleep again.

Don't get me wrong, but this went on longer than two days, or even three, like I had predicted. The burglars never showed back up. Each day I spent more time in bed than the day before. I stayed warm. Almost too warm. At some point I stopped smoking cigarettes. Not because I ran out, but because the coughing fits were coming un-prompted. There was no point. I really needed to get that piece of wood out that was keeping the door from closing. I mean, it was actually funny to me, now. The idea that I was being attacked by smoke because of a stupid piece of wood that I could never get to. I mean, irony, or something? I mean, I couldn't quite put it together how it was ironic, but there was something about it. I mean, I guess it was like a chip, or something. Like it stuck in my craw. Maybe irony is the wrong word, maybe the word was analogy? I mean, don't get me wrong, I don't want to make a bigger issue out of something that was a small issue, but it was this small thing that if only I could get rid of, I would be much happier in my life. I don't know, what do you call that? A metaphor, I guess. Like the chip was my anger or something, and if only I could get rid of the chip, I would be successful, and live a long and fruitful life, but the irony was that whenever I tried to get rid of it, I just made things worse because of the mayhem I had created by trying to get rid of it. Don't get me wrong, but, I don't know, I mean, whatever.

None of this mattered anymore. I spent five days in limbo before I decided that the next day, come whatever hell, or high-water, or whatever, I was going to light the trees on fire, and I would signal to the world that I needed help. It would probably mean that the cabin would burn too, and I would either be successful, or I would go down with the ship, as they used to say when people seemed to have dignity still. Not that dignity was a driving force, but at least it factored in when making decisions. Unlike now, I mean, when it is every man for themselves.

I spent probably my last night on earth the same way I had spent the previous, I don't know, days, weeks, months at this point, I mean, my sense of time was out the window the second I got stuck in this god-damned cabin, but I spent the last night the same way, as I had always known it, alone, hungry, and scared. I decided I would get up in the morning, and whether it was sunny or not, I would light the trees on fire and hope for the best. There was nothing else I could do. If the cabin burned down too, I would truly be fucked, but so what? I was fucked either way.

I won't pretend that the night was calm, and peaceful, and I was okay with the universe. I was not. Every time I fell asleep the mice would scream in my ears. Clattering. I would wake up coughing. Then I would find myself terrified, scared of what was coming next. Then I would calm down. Try and get comfortable, think about how maybe it would be nice to be just done with it all. Fall back asleep. Then the same thing. The mice, screaming, clattering, coughing. It was probably one of the worst nights of sleep I had ever had. But I was committed. So I made sure to keep trying. I mean, how else do you go valiantly to your death, aside from pretending that everything is alright? My only regret about it was that nobody was there to see it, how brave I was being. This only made things worse. I mean, instead of being alone, now I felt lonely. But whatever. I know it sounds dramatic, but I cried myself to sleep the last time I woke up. And then, probably around dawn, I slept quite soundly. Knowing the next time I woke up, I would at least be making a decision about my own fate. And as stupid as that decision was, I could finally pull myself up by my bootstraps. Society be damned.

Part 10

Don't get me wrong, I mean, I just glossed over five days of this mayhem like it was nothing. I mean, I don't mean to imply it was nothing, and suddenly I was on easy street, just flopping around in bed with no cares in the world. I mean, that is kind of true, but not in the way I am making it seem. I mean. I mean, I don't even know what I mean. I mean, those five days were a bust. Like, really a bust. I mean, there was just nothing to do. Nowhere to go. Nothing to eat. Nothing to think about. Just me dangling around hoping for things to change. Do you know what I mean? I mean, don't get me wrong, but I am at a loss of words about it because I don't have the words to describe it. I mean, like maybe if I had a diary or something, like to write my thoughts down or something, it would be something like:

Woke up. Put some branches in stove. No food. No help. No burglars. No Chaz. Just waiting to die. I hope somebody finds my body. Tells my mom. This world really let me down. My teeth feel soft. I think I may have scurvy. Having trouble focusing. The mice are out of control. I'm scared. Alone.

Don't get me wrong, but I didn't have any paper, or a way to write down my thoughts. But those were my thoughts. I mean, as frustrating as it might be not to know what happened in those lousy five days, I mean, it sucked to live through them. I wouldn't wish that on anyone. Not even Chaz, even though it was that bastard that got me here in the first place. Whatever. That was that. Or rather, this is that. I mean, I meant it when I said I couldn't focus, and that my teeth were feeling soft. I mean, the irony, I guess you would call it that, but the irony that I had had that orange to eat and still the scurvy was getting me? I mean, I was tired all of the time. Living in some weird in-between state. Neither fully awake, nor sleeping. Hungry. Thirsty. Hot, and then very cold. I mean, I couldn't tell you why I didn't just die. Why I didn't just give up, and let the blackness, or whatever, the thing beyond that we call death, creep in and suck my soul into the Great Beyond. And I also couldn't tell you why I knew the burglars weren't coming back. I mean, maybe I was just out of memories, and since they seemed to be obsessed with making me remember my memories, they had no reason to come around. Who knows? I don't. I mean, in the end I wish they did come back. I wished that they would have come back with the good times I had with Chaz, like when we went to that strip club and ate all the chicken wings, and he got the runs so bad that he had to go and take a shit under a parked tractor trailer in the parking lot because he was too embarrassed to do it in the bathroom, but then he didn't have any toilet paper, so he wiped his ass with a dirty rag he found on the ground, and then he didn't shit right for a week, and I had to take him to the hospital because he gave himself some weird chemical burn on his butthole, and they sent him home with a lotion, and a huge bill that depleted his bank account because he didn't have insurance. I mean, that was pretty funny. And some chicken wings would have really hit the spot.

But that never happened. I mean, the thing happened, just that the burglars never showed up with chicken wings to help me remember that. I don't even know what to say about it. Don't get me wrong, but that is what I mean when I say I don't know what to say about it. I mean, there are good times, and there are bad times, and I guess the burglars were only interested in the bad times. I mean, what the hell do I know? I mean, why did I suddenly think the burglars were in charge of everything? I mean, for all I know, Chaz was sitting down at the bottom of the mountain with a check list of indiscretions on my part, and he was somehow reading my mind, and was waiting for me to think up something new, and abhorrible that he could use to torture me? I mean, don't get me wrong, but these thoughts did cross my mind, and I did spend a large amount of time trying to dredge up some bad times that involved me and Chaz that involved food. But I never got anywhere with them. The thoughts, I mean. I mean, for the most part, all of our good times involved food, and very few of our bad times involved food. Just the cucumber, the peanuts, the cheese, and the orange, and the turkey sandwiches. And all the other times were the good times, the parties in the back yard with the grill, the steak dinners at places like Rumors in Worland, or even the Office, also in Worland. There was that time in Cody when Chaz got so drunk that he puked in the soup thing at the buffet at the Irma Hotel, and they had to call the cops, but he slipped out the back door before they got there, leaving me with a 100 dollar tab that, now that I think about it, that fucker never paid me back for, but that was more hilarious than anything. And when I got back to the hotel room he was naked and passed out in the bathtub. Turds floating on top of the water. To this day I still have no idea how he got into my room. But that was a good time. I mean, you see what I mean?

I mean, I tried. I tried to be as negative as I could in those five days. Hoping to lure the burglars back. Hoping for a little respite from my suffering. But nothing doing. I mean, all I did was dangle around, getting skinny, getting weaker and weaker. Hoping for relief. No relief came. I mean, at one point I was certain I had died, and this was my own version of Hell, but that didn't ring true. I mean, it just wasn't true. I mean, all the things I was suffering were things I had lived through already, and none of them were really that bad. I mean, if this was hell, I would have had some other degree of torture that would have made all my suffering more intense than it was. But that didn't happen. I mean, sure, I was hungry, but so what, I had been hungry before. I was alone, and helpless, but same to that too. I was thirsty all the time, but I knew how to get water, and had access to snow, that I could melt into water. I mean, what I mean is, don't get me wrong, but all of my suffering was of a very mild and ordinary sort. I mean, I was dying from starvation, yes, and I had no prospects for my future, also yes, but so what? I mean, that seems pretty same shit different day to me. Am I right?

I guess all I am trying to say is this. Those five days I spent knowing that the burglars were, in fact, not coming back, and knowing that if I didn't do anything to make my situation better myself, to pull myself up by my boot straps, I mean, those five days, there was nothing I could do about it. I was doomed, and I knew I was doomed, and because I was doomed, there was nothing for me to do but wait until the time came to make a very drastic decision about at least trying to get myself out of the scenario I was in. And because there were so many few options, or let me rephrase that, because there was nothing doing, I was left with one drastic option, and that option was to start another fire and hope somebody would see it, and maybe, just maybe, come and rescue me.

❄

Don't get me wrong, but do you play chess? And I don't mean that like an asshole. Like I am going to unleash some dumb chess analogy on you about thinking two moves ahead or some bullshit. What I mean is, in high school I joined the chess club as an alternate, thinking it would be an easy way to get credit while doing nothing but playing dumb games with nerds, and because of this, I was really bad at chess. But the one thing I learned, I mean, if I learned anything from playing chess in high school with a bunch of dweebs that took chess really serious was this. I could never tell if I was making a good move or a bad move. The only way I could tell I did a good thing was whenever the dork I was playing didn't kill the thing I moved. I mean, if I moved the horse, or whatever, into a place that the pointy thing could get me, or the castle thing, and nothing happened to it, I mean, when they didn't kill the piece, I knew I had made a good move because instead of killing my piece they would do something different, like do that thing where the king and the castle guy would swap places. And this would let me know that I was on the right track. I mean, I never won a single game, and I never learned anything else, but that is what this was feeling like. Being stuck in the cabin like I was. I mean, my whole life, actually, I mean, I always knew I was making bad decisions, but unless there was some sort of counter move from society, or whatever, work, girls, I never knew shit about what I was going to do next, and my only real pride in the world was when I would make people reconsider the moves they were making in response to the moves I was making.

Do you know what I mean? I mean, being here, in the cabin, starving to death, all because of the dumb shit I have done in my life, don't get me wrong, but that is what I mean. And here Chaz had control of the board, to put it in chess terms, but not really, I mean, he really did have all the moves, and like an idiot I was stuck trying to figure out what dumb move I could make to maybe bluster my way out of this dilemma. But I had nothing left. No way, no how. I mean, I guess that is what I am really trying to get at when I try to explain the fact that not only was I doomed, but there was nothing I could do about it. I mean, the only easy day was yesterday, right? I mean, all around me the world is moving, making choices I don't understand, and here I am, just trying to get by, and the next thing you know, it's over. Game over. You are poor because you are stupid, and because you are stupid, you are poor. Sucks to be you.

And as much as I want to defend myself, I just can't anymore. I failed. All my actions, all my maneuvering, nothing. Failure. I work, and I try. I work, and I try. I get up early. Do my job. Go home tired. Do it again, and again, and again. And nothing comes from it. And of course nothing comes of it. Why should it? The idea that you can work yourself out of this wet paper bag of commerce, and a supposed merit-based reality, it is nonsense. Nonsense! There is no dream big enough to hold everyone inside. I mean, there has to be a reason for it, am I right? I mean, I don't even know. But I have gone way too far to side of the point I was trying to make that I give up, because there is no way to solve this problem, and life, I mean, the lives that we live are only the details that get us through the day until we bite the Big One. So instead of doing a wax job about merit, and chess, and society, I think I will just tell you what happened on the day that I woke up, thinking there was no other option but to take some drastic measures that would either save me or put an end to my suffering.

Don't get me wrong, I woke up on that sixth day, weak and skinny. I had become obsessed with my teeth. They were wiggly. My gums were tender. I touched my gums. My finger had blood on it when I looked at it. I sighed. This was not a good sign. My eyes were swollen. I don't know why, but there was some last hope that the cigarettes would lure Chaz back to me and the cabin. I mean, I hadn't had a cigarette in five days. And this seemed like maybe this was the problem. I mean, I don't know, don't get me wrong, but in my mind I was thinking something like, Shit! I forgot to smoke! But also, and I mean that like I mean everything, because at this point, I was bouncing back and forth with every thought that crossed my mind, I mean, but also, I stopped smoking because I knew that the burglars weren't coming back. So, this thought, and those thoughts, had some reckoning to do with each other. But it doesn't matter, because I woke up, sat up on the bed, and lit a cigarette. The first one in five days.

I coughed, and coughed, and coughed. I did my best to blink, but the smoke still found a way to get in. I stood up, and put some more branches in the stove. I tried to shut the door, but the piece of wood was still stuck there, and I couldn't. This was annoying, but I didn't have the energy to be annoyed. I rubbed my eyes. But this was stupid because I was holding the cigarette in my hand, so all I did was get more smoke in my eyes. I put the cigarette between my teeth and bit down. This made things worse because my teeth bent, and now I was paranoid about my scurvy. I threw the cigarette to the floor, and sat down on the bed. Suddenly overwhelmed with everything. I would have cried, but I was too weak for that, I just sat there with my mouth hanging open. Looking at the door. Not the door to the stove, but the door of the cabin. I knew I would need to go outside any second now, and I really didn't have the energy to do it. Smoke rose up from the cigarette still burning on the floor. I stomped it out. Then I blinked for a while. Then I stood up. Said, *Okay, here we go.* Out loud. And walked to the cabin door.

I mean, what do you say about that? What do you say about anything? I mean, don't get me wrong, but this was a life-or-death situation. A last gasp. To put it in terms of fish dying. I mean, don't get me wrong, but this was the point of no return. I could do this thing, and be glorious in my actions, or die from fire, or starvation, or whatever there was to die from. Guilt. I mean, the idea was that I would go out back and burn the remaining trees down, hopefully someone would see it, or the trees would catch the cabin on fire, and I would end up just as useless as the goods at the bottom of the grave that I was hired to dig up. I mean, don't get me wrong, but my prospects were not looking very good. But so what? It wouldn't be the first time I did something really stupid and dangerous for a measly amount of money.

As I forced myself to walk to the door, and, I don't know the way to say it, figure it out, I caught something out of the corner of my eye. At first I thought it was a mouse. Finally! I would see one of those fuckers. And I could corner it in the corner, throttle it, tell it to stop screaming in my ears. Clattering. But that wasn't it. It was sunshine. Sun light. Sun light was coming through the good window! The clouds had broken. I went over to the good window. I want to say I ran, but I did not run. I was moving really, very slow. My hands shook as I held them in the sun's rays. I was just as drunk as Chaz was when he came to me after getting fucked up in Humphreys' room that time. The time he passed out on my floor, and pissed himself. The time that I got him transferred because I refused to pretend that he was sick. The whole reason I was stuck up here in the cabin in the first place. That, and boning his girlfriend, I mean. What with her cucumber and erotic incantations.

I looked down at my hands. I said, *Are these my hands? Is this who I have become?* I know, the sentiment was stupid, but I should remind you that I hadn't eaten in five days, and not only that, but I had scurvy now, and not only that, but the only thing I had eaten in the last, I don't even know, weeks at this point, was, a burrito, some meat, some cheese, a couple sandwiches, and a bottle of Jager. I mean, don't get me wrong, but considering, I think I was doing alright.

I stood there looking at my hands for a few moments. Forgetting what I was up to. But then clouds came and blocked the sun again, and I was shocked back into my mission. I went over to the door and opened it. My god, there was so much snow. It was a hard nut to swallow. Two in the bush style. I sighed and stood there. I didn't know what to do. I mean, I kind of knew what to do. I mean, I needed to go around to the back and light the trees on fire. The pines. And hopefully signal to whoever that I needed help. But there were mountains of snow, and I was feeling very, very weak.

I don't mean to be dramatic, but the sun came out again. This gave me energy. I said out loud:

"I'm doing it!"

"Don't do it weto!" Seneca Michael Miguel said.

"Suck it, Seneca!"

"Your funeral."

"Yeah? Tracy?"

"You are doing a great job!"

"Thanks, Trace!"

I don't know how I did it, but I pushed my way around the side of the cabin. The snow was up to my stomach. It was cold, but I got to a point where I could see the graveyard and see where the sun was breaking through the clouds. I mean, don't get me wrong, but I swear there was a single sunbeam that was landing on the grave with the goods in it. I mean, this seems foolish, but it lifted my spirits. And I was able to look around, and see what tree I could light on fire to get this action going. I mean, it would mean I would have to push myself deeper into the snow, and it would be a lot of work, and as excited as I was, my eyes felt sleepy, and my body was wimpy, but I was willing, and I don't care what you say, but the heart is stronger than the brain, so as much as I wanted to just lay down and take a rest, I went back inside the cabin to warm up and make some choices. I mean, I made that sound like I gave up, but what I mean is that I did the opposite. I went inside to retool. Knowing that I had a clear path to victory. And god be damned! I would do this thing.

❄

I don't know what to say. I mean, when I got back inside the cabin I just kind of stood there looking. I mean, I guess I had a plan. I mean, I guess. And I guess that most of my plan was to keep my spirits up. To make all this seem worthwhile. Like it was all worth fighting for, or something. I mean, I was feeling peaked. Logy. Wimpy. I forced myself to keep standing. Even though I really wanted to sit down. And I knew if I sat down, I would lie down. And if I lay down, I would sleep. And if I fell asleep, it would all be over. I don't think I had the energy to get back up again. So I stood there looking. The light went out from behind the clouds. What I mean is, the sun went back behind the clouds again. This made my heart hurt. I almost gave up. For some reason this prompted me to light another cigarette. When I did this the light came back out from behind the clouds again. I made a note of this as I stood there coughing, bent half over, nearly blind from the smoke. Saliva dripping to the floor from my mouth. I mean, don't get me wrong, but the smoking was too much. I ditched the cigarette and stubbed it out with my foot. Just then the light went behind the clouds again. I said, *Interesting*. Out loud. As much as I didn't want to, I lit another cigarette just to check. Don't get me wrong, I mean, this seems a little dramatic, but when I lit that cigarette, the sun came back out. From behind the clouds. Typical, right? I mean, what the fuck. I mean, here I was, sick as a dog, starving, looking for any sort of relief, and the only thing that was keeping the sun shining was the cigarettes I was smoking. Which were making me sicker every time I lit one. I mean, what do you do with that information? It seemed so stupid. So, since I am a scientist, I gave it one more try. I dropped the cigarette I was smoking to the floor. Put it out with my foot. Then, just like that, no more sun. I mean, third times a charm, right? Am I right? I mean, as nasty as it was, I lit another cigarette. The sun came out. And that was that. I guess I now had control of the clouds. Whatever that meant.

I stood there looking. Smoking. Trying to focus. I knew I needed a long branch to light the tree on fire to get this whole thing in motion, but I didn't have any long branches. I had broken them into bits long ago. Weeks ago? Months? I mean, I knew it wasn't months but it felt like it could be months. I mean, don't get me wrong, but it felt like I had been stuck in this cabin for ages. I stared at the branches for a while. Did some deep lung coughing, you know, just to get the blood flowing. Don't get me wrong, but that is a joke I just made. I mean, the coughing was becoming quite severe. I mean, I guess it was the cigarettes, but I think it was also the smoke from the fire all this time, you know, the god-damned door wouldn't shut. I really needed to get that branch out that was keeping the door to the stove from closing. But there was not time for that now. But also, I mean with regards to the coughing, I think my body was giving up, or maybe the opposite of that. I mean, like maybe it was trying to tell me something. Like, I don't know, that I was sick, and I needed to do something about it, like not smoke, and maybe eat some food, and drink some water, and maybe not keep living in this stupid cabin up on top of this mountain in Wyoming. But whatever the reason was, I was coughing constantly. And not in a good way. Don't get me wrong, I mean, I don't know if there is a good way to do some coughing, but maybe there is. I can't think of any, but you know, I am a man of science, remember, so maybe I won't just discount that idea outright, but I can't think of any good for a body coughing can do. But maybe I am looking at it wrong. Like maybe coughing is the lungs' way of sneezing like the nose does? So maybe all coughing is good. The way that all sneezing is good. I mean, I take that back. Sneezing under water is really painful. Which, I don't know, maybe that is bad sneezing? But this is not my point.

Don't get me wrong, but I don't know what my point is. I mean, aside from the fact that I was coughing like a fool. And I couldn't stop smoking because the light would go away. So I stood there coughing, trying to stay focused. Looking. Looking at the branches. Trying to come up with an idea. I mean, don't get me wrong, but no ideas came to me. I decided to go back outside and have another look-see. Maybe the solution would present itself. I mean, I have always adhered to the dictum that you should give up first and the solution would present itself, but this was not the time for that. These times were times for action. So I went back outside to have another look-see.

I followed my trail around the cabin. The cigarette still burning. I was holding onto it as tight as possible. Not wanting it to go out. I would take a puff every now and again. Just to keep the cherry burning. Then I would get a coughing fit, and would have to stop. Flashes of white light kept erupting in the corners of my eyes because of this. But whatever, I had to ignore this. I had to keep going. So I kept going. Coughing and coughing and coughing. I got to the end of the trail I made, and looked out across the field of snow that was between me and the tree closest to me. The one that I wanted to burn. Or the one that would get the burning going. There was a lot of white that needed to be traversed. I stood there looking. My heart racing. I mean, that was another thing that was going on with my body that I forgot to mention. My heart was beating like a hummingbird's. And not in a good way. I mean, I am not sure that a hummingbird's heart beating that way is a good thing or not, but when you are a large animal like me, a human, or whatever, I don't think it is such a good thing. And much like the coughing, I wasn't sure what was causing it. The lack of exercise? The lack of food? The cigarettes? The anxiety and stress of the situation? I mean, whatever, but my heart was beating like crazy, and it scared me. That, and the light flashes out of the corners of my eyes, and all the coughing. I mean, don't get me wrong, but I was starting to get scared that I might just drop dead. And at first, I found this startling. I mean, I guess that is the word. Maybe the real word is disconcerting, but whatever, at first this scared me, but the more time I lived in this state of mild panic, and easy terror, the more accustomed I became to it. And frankly, I was starting to enjoy the idea that I might just die at any second. I mean, don't get me wrong, but it was a little thrilling. I stood there looking. Trying to focus. Trying to keep the cigarette lit. Coughing. Vibrating. Half-scared, half-exhilarated. I mean, whatever. I had a job to do. And damn it all, I would get the job done. Boot-straps and all.

Don't get me wrong, but the next thing I did was kind of dumb. I mean, don't judge me because it did need to happen, but I did it in such a stupid way that I don't know what to say. I mean, I think this story would be over had it not worked out the way it did, and it very well should have worked out differently, but it didn't. I mean, I guess I got lucky, but whatever. I mean, I needed to get to the tree that was the linchpin to my plan, and there was no way to get to it aside from walking over to it. I mean, I feel like I established that, right? I mean, you understand that I need to get to that tree, am I wrong? I mean, I guess it doesn't matter what you think, but I guess I am telling you. I needed to get over to the tree. And there was no easy way to get there aside from just walking over to it. But there was a field of snow in between where I was standing and where I needed to go. So, I mean, don't get me wrong, I mean, I pretend that there was another way to do this, or at least I implied that, but I guess what I mean by that, is that, I mean, I don't even know, I mean, I guess what I could have done instead of doing what I did was a simple thing that would have saved me from the misery that I befell onto myself. I mean, don't get me wrong, I mean, I could have gone back into the cabin. I could have warmed myself up, as much as possible. I could have wrapped myself in blankets, and done whatever else to keep myself warm. I could have put my gloves on. I could have, oh, I don't know, done anything aside from what I did, which was this. I lit another cigarette, since the one I was smoking had gone out. I put my hands in my pockets, looking for my gloves. I must have left them in the cabin. I held the cigarette in between my lips, squinted, and started walking.

The snow was waist deep at first. Then it got up to my chest. I pushed forward. The cigarette smoke burning my eyes. My hands in my pockets. The snow doing its best to keep me from moving forward. I kept pushing. Sometimes I would have to stop, turn around, then turn around again, and run into the snow. It went on like this for some time. The snow became a little more powdery, but much, much deeper. Before I knew it, the snow was up to my neck. I kept pushing. The cigarette burning my eyes. My body turning to ice. My hands in my pockets. But I did it, I kept pushing. And just as I got to the bottom of the tree, I dropped down below the snow. My head went under. The cigarette went out. I scrambled to get out. My hands came out of my pockets. My fingers were instantly frozen. Snow went down my coat. I got mixed up, and went a few feet in the wrong direction. When I finally popped my head out of the snow, like some idiot submarine periscope, I was way off track, and had to make a new trail to get back to where I should have been. I could barely see straight because the snow that fell into my coat was ghastly. The sun had gone behind the clouds again. And as I started to panic about how cold I was getting, I managed to look up at the tree that was the main goal of this horribly stupid adventure. Don't get me wrong, but the branches were way above the ground. I mean, they looked so close to the ground from back at the cabin. I mean, I guess there was a hill or something that was under the snow. I guess I made a note of this, and followed the trail I made back to the cabin. I mean, I don't know how I did it. I mean, I know how I did it, I walked there, but I don't know where the energy came from. Maybe it was the prospect of eminent death, or whatever, but I got back to the cabin as quick as I could. And instead of stripping naked, and warming myself up, I tried to light a cigarette, because for some reason the idea of the sun giving up on me was way worse than freezing to death.

Don't get me wrong, but I couldn't do it. I couldn't get the cigarettes out of my pocket. I panicked. My hands were useless. For some dumb reason I thought it would be smart to heat them up by slapping them on top of the stove. I heard a sizzling, and then felt a pain I never experienced in my life. I pulled back as fast as I had put my hands on the stove in the first place. There were two white hand prints on the stove. I looked down in horror at the missing skin from my hands. I stood there staring just long enough to realize what I had done. Then I felt a slight tingling. I laughed for some dumb reason. Then everything just drifted away in silence.

I mean, I must have been out of it for quite some time because I woke up wet. I mean, the snow had melted inside of my coat, and steam was rising off of my body. My hands stung, and the wooden floor felt like concrete. I don't know how I did it, because I could barely use my fingers, but I managed to get all my clothes off. Including my boots. I got everything off. My pants. My long johns. My two pairs of socks. My overalls. All my shirts. I mean, in the end I stood there naked. My hands stinging. My body reeking. Don't get me wrong, but it had been quite some time since I had showered. The smell was a mix of dog shit and rotting garbage. Plus some other earthy smell that had a few raccoon notes to it. My genitals were little nuggets of hard skin. Brown and purple. Surrounded by black pubes in great contrast to my almost translucent white skin. I was startled at how skinny I had become. Not that I thought too much about it. I mean, my starvation was the least of my worries at the moment. But I did notice. Bones were poking out everywhere. My hips especially. My feet looked gnarly and scary. I had to ignore them. I stood there shivering until

I got a whisper of a thought together, and went to the bed and grabbed a blanket. I put it over my shoulders. My hands were on fire. I mean, I really felt like an idiot at this point. I could barely move my fingers. They just stood there, jutting out from the ends of my arms like red priest guys from some horrible game of chess you would play with the devil. I mean, you would never win, but you would be stupid enough to suggest it. Then he would own your soul or something, and you would be left to wander in purgatory with chess pieces for fingers, or something stupid like that. I mean, that is a dumb analogy, but that is what my fingers looked like.

Don't get me wrong, but it took me forever to warm up. I mean, I was shaking like a reed. What, with my hummingbird heart. I couldn't stop coughing. My eyes were doing better because I wasn't smoking, but this just reminded me I should be smoking. I mean, the sun was still behind the clouds because of this, but I mean, I don't know. I guess I had bigger problems at the moment. But this made me nervous to think about. I mean, time was disappearing fast. I was burning daylight. And I was starting to get scared that I wouldn't last much longer. I mean, if I couldn't do this thing now, when the time was right, and if the sun never came out again, and I was left to wallow in my misery for another day, just one more day, I mean, don't get me wrong, but I was afraid I wouldn't make it. But whatever. I mean, my hands were useless now. Or at least it seemed. Every time I tried to make a fist the stinging would start at my fingers and crawl up my arms and go straight to my soul. But not in a way like I just described, like it was a cause-and-effect thing, but more like lightning would go through my body in an instant. And I would be left panting, and coughing, and bent over, vibrating like a hummingbird. I mean, don't get me wrong, but when I said I was an idiot for pushing through the snow in the way that I did, I mean, this is why. I mean, a stitch in time, or whatever. I mean, I did also have this thought that all the work I did today, the pushing forward in the snow, to make a trail to the tree that was taller than I thought, I mean, what if it started snowing again? What if I was laid up overnight, and all my progress was for nothing? I mean, what would that mean? To work so hard on something, only to get nowhere? Only to go back tomorrow and do it again? I mean, am I right? That would suck. Life doesn't work that way. Right? I mean, you work hard, and everything you do adds up to progress for your future. Right? I'm not wrong, am I right? Yeah, okay, I am fucking with you again. It doesn't work that way. You can work as hard as you want, all your life, but that doesn't mean shit if all the cards are against you. I mean, I feel stupid for bringing the devil into the mix, but that thing with the fingers, I mean, if you don't have luck on your side, you are screwed either way. I mean, whatever, as much as I wanted to move forward with this plan of mine, I was kind of screwed. I was freezing and I needed to deal with it. Right now. Right here. And as much as I wanted the sun to keep shining on me, I would need to deal with my body first. And that meant getting warm again. And the problems with the future would have to wait. Even if I wished that wasn't true.

Part 11

Don't get me wrong, but I stood there like an idiot, freezing, for quite some time. My hands hurt. My skinny knees knocked together. The blanket I had draped over my shoulders was really scratchy. I hadn't noticed how scratchy it was before, because I was always wearing all my clothes whenever I was under it. I looked over at the other blankets on the bed. They seemed to be the same material. I didn't even bother testing. I mean, what was I going to do? Get a different blanket to get more cozy? I mean, I felt so stupid that if I had a whip or whatever, I would have flagellated myself. Penance, or whatever they call it. I mean, to that end I started to focus on my fingers. Trying to get them to move again. I mean, I forced myself to feel every ounce of pain coming from them. I mean, I would start to ball them, the fingers, into my palm, scream out in pain. Nearly cry. Then release. I mean, I had so much self-hatred that I was able to make some pretty quick progress. The more I moved my fingers, the easier it was to move my fingers. The only problem was when I would stop. I mean, the pain would get worse, and I was back to square one. I mean, the only real solution I could think of was to just grow accustomed to the pain. To try and work through it. I mean, don't get me wrong, this wasn't much of a plan, as far as plans are concerned, but what else could I do? The day was slipping away from me at an alarming rate. I mean, I don't know what to say, don't get me wrong, but, whatever.

When I gave myself enough pain to start to forget how stupid I was, I did the other stupid thing that kept me going, I bent down and found my cigarettes in my clothes. They were wet from the snow that fell into my pockets. The snow had melted. Making the cigarettes wet. I sighed. Went over to the cooler and got a fresh pack. It took a lot of doing, and a lot of painful moves in order to open them. They had that little plastic tab that I had to unwind in order to get inside. And since my fingers were almost entirely useless, I had to use my teeth to pull it. But this involved holding the package of cigarettes with my hands. Which, don't get me wrong, but this was nearly impossible. I mean, I had to hold the cigarette package in between the palm of both of my hands, and use my teeth to pull the piece of plastic. Then I had to do this again to open the lid of the package of cigarettes. Then I had to do this again to remove the piece of paper that was covering the cigarettes. Then I had to bite a cigarette out of the package. Then, don't get me wrong, this was the hardest part of all, I had to light the cigarette. I mean, I don't even really know how I did it. I mean, I couldn't use the lighter, because that involved my thumb, my fingers, and the palm of my hand. The only other option was to get a branch lit, and then use that to light the cigarette. But all the branches were short stacks. I mean, I don't know when I started calling them short stacks, but I think it was at some point when I realized I would need a longer stick to start the tree on fire that would maybe save me from this dilemma I was in. I mean, don't get me wrong, it was either that, or I was calling them short stacks this whole time and I never noticed until this very moment when I really needed a longer stick but couldn't find one. But, I mean, I don't know, I somehow managed to light one of the sticks, I mean, I know that I used the in-betweens of my fingers to hold it, and I remember it hurting quite a bit, what with my hands being burned so badly, and getting them so close to the fire, but I must have blacked out, because when I came back to knowing what was going on, I had a lit cigarette in my hand. I mean, I was coughing like crazy, maybe that is what brought me back, but whatever, I mean, I lit the cigarette, and that is all that mattered.

Don't get me wrong, and I know this sounds dramatic and unlikely, but just as soon as I was aware of the cigarette burning, the sun came back out. I mean, it sucked. The smoke from the cigarette was intolerable. And I was coughing like a donkey, but the cigarette did do the trick. And I suppose I was glad because of it. I mean, don't get me wrong, but I was exhausted. I was still shivering. My genitals were still tiny, brown and purple chunks of skin floating in a sea of pubes, and I really didn't think I had it in me to dry my clothes out and get them back on. But at least the sun was shining. Am I right? I mean, I say that now, from the comfort of distance, like it was all some funny games, but at the time I actually felt more despondent because the sun came out. I mean, it meant that I needed to act. And I needed to act quickly. I mean, I had no idea what time it was, but in my heart I knew it was early afternoon, and the sun would be setting again soon. If I didn't act now, night would come, and who knows what tomorrow would bring. I mean, if it started snowing again, I was fucked. My whole nearly freezing to death and stupidly burning my fingers off would be for nothing. And since I didn't have much fuel left in my tank, I mean, life-wise, I mean, who knows? I may be dead by morning. And that didn't seem like a very good thing to happen to me. I mean, not this late in the game. When I was so close to achieving my goals.

Whatever. I mean, don't get me wrong, but once again I pulled myself up by my bootstraps, and started gathering my clothing from the floor. I mean, in order to see what was soaked, and what was merely wet. I mean, this simple task was excruciating. I mean, what with my fingers being useless, and the cigarette burning in my eyes. The coughing. The exhaustion. The hunger. The bad smells, and the fear that the sun would go away, or that night would come before I could do the thing that needed doing. I mean, I tried to stay focused, but everything was a giant drag. The inertia was incredible. I mean, I found my socks first thing. They were wadded up, and wet, but not soaked. I spent what seemed like hours, but was probably just minutes, draping them over the open door of the stove. It was gross. I had to use my teeth to unwad them. And, I mean, weeks, I guess, of the same socks inside the same boots, I mean, they stank, and were crusty, and tasted like mushrooms soaked in a middle school boys locker room. Both salty and sweet. But with some greasy film that stuck to my lips. I mean, I don't know what to say, but yuck. After I did this, I was winded and had to take a break. I made sure the cigarette was still going. This made me cough like crazy. Which made me tired. Don't get me wrong, but I almost got into bed. I didn't though. I took my break, and then started gathering my other clothes. My long johns were only damp. Which was nice. I spent a year putting them back on. Which was painful. I mean, I couldn't use my teeth, and I kind of had use of my knuckles at this point. I mean, not so much my knuckles, as I could make scissors out of my fingers, kind of, and with a bunch of pain I was able to connect my knuckles as little pincers to pull my long johns up to my waist. Which made me feel better. I didn't have to see my shriveled genitals anymore. I mean, not really, they were poking out underneath the fabric, but I didn't have to look at their brown/purple sea of pube nature anymore.

After I got my long johns on, I took another break. I had to get another cigarette going because the one I was smoking was about out. Luckily, I noticed before it was too late, and I was able to light the next one off of the one that was burning. But this caused another coughing fit, which made my stomach hurt, and I couldn't tell exactly, but I think I was now coughing up blood. I mean, I spat onto the ground, and the spit was as brown as the floor, but this might have been just a trick of the light, I mean, either way, if I got out of here I was going to have to go see a doctor, I mean, don't get me wrong, but smoking or not, the amount of coughing I was doing wasn't healthy. And I don't know why seeing my spit come out brown gave me a shock of anxiety, but it did. I mean, it is one thing to be dying from starvation, it is another thing to be dying of cancer while you are dying of starvation. I mean, I don't know about you, but don't get me wrong, the will to live is pretty strong, I mean, I guess it is good to hold onto hope as long as you can, but the idea of being sick beyond just the sickness that is your immediate sickness, I mean, I don't know, I mean, I can understand how easy it is to give up hope when you are in a hopeless situation. I mean, it's a different thing to try and thrive in a situation when you know you are fucked even if you are successful in your endeavors. You know what I mean? I mean, whatever, I guess I was coughing up blood now, and I was trying to ignore it, but it made my asshole hurt with fear, and it took all of my energy to put this reality at the back of my mind, and just move forward.

I mean, whatever. I was able to ignore my new predicament by focusing on my next move. Which was to get my shirt, and my other shirts. I mean, this was a simple task, luckily. All three of them were just damp. I mean, kind of. Damp enough to just put back on, and let them dry out on my body as I stood there next to the stove. I mean, they were easy to get on. The only hard part was keeping the cigarette from burning out, which I solved by holding the cigarette in my lips while I put one arm through the arm hole, and then transferring the cigarette to my hand, and getting my head through the neck hole, and then getting my other arm through the other arm hole. This was exhausting. I had to do it three different times. But in the end, I had all my shirts on. I took a break and coughed for a while. Making sure the cigarette stayed lit. By the end of my break I had to light another cigarette. Which I did by lighting the new cigarette off of the still-burning cigarette.

The next thing that I needed to put on, or dry out, or whatever, was my pants. I looked down and sighed. They were button-up. I almost cried, but I instead took a minute to assess my warmth and think about the future. I mean, I had the overalls, and the coat. Both of these things had zippers, which, I mean, I decided I could manage, but the pants seemed too daunting. Don't get me wrong, but I was getting warm again. The shirts were getting my torso nice and toasty. The long johns were keeping my legs warm. The socks were steaming their stink into the air, and were probably ready for my feet. I mean, I thought about how warm I would need to be outside, and I decided that I could just wear the overalls, and I didn't need to put my pants on. I mean, I don't think I was going to have to push through five feet of snow again,

I mean, if the stupid trail I had made to the tree I was going to light on fire was the same as I had left it. I mean, don't get me wrong, but there was no way I could get my jeans on. So I ignored them, and tested the overalls for wetness. They were pretty wet. Like too wet to put on. This made me frustrated. I checked the coat. It was also pretty wet. Too wet to put on. I mean, I would need to dry them out. And there was no easy way to do this. I took the stinking socks off the stove door, and put them on the bed. Then I draped the overalls over the stove door. I mean, this would have to do. I didn't know what to do about the coat. I mean, I decided to put my socks back on. I would decide what to do about the coat after that.

Don't get me wrong, but the socks sucked. I mean, without the use of my fingers they were just as hard to get on as they were to unfurl. Except now I couldn't use my teeth. I mean, there was nothing I could do except just suck it up and use my hands. But this was rather painful, and took a huge amount of time. I burned through two cigarettes before I was wearing the socks again. And sadly, they were still very wet. But what can you do? I mean, I guessed I still had some time. Not only that, but it would be awhile before the coveralls would be dry enough to put on, and not only that, but the stupid coat needed to be dried out, and after that, I mean, my boots were going to be the biggest struggle of all.

I mean, I spent some time flipping the overalls, drying them out. Getting them to steam, and then flipping them. All the while coughing, and coughing, and coughing. Spitting blood that I was ignoring. Taking breaks to see if I could get my socks dried. I mean, like lifting my feet up to the stove. Then turning around, and putting my feet behind myself, in the air, or whatever, trying to dry the bottoms. Eventually I decided to just fry my coat on top of the stove to get it to dry out. Which worked out, mostly. I mean, the thing would sizzle for a few, then I would flip it, steam would come off, then I would flip it again. I mean, I could tell I was burning the thing. Ruining my coat, but whatever, time was important. And this is all I could do. I mean. I guess you can judge how much time this took because I smoked nearly seven cigarettes doing this. I mean, if that means anything. And in the end, I was able to put my overalls back on. My coat too. I mean, they were still damp, but I would warm them up from the inside, I decided. And what else was I to do about it? I mean, I was certain it was nearly three in the afternoon at this point. Maybe later. I mean, since I was smoking so much the sun was really going now, and this was different light than all the days of snow since I had come to the cabin, so I wasn't positive, but I was pretty certain that the day was coming to an end, but not like it was dusk, I mean, more like it was the last good hour or two before sunset. I mean, I was doing alright, considering. The only issue, or issues I had remaining was the problem of my boots, the problems of my burnt hands, and the problem of how the hell was going to set the trees on fire like I had planned. And frankly, I was starting to get nervous about how late it was. I mean, what is the point of lighting a fire for the world to see when it is too dark to see the smoke? I mean, if I didn't light this fire soon, it would be pointless.

Don't get me wrong, but my boots got on easy. It was tying them that was impossible. I mean, in the end I just tucked my laces in as good as I could and hoped for the best. I mean, they were a little floppy, but what could I do? I didn't have any time to think about it. I stood there coughing, getting as warm as I could. Making sure my cigarette stayed lit. Hoping the sun stayed out. Thinking, or trying to think, I mean, trying to stay focused, trying my hardest not to get into bed and sleep away all my misery. I mean, this was starting to be the true test of what I was doing, my exhaustion. I mean, I was dead on my feet, as they say. I mean, I could barely keep my eyes open, and the cigarette smoke wasn't helping. I had to slap my face a couple times to wake up. And this worked pretty good, I mean, mostly because slapping my face hurt my hands more than it hurt my face, but whatever, I mean, I was fading fast. And the sun was fading fast. And if I didn't act soon, all of this would be for nothing. I mean, I did my best to shift gears, but all that meant was that I sat down on the edge of the bed and slowly nodded off. The thing that woke me was the cigarette I was holding between my lips burned me, and suddenly I was standing up again. The cherry from the cigarette was burning on the ground. The butt still in-between my lips. There was a puddle of water dangerously close to the cherry. I dropped to my knees, a fresh cigarette in my mouth. Stabbing it into the slowly fading cherry. I puffed, and puffed. Don't get me wrong, but I got lucky, and the cigarette caught fire, but I was now wide awake. Coughing, and coughing, and coughing. I spit on the ground as I knelt there. I mean, I wasn't really kneeling, I mean, it was more like I was on my hands and knees, but I was trying to stand up. But this time I could really see that there was blood in my spit. And this made me very tired. I mean, don't get me wrong, I ignored it, but I was very disheartened. I managed to get myself up. And, I don't even know, I managed to stand next to the stove one last time. Making sure I was dry enough, and warm enough to get out there and do my best to try and save my life, even though I was starting to wonder if my life was worth saving.

Don't get me wrong, but I went outside. To gauge the situation. I mean, the sun was burning bright in the Eastern sky. Or whatever poetry you want to make of it. I mean, it was kind of crazy. The first time since I had been in the cabin the sky was clear. And it wasn't freezing. I mean, it was freezing cold, I mean, I could see my breath, but with the sun being out it was a different type of freezing. I walked over to the beginning of the trail where I had pushed through five feet of snow, and up to the tree I had designs on. I mean, the trail was still there. I mean, it was kind of surprising. I mean, I guess I figured the walls would collapse, and I would have to do the thing all over again. I mean, that was the nature of work in my experience, I mean, if anything is worth doing you do it twice, or whatever. I mean, that is the nature of all business, if I understand it right. It not so much a service you provide, it is more like the idea of a service that you are providing. I mean, that is what they call overhead, am I right? The fact that you will fuck the shit up in the first place, so you need enough money to fix the thing you are inevitably going to fuck up? I mean, that is the whole reason they can pretend job creation, and hourly wage, right? And by they, I mean the people that get a huge tax break for having businesses that are just fucking shit up all the time in order to fix the shit they fuck up? I mean, who am I to buck the system? I mean, I was kind of disappointed that my trail was still there. I mean, it was almost a failure on my part that I didn't have to do the job twice. You know what I mean?

Whatever. The sun was shining. The job I did, as stupid as it was in the first place, was still good. I walked over to the tree. Looked up. I mean, fuck. There was a lot of distance between the first tree branch and the ground I was standing on. I mean, there was no way in hell I was going to get a stick of wood long enough to light those first branches on fire. I mean, I would need to think of something different. I mean, there must be a different solution. I mean, I needed to think of one. Like, right now, and right here.

Don't get me wrong, but I stood there looking at the tree for a while. Trying to stay focused. A bird flew over. It was a robin. It landed on the branch I was looking at. I don't know why, but I yelled up at the bird. I said, *Yo bird! What-cha thinking?* The robin flew to another branch. Then it made noise. I mean, because of this I was suddenly back on the oil field in the hottest summer I knew of. Standing under a derrick. The waterhead rotating up and down. Like a road runner drinking from a puddle. I mean, I don't know if they call them waterheads everywhere, but we did. I mean, by we, I mean me, and Chaz, and Humphreys. I mean, at the time I hadn't ever worked on a derrick before, so I had no frame of reference, but I was standing there, while White was up about fifteen feet from the ground, trying to fix a leak or something. And because he was working off the ground, he needed a guy to help him by giving him tools from the ground. I mean, he called it a ground guy. He needed a ground guy to help him. I mean, for some reason he asked me to help him. Like I was the ground guy.

I mean, whatever. My point is, as I was standing there helping White fix the leak, I had a bag of tools at my feet. White was up on the derrick. The waterhead going up and down. He yelled to me, *Give me the three quarters dog bone!* I grabbed the wrench, and tried to throw it up to him. Overhand-style. The wrench flew off into the sagebrush. I scurried over to get it. Brushed the dust off, and went back to where I was standing. I tried to throw it again. This time it wanged off the derrick, and landed in a puddle of oil. White yelled down, *Hey idiot! Throw it up underhand!* I had to wipe the wrench down with my t-shirt before I tried again. This time the wrench flew up, floated for a second, then landed in White's hand with no problem. He was able to do what he was up there doing, and I had learned a thing or two because of it. But watching this robin flying around from branch to branch gave me the same feelings of what it was like being White's ground guy. I mean, maybe I couldn't use a big long stick to start the tree on fire, but what if I used a series of burning wrenches to get the thing lit? I mean, White was pissed at me when he got down from the derrick, I mean, he said as much, I mean, he said, *You suck at this.* And I was never the ground guy again, but the robin reminded me that at one time in my life I was still able to try to do good, even if it meant failure from a chain-smoking bully that only cared about making me feel bad. I mean, I don't know if that was White's intention, but that is what happened. So, screw that guy, but whatever, I now know how I would start the fire. I mean, get bent, White, I can be my own ground guy from now on.

Don't get me wrong, but I went back to the cabin to gather a bunch of branches. I had plans to throw them up in the tree like three quarter dog bones. I mean, some of them would stick. Am I right? I mean, I didn't have any other option. Time was burning. I would either do this now, or, I don't know, not do it at all. Hope for the burglars to come back? Maybe Chaz would show up, tell me it was all just a big joke. Bring a doctor. Put me on oxygen. Get me down the mountain. Feed me some pizza. I mean, I don't know. Give me a bath. All my options were pretty limited at this point. But whatever. The bird said this was the thing to do. I mean, I think I would just listen to the bird.

I mean, I stood there in the cabin, next to the stove, smoking a cigarette, and coughing like a fool, trying to figure out how to get a stack of sticks lit so I could throw them into the tree, underhanded. I mean, my hands hurt like hell. Don't get me wrong, but this was kind of a big problem. I mean, I was running out of ideas again. I stood there long enough, trying to focus, that I had to light another cigarette. I lit the new cigarette off of the old cigarette. This made the sun come out some more. I mean, the only thing I could think of was to put the branches in between my fingers, like cigarettes, and hold them that way. Then I could light them, hopefully, then I could get them to the tree, hopefully. I mean, I tried it with one, and it worked, so I did this with four branches in each hand. Don't get me wrong, but this took some doing. Some very painful doing in fact. But I did it. And I was able to get them all lit. Like an idiot I got to the door, and realized that I couldn't open the door because my hands were useless, and I had burning sticks in between my fingers. Not to mention, my cigarette was nearly out now. I went back to the stove. Dropped the burning sticks on top of the stove. I mean, I guess I was thinking I would try to get them back in between my fingers, but this was a stupid idea. All the branches just fell out of my hands, and made a crisscross on top of the stove that I couldn't pick back up. This made me sad. Don't get me wrong though, I didn't give up. I wanted to. But I didn't. I went over to the door, opened it. Somehow. I mean, I used the palms of both of my hands to turn the doorknob. And it hurt. But I did it. Then I went back to the stove. I lit four cigarettes, and held them in my mouth, all at the same time. Just in case. I coughed and coughed and coughed. But whatever. Then I got another four sticks burning per hand. Sticking out from in between my fingers like cigarettes themselves. Then I was ready to go. I walked out the door, smoke coming from my face, from my hands. I must have looked like an idiot pirate, because I felt like an idiot pirate. My eyes red and burning. Tears streaming down my face. My boots sloppy and untied at my feet. I don't know what happened to my stocking cap, because it was gone now, and for some reason I just noticed, but whatever.

Don't get me wrong, but it took some doing to get back to the tree. It was hard to see, and I was coughing and coughing and coughing. But I did get there eventually, I mean. And when I got there, I proved myself to be an idiot one more time because I had no idea how I was going to throw the burning sticks up into the tree when all the sticks needed to be in between my fingers. I did my best to do a throw, but all the sticks just went everywhere, and none of them landed in the tree. I mean, this kind of hurt my feelings. But I was still optimistic, I mean, I don't really know why I was still feeling positive, but whatever, I was. I mean, don't get me wrong, but I had no choice at this point. I had wasted so much time on this ill-conceived plan that I was in it to win it now, I mean, as the kids say. I mean, I dropped three of the four still burning cigarettes to the ground, keeping one lit so the sky stayed lit, and walked back to the cabin. When I got inside, I went over to the stove and found the metal bucket that I had used to make a helmet when I was trying to fight the burglars. I used this to hold the sticks I was lighting on fire. I mean, it worked okay, and in the end I had a pile of burning sticks in the bucket. I used the cigarette I was smoking to light another cigarette, and then put the handle of the metal bucket around my wrist, and walked back to the tree I was trying to light on fire.

When I got back to the tree, I put the bucket on the ground. I took a deep breath, and picked up a burning branch from the bucket. This hurt like hell. But I had no choice. I threw the burning branch underhanded up into the tree. It was amazing. I mean, I was amazed. The first branch got snagged on a branch. I could see it lighting the needles on fire. I decided this wasn't going to be enough, so I threw another one up. Underhanded. This hurt like hell as well, but the burning branch landed on a different branch with fresh needles to burn. Suddenly I was all sorts of successful. I mean, don't get me wrong, but I was getting cocky. I kept throwing burning branches up. With various success. But, I mean, by the time the bucket was mostly empty, I mean, there was some burning coals and debris or whatever, but by the time the thing was empty the tree was very much on fire. Like really on fire. Like shooting flames 20 feet into the air on fire. I smiled for the first time I can remember.

I mean, I celebrated. In a way, I mean, I lit another cigarette off of the cigarette I was smoking and watched the tree burn. I mean, at first, I just stood there, coughing, and smiling, then burning debris started falling on my head. A coal got stuck in my hair because I wasn't wearing my stocking cap, and burned a hole in my skin, and caught my hair on fire. Which sucked. I had to drop to my knees. Somehow remembering to remove the cigarette from my mouth, and gave myself a swirly in the snow. Which gave me an ice cream headache, which hurt like hell. And the hole in my scalp made my soft and wiggly scurvy teeth feel like lightening was striking them. I mean, I reached up, and could actually feel the hole. I could feel my skull. This made my eyes do a weird thing, and for some reason, I mean, being the idiot I was becoming, I just stood there worried, but then a burning branch fell to the ground right next to me, so I hauled ass back to the corner of the cabin that was closest to the burning tree. I mean, I stood there admiring my handy work. Smoking. Coughing. Worrying about the hole in my head. I mean, don't get me wrong, but a sense of satisfaction and relief washed over me. I sighed, and nearly fell asleep. I mean, I hadn't realized how tightly wound I was. But I forced myself to refuse the sleep that was coming over me. Which made me feel dizzy with anxiety. I mean, like my body was about to shut down, like a computer shuts down, and that maybe I was suddenly dying because I had accomplished everything I was supposed to do in life, but then I realized I wasn't breathing, so I took some deep breaths, I mean, not really, I took some breaths, they weren't deep, and they made me cough, but I tried, and this made me less anxious.

Don't get me wrong, but I stood there watching the tree burn. Kind of happy. I said:

"Pretty good fire, eh Trace?"

"You are doing a great job, Donkey!"

" Thanks, Tracy. Seneca?"

"Well, weto, I have to hand it to you, you are a moron, homey, but you lit a good fire."

"Well, hell, Seneca, I love you too."

"Now don't get carried away weto."

Don't get me wrong, but as we stood there watching the tree burn, I heard the sound of a snowmobile off in the distance. It was faint, but it was there. Or at least I thought so. I asked Seneca Michael Miguel if he heard it too. He said, *Sure as shit, homey.* I didn't know what to do. I mean, were the burglars coming back? Was this a different snowmobile, maybe one that Chaz was riding, coming back to rescue me from this hell I was living in? I mean, I had no idea. And I didn't know what to do about it. I mean, should I hide? Would the burglars brain me again? I mean, the timing couldn't be worse, but if it wasn't the burglars, the timing couldn't be better. I mean, I guess. I looked at the burning tree. It was starting to catch the other trees on fire now. And if my calculations were correct, the trees would all burn all the way around the cabin, around the graveyard, and come back in a horse shoe, and end up back at the cabin on the side that the burglars usually came from. I mean, don't get me wrong, but what would they do if they came, and the whole woods were on fire? Would they just turn around? Go back and get help? Just leave me here to my own misery, to starve to death in a burned-out patch of mountain?

I mean, don't get me wrong, but I had no idea. And I had no idea about what to do about it. Hide? Greet them? Try and steal their snowmobile again? I mean, they seemed pretty far off, but because I could hear the snowmobile, they were close enough for me to hear them approaching, which meant that they were kind of close.

I mean, I didn't know what to do, so like normal, I did nothing. I lit another cigarette, from the cigarette I was smoking. I coughed, and coughed, and coughed. I watched the trees light each other on fire. I made sure the sun was still out. It was. The smoke from the fires was getting pretty intense. I mean, as stupid as my plan was, I was starting to think it just might work. I mean, I didn't have anything else to do, so I just stood there. Waiting. Watching the fire. Watching the sky. Listening to the snowmobile approaching. I mean, I was nervous, but hopeful. Plus coughing. My head hurt where I burned a hole in it. I could smell burned hair. My hands hurt like hell. My legs were cold because I wasn't wearing my jeans. But aside from this, I was doing all right. I mean, as far as all things were concerned, I had just pulled myself up by my bootstraps for real this time. I mean, even if it meant nothing would come of it, I had worked my hardest, and my hard work was starting to pay off. Or so it seemed.

Part 12

Don't get me wrong, but I don't really know how to describe the next thing that happened. I mean, aside from watching the trees burn, and listening to the snowmobile approaching, everything else happened in such a flurry that I still am having trouble processing it. I mean, not to get all philosophical and what not, but there are times in your life when nothing makes sense, and it takes you months, years, decades to understand them. I mean, don't get me wrong, but this was kind of one of those times. And I mean, I don't mean to be dramatic, but I mean, it was like I was looking left, and then a freight train hit me from the right, or something stupid. I mean, I am bad at analogies, but this is what it felt like, I mean, sometimes when you are given soft avocados, you have to make guacamole, or something. Life, I mean, it is kind of unpredictable. I mean, kind of. But if you ever find yourself stranded in a cabin on top of mountain in Wyoming, maybe you will think of me, and this account will be useful to you. I mean, I am not holding my breath, and don't get me wrong, I made some pretty dumb choices, but you win some, you lose some, am I right? Whatever. All I am saying is that sometimes you juke when you should jive, and this time was one of those times. Let this be a lesson to you.

Don't get me wrong, but for some reason I went back into the cabin and opened up the cooler. I put the remaining packs of cigarettes in my pockets. Just in case. I mean, that is what I told myself, just in case. I looked around in the cabin. Looking for what, I couldn't tell you. Something. Anything that would be useful. I mean, there was nothing there. Just dirty scratchy blankets, and a cooler. A bed. My button-up jeans on the ground. I found my stocking cap. It was on the bed. I put it on. Then I took it off. I felt the hole in my scalp. This hurt my teeth. I put the stocking cap back on. I put a few more branches in the stove. I tried to shut the door. That stupid stick was still keeping the door from being shut. I would have to deal with this at some point. I mean, I guess, but now was not the time. I lit another cigarette off of the cigarette I was smoking. I coughed, and coughed, and coughed. I spit on the ground. My spit wasn't even brown anymore. It was just blood. I sighed. I could hear the snowmobile approaching. The sun was still out, but now there were shadows from the smoke coming from the burning trees outside. I mean, I don't know why, I mean, my hands hurt like hell, but I decided to make the bed. I put the pillow in place, and then draped all the blankets over it. The bed, I mean. I made it look real nice, in fact. I mean, if there was a broom I would have swept up. I mean, I picked up my pants from the floor, and folded them. I put them on the bed. I organized the rest of the branches. Into a neat little pile. I coughed for a while. Then I took a break, and sat down on the bed. This was stupid. I got very tired. I almost laid down. I didn't though. I stood up. I shook myself awake. Made sure my cigarette was still burning. Then I looked around one more time. The cabin seemed tidy. I said my goodbyes. I mean, I didn't know if I would be back or not, but this seemed like an appropriate thing to do. Then I walked out the door. I mean, that was that. I guess. I shut the door behind myself. Thinking it would suck if I had to open it again, but whatever, I would deal with that later.

Don't get me wrong, but I walked around the side of the cabin. I could see that the trees that were burning were now about halfway around the cemetery. The snowmobile was getting closer. The sun was still out, but I could see that dusk was approaching. I mean, maybe, or maybe not. I mean, the smoke was starting to obscure the sky. Meaning, I mean, that instead of clouds of clouds, it was now clouds of smoke that were making things dark. Which was a good thing. I mean, I could only hope that somebody was seeing this, and maybe they would send somebody to come investigate. Or, I mean, who knows? Maybe the snowmobile wasn't the burglars, or Chaz, but some Forest Service guys coming to see what was happening, right? I mean, I don't know, but why not. I pushed myself through the snow all the way to the grave that said Miguel on it. The one with the goods inside. I don't know why I did this. I mean, I guess that maybe there was still something to do about it. I mean, in a way there was still a chance that the burglars would show up with a pick-ax, and, oh, I don't know, a blow torch, and we could get down to the bottom, and find out what this thing was about all along. I mean, aside from my frail state, my hummingbird heart, my wriggly teeth, and my complete lack of sustenance, I mean, I still had hope that I could get my hands on the goods, one way or the other. I mean, I guess, I mean, this is the job I was hired to do, right? I mean, I couldn't just let it go. Am I right? I mean, I know I am right, because that is what I did, I pushed myself through the snow, and stood next to the grave marked Miguel. Looking. Listening to the sound of the snowmobile approaching. Watching the smoke from the trees go into the sky. Watching the trees burn. Smoking and coughing. And coughing, and coughing. I mean, I might not be going anywhere, so, I mean, it was probably best to let things come to me. Don't get me wrong, but am I right?

I stood there looking. My legs cold. My hands hurting. My head hurting. My teeth wimpy. My stomach empty. Smoking, coughing. Listening to the snowmobile. The trees burning around me. Smoke billowing into the air. I mean, I didn't know what to do. I mean, not really. All I could do was wait. And waiting is hard. I was starting to get warm. The fire was getting close. I mean, I didn't mind so much. I mean, I guess what was really starting to bother me was that the trees were getting loud. Their burning, I mean. It was keeping the sound of the approaching snowmobile from reaching my ears. I mean, I thought about going back, and around the cabin to get a better sense of what was happening, but the heat from the burning trees was nice, and I was feeling very tired, so I stayed where I was. Hoping for some sort of sign as to what I should do. Nothing came. So I lit a new cigarette from my old cigarette, hoping to keep the sky open. Hoping to keep the signal going. Hoping to maybe get a rescue moving. I mean, snowmobile or no snowmobile, I still needed to let the world know that something was pretty fucked up, and it needed to be investigated. I mean, society wouldn't just leave a guy stranded like this, I mean, am I right? I mean, I worked so hard my whole life, I feel like somebody was maybe missing me, right? I mean, even if it wasn't me specifically that they were missing, they would send somebody to come help me even if it didn't make a difference who I was. Am I wrong? America wouldn't leave me stranded in my hour in need. I mean, not on purpose, right? I mean, politics stop when we see people suffering, right?

Don't get me wrong, but I am joking. My only hope was that I would create such a huge emergency that nobody could ignore it. But then if that happened, I think the burglars, or whoever was on that snowmobile would turn around, and go back home, so it was a kind of double-edged thing. I mean, take the little help you can get, or burn it all down so you can maybe get the larger help for you, and everyone else. I mean, I guess this was the dilemma, however, at the moment neither of these things mattered. I was doing both. And, I guess it was more like, which one would come faster? The snowmobile, or the forest fire. And, quite frankly, it was looking like they would both arrive at the same time.

As I stood there waxing poetic, a funny thing happened. Don't get me wrong, but it started to get really hot. Like the snow started melting. I mean, I didn't notice at first, but suddenly the snow on top of the cabin started dropping in sheets off of the roof. Which startled me. I jumped back. Then I saw steam coming off of the roof. I guess I was distracted because I hadn't noticed that the trees had burned themselves all the way to the cabin on the side where the burglars came from. I mean, it must have been pretty hot by the cabin on that side because the cedar shakes were starting to buckle. They were making a noise like broken piano keys as they sprung up from the nails that held them down onto the rooftop. I mean, it sounded like this, Ploink! Plink! Plang! Doink! Bonk! Bedoink! I mean, I was startled, and then I was nervous, and then I got really nervous. My hummingbird heart started pounding. I got shaky, and I gave myself the hiccups because of it. I mean, now I was coughing, and hiccoughing at the same time. Which was annoying, but what could I do? I mean,

I thought about going back around to the other side of the cabin when the original tree I had lit on fire fell down at the exact spot where the trail led back. I mean, this was not good. I mean, the tree was still on fire. And it started burning the corner of the cabin that it was touching. I mean, I sighed, and decided to make a move towards the other side of the cabin. The side that the burglars would usually come from. But the trees were burning like crazy at that point too. I mean, don't get me wrong, but I suddenly found myself trapped. I mean, I guess I had one option left, and that was to go and try and break through the good window, and get into the cabin that way, but these dreams were dashed when I noticed that the entire inside of the cabin was on fire now. I mean, I don't know how it happened, I mean, it was either the original tree that did this, or more likely the fact that there was that stupid piece of wood that was keeping the stove door from closing, and by adding a bunch of new branches to the stove before I left the cabin, I had accidentally set the cabin on fire, I mean, of all the stupid moves I had made since deciding that I should start the trees on fire, I mean, this move seemed the most likely. I mean, I had no desire to break a window to get into the cabin, only burn to death inside of it. I mean, not that I made this decision in a rational matter, but I realized I was fucked, and there was no reason to try and get to safety through the cabin at this point. I mean, I was trapped, and that was that. My only hope was that I could wait the fire out, and not burn to death in the graveyard, standing next to the grave that held the goods. I mean, I did feel kind of safe where I was standing. But at the same time, I was worried about the burglars coming to do who knows what, riding the snowmobile. I mean, who knows, maybe it was somebody else, but I was starting to doubt it.

And since the fire was so loud, I had no idea how close they were. I mean, I didn't know what to do, so I just stood there, watching the snow melt. Smoking. Coughing. Hoping for the best. But starting to get really freaked out. I mean, I was trapped, and it was getting really hot.

Don't get me wrong, but I had to take some of my clothes off. First my coat came off. Then my stocking cap. Which reminded me of the hole in my scalp. I mean, I smelled my burned hair. I touched my skull. Which made me nervous. Then I had to kick my boots off. Which was lucky that they weren't tied. But standing in the snow while I removed the overalls was brutal. I mean, I don't know how I did it, because before I knew it, I was back in my boots, standing there in my long johns, and shirts, wearing my boots again, fire heat coming from all sides, smoke above me, my cigarette having burned out, the sound of the snowmobile getting closer, loud enough now to sneak through the sounds of burning wood. I mean, the snow around me was melting at an alarming rate. I mean, I thought it was a joke, I mean, it turned from snow to running water in moments, seconds, I mean, suddenly there was grass, and dirt, and I don't know, rocks. I mean, all of everything was turning to water, and rushing down the mountain, down, and through the cemetery. I mean, just like that, I was standing naked, coughing, and coughing, and coughing. I mean, I had torn my socks off, my long johns, all my shirts. I had to look at my genitals again. But this time they were larger, and robust. I mean, because of the heat they were back to normal. Plump. Not so much brown and purple, but more like pink and dangly. I mean, I was still skinny, and stinking, but I wasn't as embarrassed as I was before. Whatever that means. I mean, things were getting weird, and water was now rushing over my feet — warm, dirty water. And something was happening with the grave with the goods in it. I mean, the ice on top was starting to protrude. And was melting at an alarming rate. I mean, I myself was getting really hot. Like the hottest summer I had ever lived through, hot, and I thought about lying down on the ice coming up from the grave with the goods in it, and maybe riding it down to the bottom of the mountain, but that time came, and went, and the only thing that was left in the grave was wet and brown. And, I don't even know what to say, but it was looking pretty inviting, that grave. I mean, the grave looked cool, and inviting. I mean, enticing. I mean, don't get me wrong, but I was resisting getting in it, I mean, I could still hear the snowmobile approaching, but I was running out of options about getting out of the heat from the burning trees. I mean, I looked over at the cabin. The cabin was on fire. All of it. There was no going back to that. I mean, I either jumped in the grave, or I tried to run through the wall of burning trees. I mean, in the end there was only one option, really, and that was to jump in the grave. And, I mean, don't get me wrong, but I was already naked, so, I mean, I was ready for the drink.

I won't lie to you, I mean, I didn't have any options left. I slipped into the grave. The water felt cool, but somehow dry. I mean, it didn't even seem like water. Don't get me wrong, but I ignored this. I mean, I didn't completely ignore it, I was aware of it, but there was nothing I could do about it. I mean, maybe the water was cool steam or something. I mean, maybe some weird physics happened, you know, because I was in a grave yard or something. Or like the snow and ice was melting so fast that it was living in some weird condensate, or whatever they called it when liquid acted like gas. Or the other way around, or whatever, but I don't mean to be giving science lessons at the moment. I stood in the grave, my body under the water, or what was supposed to be water, my head poking out. I was standing there, just looking around. Watching the trees burn. Listening to the snowmobile approaching. I mean, my head was hot. I could smell my hair burning. I reached up, and rubbed my scalp. All the hair fell down on top of the water, and just floated there. I mean, don't get me wrong, but I was bald now. The hole I burned in my scalp before, when I was standing under the burning tree really hurt. Because of the heat. I mean, I don't know if it was because of the weird water, or being so low to the ground, but the rest of my head was doing okay. I mean, not burning. I mean, aside from my hair burning off, my head was doing okay. I mean, don't get me wrong, but I just stood there looking. I turned around and looked at the graveyard. All the grave stones were buckling now. Falling over. Michael, Miguel, Miguel, Michael. Dropping to the ground. Some of them breaking on impact. The ground buckling. I could see coffins start to pop up. Then the coffins would pop open, revealing skeletons in suits. Smiling at me. I mean, one in particular popped out, and waved at me, or it seemed. I mean, I guess that is how you would describe it. Waving at me, smiling, wearing an old-timey suit. I want to say the skeleton was wearing a top hat, but that can't be true. I mean, I must have dreamed that detail up, or something. But whatever. I mean, don't get me wrong, but this didn't creep me out, it was actually kind of funny at the time. I remember laughing about it, and saying, *Well hello, Mr. Lincoln, how do you do? Hot enough for ya?*

There was a noise from the place the snowmobile was coming from, so I looked over. Just then the snowmobile jumped through the burning trees and came barreling towards me. I had to drop down into the weird water to avoid getting my head tractioned. Skied? Run over by the snowmobile. Then it jumped over the grave. I looked up through the weird water, and could see it. I popped my head back up. There was three people on the snowmobile. What looked like the two regular burglars, and a third kind of short and plump little guy. I mean, my heart jumped. It surely seemed like it was Chaz. I mean, shit, here I was stuck in this grave with the goods in it, the fire blaring all around me, and had I just waited a few extra minutes instead of burning the forest down, I might have been saved. I mean, I say that like I know it, but it certainly seemed like Chaz on the back of the snowmobile. But what didn't make sense is why they tried to run me over and then rode off into the other end of the fire, only to disappear into the distance. I mean, what was that about?

I mean, I stood there looking. Listening. I could kind of hear the snowmobile, I mean I think I could. Then I know I could. Then I know I really could because I could see it coming back. Then it was really coming back. Then it was about to run me over again. Then I ducked down into the weird water, and watched it blast over me again. Then it disappeared the way it had first come. I mean, what the hell were these guys doing? I mean, why didn't they stop if they were trying to save me? And if maybe they actually wanted to run me over, why didn't they just stop and put me out of my misery? I mean, don't get me wrong, but what the hell? I stood there looking some more. I mean, I was trying to stand there looking, but don't get me wrong, it was getting hotter by the second. I mean, my body was still cool, hanging out in the weird water, but my head was getting hotter. Too hot, I mean. I mean, I had to stop looking. I mean, don't get me wrong, but I couldn't take it anymore. And not only that but it was starting to get really smoky. My eyes were burning. And I was really regretting starting this fire now. I mean, even if I was able to outlast the fire, which didn't seem possible, I had missed my chance to understand what Chaz was up to. I mean, he had come up with the burglars this time. I mean, maybe it would all make sense. Or, whatever, maybe they had some food at least. I mean, I didn't see that they were carrying a cooler or anything, but maybe one of them had a backpack filled with summer sausage or something. Some crackers, and some American cheese. I mean, just thinking about this made me really hungry. But what could I do about it? I mean, I held my breath and dunked my head under the weird water. Which cooled my head. But, don't get me wrong, the water was very dry. And I don't know why, maybe I just decided to be done with it and drown, or something, but I held my breath for as long as I could, and instead of going up for air, I just decided to take a breath. To suck the weird water into my lungs, and, I guess, drown. But, I mean, don't get me wrong, that didn't happen. I learned that I could breathe the weird water just fine. I mean, by just fine, I mean, I could breathe the same as normal, but under water. Do you know what I mean? I mean, the water was air, I guess. Or whatever, I mean, I didn't drown. I just floated there under the weird water, breathing just fine. I mean, it didn't kill me.

I dangled there for quite some time. Kind of floating. Breathing in the weird water. Not knowing what to do. I could still hear the fire burning. The trees crackling. Other water rushing by. The snow melting. I mean, everything was muffled, but I could hear it. Then I heard the snowmobile coming. I poked my head up out of the weird water, and had a peek. It was coming straight for me. The same as before. I ducked down again. Waiting for them to drive over the grave again. But this time they didn't. The snowmobile stopped. Then I heard some screaming. Then, just like that, three people jumped into the grave I was dangling around in. Breathing the weird water. I could see them clearly. The two burglars, and Chaz. I mean, I thought it was Chaz. I mean, judging by the shape of his body, he was wearing a helmet, but not the full body suit the burglars were wearing. I mean, I don't know how it happened, but the grave was kind of cramped when I was in it alone, but now it was bigger. I mean, much bigger. Like it was suddenly a large room filled with weird water. The air was white, I mean, the weird water that was air, was white. Like smoky or something, but not. I could see everything clearly, but there was a haze, I guess, but not really. I mean, I don't want to give the impression that it was like some smoke machine spitting out spooky Halloween vibes, or like, I don't know, dry ice, or something, but the air was kind of smoky, I don't know how else to describe it. I mean, it was like I could see the molecules, but not really. And everything had this white glow, I guess, or kind of. I don't know. Don't get me wrong, I don't know how to describe it, and since I am telling the story, I am not going to try anymore. All I can say is that it was kind of smoky in the grave, but not really, and the small grave turned into a big room somehow. I mean, don't get me wrong, you can take it or leave it. Or whatever.

I mean, say what you will, or don't get me wrong, or, I mean, or, I am just saying, but when the two burglars and Chaz jumped down into the grave they seemed pretty freaked out. I mean, I don't think they trusted the water, but they could see that I was doing just fine. And instead of just going with the flow, or whatever, I could tell that they were holding their breath. I yelled out to them, surprised my voice was working in the weird water. I yelled:

"You can breathe! I can breathe! You can too!"

Chaz was the first one to believe me. I mean, I guess, either that, or he was the first one to take his helmet off, because he was. I mean, Chaz took his helmet off, and yes, it was indeed Chaz. He kind of smiled at me, I mean, I guess that is what you would call it. I mean, it was more of a sneer, but whatever, I am splitting hairs here. Then one of the burglars looked at Chaz, and decided he was doing alright, so he took his helmet off. It was Humphreys. Then the other burglar took his helmet off. I mean, don't get me wrong, but it was White. I mean, for fuck's sake. When I saw this, I tried to run over and strangle everyone. But because I was so weak, combined with the weird water, I just kind of did some stationary bicycle move that made me look like an asshole. And, I guess because everyone is a comedian, they just laughed at me. Which made me upset, but whatever, there was nothing I could do about it. So I just dangled there glaring at all three of them as they laughed at me. Then a moment passed, and I regained my composure, and said:

"What the fuck you god-damned maniacs!"

"Oh relax, Donkey, don't blame us, man, blame society." This was Chaz speaking. His sneer was more of grin now.

"Oh, yeah, society, huh? I should throttle you where you stand."

"Give it a try, you wimpy worm. Look at you, you couldn't strangle a mosquito, what with your tiny dick, and your skin and bones."

"Fuck you, Chaz, you made me this way."

"I made your tiny dingaling, really? I did that?"

"Oh, fuck off, that's not what I mean, and you know it. What the fuck, man! I been starving up here for weeks. That's on you, not me."

"C'mon, Donkey, don't blame Chaz, you know what you did." This was White, he was lighting a cigarette, and talking out of the corner of his mouth.

"What I did? I mean, don't get me wrong, but what the fuck did you guys do! You think this is okay shit? Leaving a dude stranded to starve like this?"

"You did sleep with his gal, Donkey." Humphreys had some strange device that he was snorting from. He handed it to me. I don't know why, but I did a bump. This woke me up. And made my hunger go away. It also shrunk my genitals.

"My god, can they get any smaller?" Chaz was making fun of me again.

"Fuck you, Chaz. I've seen your things, I wouldn't be noticing stuff if I was you."

"Yeah, well, let me get my magnifying glass then we can talk."

"You're a dick."

"Can't say that about you, right guys?" All three of them laughed. I got so embarrassed that I tried to get out of the grave. Somebody pulled my leg down before I got to the surface. Then White said:

"Ah, c'mon, Donk, we are just fucking with you, have a sense of humor."

"Yeah, man, we're here to get you out." Humphreys said.

"Yeah, just apologize, and this will all be over." Chaz said.

"Yeah, man." White said.

"Apologize for what?"

"Oh, I don't know, you could start with the fact that you got me fired, and then you slept with my girlfriend."

"Bullshit, Chaz. Lorinda slept with me, I didn't sleep with her. It was poor form, I agree, but she is not innocent in the bigger scheme of things."

"Dude, just apologize!" White yelled.

"I won't! I refuse! You dudes trap me in this cabin, and nearly starve me to death, and now it is all on me? I don't blame society, I blame you motherfuckers. I mean, this shit has got to be illegal. I mean, I am calling the cops the second we get back to Casper."

"I don't think we can get back to Casper anymore, Donkey. This is last place we can get to." Chaz said.

"What the hell are you talking about?"

"This is the end of the road, man. You can apologize, which would be nice, but you have gone too far. There is only one way out of this grave, and it is down there." Chaz pointed to the ground.

"What does that mean? We are already in the ground, we can't go any further. I mean, do you plan on killing me if I don't apologize? I mean, I am sorry. I didn't mean it when your girlfriend boned me. It felt pretty good though."

"Yeah, no. I don't care about that. I mean, I wish you wouldn't have boned her, but that is whatever, what I mean is, don't get me wrong, but there is no way out of this grave. The only thing that will save you is to get the goods, and those goods are down below."

"Why are you talking like me, Chaz? I guess you are mocking me now?"

"I mean, I don't know, maybe. All I am saying is that there is only one way out of here, and I think you know what that means. I mean, don't get me wrong." Chaz kept pointing to the ground.

"Yeah, okay, I mean, but what do I do?"

"You have to dig, Donkey." Humphreys said.

"Dig, weto." Seneca Michael Miguel said.

"Seneca! When did you get here?"

"You are doing a great job, Donkey!" Goil Tracy said.

"Oh, Tracy! Thank you."

"Just dig, man." White said.

"You can do this." Chaz said.

Don't get me wrong, but I started digging like a fool. Like a donkey. Like a hairless, starving to death, and naked, and stinking donkey. Trying to get at the goods. For some reason I started yelling:

"Tortilla! Tor-tilla! Tooor-tiiilla!"

Like I was digging for tortillas because that was the food I only ate. Like I was a donkey that only ate tortillas. Like my voice even sounded like a donkey. And when I finally got to the goods a good feeling came over me. And, don't get me wrong, but I enjoyed it. All my suffering went away, and I was one with the Universe. I mean, don't get me wrong, but as I held onto the goods, and the goods pulled me into the abyss, I turned around and could see all of the smiling faces of all the people that had done me wrong my entire life. I let go of the goods for a second. I held out my hands, both of them, the pain from me being an idiot and burning them on top of the stove was gone, I curled my fingers into a double barreled middle finger, and yelled:

"Fuck you!"

Thanks to:

Miette Gillette
Tina Satter
George Truman
Scott Halvorsen Gillette
Shane Foote
Jack Warren
Die Bangst

About the Author

Joey Truman is a writer from Worland, Wyoming. He moved to New York City when he was 19. He has twice taken a Greyhound bus from Denver, Colorado to NYC. By himself. Which is a 57 hour trip. He has written many novels. Among them are:

Moveable Rooms (2022)
Sequestered (2020)
Etiquette (2020)
Killing The Math (2019)
Parlay (2018)

He is now living in Vermont with his best friend who has curly red wires for hairs. Eventually when the plague is over, he will spend some times in Vermont, and some times in Brooklyn.

About the Publisher

Whisk(e)y Tit is committed to restoring degradation and degeneracy to the literary arts. We work with authors who are unwilling to sacrifice intellectual rigor, unrelenting playfulness, and visual beauty in our literary pursuits, often leading to texts that would otherwise be abandoned in today's largely homogenized literary landscape. In a world governed by idiocy, our commitment to these principles is an act of civil service and civil disobedience alike.

For more issues of *Donkey* please visit whiskeytit.com/donkey or write the publisher at miette@whiskeytit.com